A novel by Jacob Oritt

Artwork by Jose Corkhill Rivera

This book is dedicated to the two most amazing people in my life: my parents. Jeff and Kristi Oritt gave me an incredible upbringing, filled with love, kindness, and never ending support. It is because of them that I am the man I am today. I am forever grateful to you both.

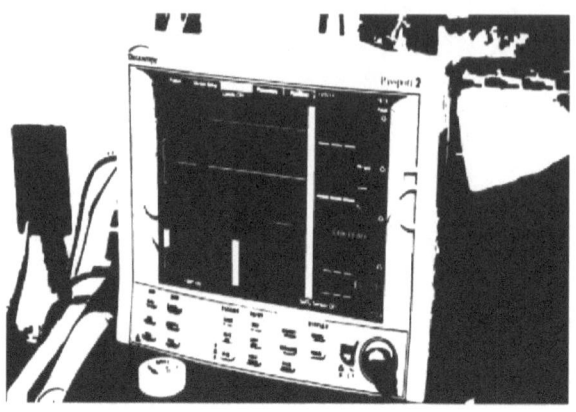

Prologue (The Year 2009)

The patient was perfect. And she died anyway.

With the barest hint of a smile on her lips, enough to reveal a single dimple.

Without a hint of a crease to furrow the skin of her forehead, showing a lack of pain.

A final, soft exhalation as her body sank down ever so slightly into the hospital bed.

She departed, gently, into that good night.

The doctor standing over her cursed, hurled the defibrillator paddles against the far wall. The resounding *crash*, paired with the violent temper of the doctor, sent the two attending nurses scurrying from the room like a pair of frightened mice.

"Why?" The doctor implored, empty hands outstretched over her head, begging to a God she barely took time to believe in, despite the gold cross hanging around her neck. *"Why?* What caused this?" She whirled on the recently emptied vessel on the hospital bed. "There's nothing wrong with you! You shouldn't have died! *Why do you all keep dying?!"*

The patient was only 15 years old.

Part 1: A Blessing (The Year 2003)

1

    My name is Annie, and I was born in 2003 on the morning of a new year.
    They tell me that I am a twin, but I have never met my twin sister. Now I know I never will, at least in life, although I strongly believe that I will meet her again one day in whatever comes after this consciousness.
    They also tell me that when I was born, I was the sickly of the two twins. A sickness passed on from my mother, who did not long survive the birthing. The doctor who delivered me seemed morbidly positive that I would follow my mother into the black, but after doing blood work on my twin, the doctor discovered something miraculous: my twin, who was born just as perfect as could be, had one spectacular abnormality.
    Her thymus gland. More specifically, the thymosin hormone within the thymus gland that stimulates the disease fighting T cells.
    Under a microscope, my twin's thymus gland was a genetic abnormality, and stimulated the development of T cells at an

accelerated rate beyond what medical science had ever seen before. They seemed to be a wildfire of life, of healing.

You see, my twin's thymus gland didn't just produce T cells. When normal white blood cells, called lymphocytes, passed through her thymus gland to be transformed into T cells, the new cells didn't just rush out into the body to aid in the fight against autoimmune disease. Rather, they became a kind of cellular chimera, rushing to any singular part of the body that needed help with maintaining full, healthy operation. It made absolutely no sense.

But it happened.

A blood transfusion was performed, the blood of the healthy twin filled with the abnormally strong T cells poured into the blood of the sickly. And I healed.

No.

I *transformed*.

My skin, mottled and scaly one night, was pink and glowing before the sun rose on a new day.

My bones, brittle and weak, became dense, nigh unbreakable.

My heart, weak and feeble, grew stronger with each pump in my tiny chest, sending that life-saving blood through my veins at an ever faster rate.

Within a single day, *both* twins were healthy, and *both* twins possessed radically altered thymus glands with accelerated replication properties.

And then, that second night, as I drew in breath in my 25th hour of life, my twin was stolen from the bed next to me in the NICU by my father.

My twin, whose name was Grace.

My father, the surgeon who had delivered us, and saved my own life with the blood of my sister. My father, the brilliant surgeon and geneticist, whose intellect had taken him to the peak of the medical field, and whose actions that night made his very name anathema within the field that had given him fame.

Calvin Michaels.

2

My time in the NICU was extensive, not because of my poor health, but because I had nowhere to go. No extended family to come pick me up and give me a home. I was given the nickname Orphan Annie my second night there.

The doctors in that hospital took advantage of the time I spent there. After seeing my health transform overnight, coupled with my own new, miraculous accelerated thymus gland, every person in a white coat that heard of me wanted to study me. Blood was taken and analyzed by every department there. My blood, which had at first been identified as AB negative, was re-labeled as AZ blood, the first of its kind. So named because it could be used to treat anything from A to Z, within my body.

Cardiology wanted to see if my blood could be used to help with blood transfusions for people with congenital heart conditions to improve their vascular system.

Accident and Emergency wanted to culture samples of my blood once it had been taken outside of my body, to see if it could be encouraged to replicate and diminish the need for outside donor blood, therefore saving more victims who were brought in with serious blood loss.

Critical Care wanted to see if the AZ cells in my blood could be used with their patients who had serious diseases with no known cures, such as AIDS or the Ebola virus.

The list went on.

Most of the doctors got nowhere with their tests. But I wouldn't know the reason why for years to come.

I would end up staying a grand total of 5 months, 14 days, and 19 hours in the NICU. All of the doctors came to see me as a kind of surrogate child, a 'miracle baby', and when it came time to look into foster care, I had dozens of advocates who wanted to ensure that the family I ended up with would be in it for the long haul, not just become the first in a long line of foster homes, as so often happens to other children in 'the system'. I will be forever thankful to the hospital staff of Primary Children's in Salt Lake City, Utah, for they matched me with a family that gave me all the love anyone could ever ask for.

On June 15, 2003, my new parents took me home and introduced me to my new siblings.

Orphan Annie was no more. Now I was Annie Oritt, the youngest of 4 children. My life truly began that day.

3

"I know that children can start talking as early as 6 months, but everything I've ever read - or that we've experienced, for that matter - says that full sentences and real language acquisition doesn't happen for, what, a year and a half? Two years? How old was Madeleine when she spoke her first full sentence, and not just random, multi-syllable prattle?" Jeffrey Oritt, Attorney at Law, asked his wife Kristi, English teacher and hospital volunteer. My new parents.

Kristi shook her head in wonder, looking down at me with wide eyes. "18 months at the *earliest*. And this girl, our new daughter, is barely 6 months old!"

"I definitely didn't imagine it? Annie just thanked us, in perfect English, albeit with slightly soft enunciation, for adopting her."

I stared up at them from the pink crib that had been waiting for me when they had brought me home 2 weeks ago. From my vantage point they looked larger than life. Father, with his strong jaw and broad shoulders, seemed powerful enough to heft the world upon his back and carry us all. Mother, thick raven hair framing a beatific face, appeared as though she could cure pain with the power of her smile.

"Yes, I did," I replied to them in a voice that seemed too childish to mine own ears. I hoped it would mature quickly, but according to the doctors at the hospital I had so recently left, my vocal chords, while they were developing at an accelerated rate (like everything else inside of me) still had a ways to go. As it was now, I was irritated with the slight lisp that marred my pronunciation.

Father jumped, startled. Mother's eyes widened.

"You really are a miracle, aren't you?" Mother whispered, reaching down to stroke the fine blonde hair that wisped up on my head.

I frowned. I had heard that term many times at the hospital, but it didn't seem to match with what I felt inside. "I think," I said, straining to keep that irritating lisp out of my voice. "I'm just a baby."

My new parents laughed, and it was music to my ears.

4

Soon after being brought home, I met my three new siblings.

Alex, the oldest and biggest, was 25, and worked as a male model in Miami, Florida. He showed me on a map where this was in relation to my home here in Salt Lake City, and due to the size of the map, it looked less than a short walk away. When I pointed this out, Alex laughed and explained to me that a map took the world and made it smaller and easier to understand. I filed this information away as 'important'. I also noticed that Alex seemed to be dressed more ostentatiously than the other members of my new family. Mom broke in with a laugh and told me it was because Alex had something called 'style'. Alex grinned and gave me a wink, crossing his arms over his chest.

Jacob, the loudest of the family, was 18 and had just graduated from a place called 'high school'. His voice sounded booming to me, but in a pleasant way. I decided I liked him from his voice alone, even if he didn't seem to have as much 'style' as Alex.

Madeleine, called either Maddy or Mad depending on which member of the family was addressing her, the only girl in the family until I came along, had just turned 12, and she had the most beautiful red hair I had ever seen. Before she even opened her mouth to introduce herself, I was already reaching up to grasp at her fiery locks. She laughed, and I decided that I liked her, too. She seemed like a kindred spirit in a way I didn't quite understand yet.

At that point, surrounded by these friendly giants that were crowding around my crib, I started to yawn. I suppose that even for a mind that was developing as rapidly as mine, there was still such a thing as sensory overload.

Mother and Father, whom I noticed the other three kids calling Mom and Dad (another point that I filed away) noticed and started shooing my new siblings out of my room.

"Let's let her get some sleep," Mom said to them as they left. "This is all so much for her to take in."

"But did you see *how* she took everything in?" Alex, the biggest one, replied with awe in his voice. "I swear, as soon as I showed her that map it was like she was already memorizing-"

Then the door shut, and I fell deeply into dreamless sleep.

5

For a while, time seemed to speed up. The year 2003 vanished in the blink of an eye as I integrated into my new life. I spent my days within that house with my wonderful family, absorbing everything they shared with me.

My first interest was maps. Ever since that day I met Alex when he showed me a map and explained how Utah and Florida could look to be so close and yet truly be so distant, I had an insatiable curiosity to know more about the world.

Mom, being a teacher, had access to the most amazing things! She brought home geography supplies from her school and explained them all to me. It started with maps of Salt Lake City, the place where our house was. Then the entire state of Utah. Then the United States of America, which is called a country and is defined by a border wrapped all around it like the string around a present. All of the people within this border, Mom explained, were called *Americans*.

That seemed silly to me.

"You said people are called people," I pointed out, proudly using my voice that didn't have a lisp anymore.

Mom laughed. I loved her laugh. "*People* is an all-encompassing term. *American* is a smaller term, meaning people just in this area." She pointed at the map she held in front of me, a map that contained all of *North America* which was called a continent. "You see, this border here is The United States of America, and the people inside it are called Americans."

I pointed with a finger that was too chubby for my taste at the place above the United States. "What about that?"

"That's called Canada, and the people there are Canadians."

I pointed at the place under the USA. "That one?"

"That's Mexico, and those people are called Mexicans."

I shook my little head. "But the big word for all of us together is people?"

Mom smiled and kissed the top of my head. "That's right."

I frowned again. "Having two titles is redundant. We should all just be people, because that means we're all the same."

"Your dad and I agree with you, but many people in different parts of the world like having separate names," Mom explained. "It has to do with how people identify themselves, and their individual cultures."

"Redundant," I said again, firmly. "Can we call someone and ask them to change it?"

Mom sighed. "I wish it was that easy, Annie. You have a beautiful perspective that I would like to share with the whole world."

I resolved, then and there, that I would do just that.

I was just about to turn 1.

6

New Year's Day, 2004. My first birthday.

At my insistence, no one in my family got me what I termed "baby gifts".

Mom and Dad gave me a gorgeous globe of the Earth, with bumps and ridges that denoted mountain ranges. It also had the names of all the major states, countries, and continents. These names were etched with gold leaf and made the globe shine. I was so entranced with it that I could barely tear my attention away and accept my other gifts.

Big brother Alex gave me the tooth of an alligator, which are native to Florida and other parts of the south. I promised him I would learn about animals after I finished learning geography.

Loud brother Jacob gave me a picture book about celestial bodies, and informed me that the Earth we lived on was called a *planet*, and there were many others in our solar system. I promised him I would learn all about space.

Beautiful sister Maddy gave me a telescope to go along with Jacob's picture book of planets. I immediately started looking at everything through it to see what things look like up close. It turned out that faces, when looked at through a telescope, are decidedly weird.

Then we had cake. Cake is VERY good. Why don't adults eat cake after every meal? I think I'll ask for cake more often.

After my first birthday party, I was very tired. Tired but happy, and filled with love.

Mom carried me back into my room and lay me down in my crib.

"You know," Mom said. "You're growing faster than we expected. I think you might need your own real bed soon."

I was elated! "Like an adult? Will I be an adult soon?"

Mom smiled, but her smile seemed...worried? "I think you just might. Annie, I was wondering if you would give ME a birthday gift."

I frowned. "But it's not your birthday. Is it?"

"I know. We could call this an early birthday gift for me."

"I would give you anything, Mom," I said promptly.

Her smile grew. "Would you be ok with going back to the hospital again? Not to stay, just to have a few tests done. Just...to make sure everything is ok."

"Am I not ok? I FEEL ok."

"Oh no, you're perfect!" Mom quickly assured me. "You're just growing and learning so much faster than other children do. Your dad and I just want to make sure that everything is growing the way that it should."

I thought about that. "Your logic makes sense. The other children I see on the television seem fairly slow of thought. Hardly any of them can talk yet! Maybe the doctors can figure out how to make those other children smart like me, and then they can be my friends!"

Mom smiled that worried smile again, leaned down, and kissed my forehead. Her hair fell across my face and tickled my nose, and I giggled. "That's right, baby girl. That's exactly right."

7

The next morning dawned bright and cold. Salt Lake had been hit by a storm in the middle of the night, and the whole of my world was covered by a shimmering blanket of white. Before we could leave for the hospital, Jacob and Alex had to brave the elements and shovel the driveway. I sat in the living room in front of the big picture window and watched them. And listened to them, too. I learned a few new words that I don't think Mom and Dad would have been thrilled to hear. I filed them away regardless.

A short while later I found myself bundled up head to toe and buckled into Mom's little blue Subaru, which is a kind of car that comes from a place called Japan (which I found on the other side of my globe; it seems quite far away). Jacob and Alex had done a good job of shoveling the driveway, and we didn't even slide once as we reversed out onto the street.

I was curious about the main streets being shoveled clear as well. "Mom, did Jacob and Alex get up early and shovel the streets, too?"

Mom laughed. "No, Annie, I don't think we could have gotten that much physical labor out of them no matter how hard we tried. The city takes care of things like that, using trucks that have big metal shovels on the front. I'll point one out if we pass one."

My eyebrows drew down as I thought about this new concept. "So, whenever there is an issue in the city, the city just takes care of it?"

Mom nodded, eyes intent on the road as she drove carefully up the steep slope that would take us to Primary Children's hospital. "That's right. The word for that is 'infrastructure'. It's the inner workings of a society that keeps all the nuts and bolts turning in the right direction."

I processed this. "What if something happens that the infra...infras...infrastructure doesn't have an answer for?"

"There are people whose job it is to figure those things out. To always make sure that if something happens, anything at all, our society can still function normally. And if something new pops up that hasn't happened before, these people get together and come up with an answer together."

I loved it when Mom got into 'teacher mode'. She always had an answer for me, and it just drove my curiosity into new places. But before I had the chance to ask another question, I was interrupted by the sight of a monster truck with a huge shovel that looked like it was coming straight at us from up the street. The shovel was level with the street, pushing a tidal wave of snow in front of it at an angle. It was absolutely entrancing.

"Look Annie, there's a snowplow!" Mom said enthusiastically. "It's keeping the streets clear for us so that we can go about doing all the things we need to do."

I nodded, full of self-importance. "Yes, Mom. Infrastructure. I know about these things."

Mom burst out laughing, and my happiness grew and grew.

8

We arrived at the hospital shortly thereafter, and Mom pulled the Subaru into a spot close to the main entrance. As she unbuckled me from my special chair in the backseat, I saw that her earlier smile had slipped, and was in danger of falling all the way off of her face.

"What's wrong?" I asked, suddenly worried that something was happening that I didn't know about.

"Nothing, baby, I promise," she replied without hesitation, and her smile firmed up again.

But the worry was still there, hiding, behind that smile.

A cloud slipped across the sun, and the day was bathed in shadows. Premonition folded itself upon me, and stole my breath away for the space of a moment. Then the cloud passed by, and so did the feeling of complete unreality. What mattered was that Mom was here with me, and no matter what happened, things would be fine. I held onto that thought as she carried me through the main entrance, and back into the sterile, pastel-colored world that I had been born into.

"May I help you?" A thickset, matronly woman with kind eyes asked as Mom walked us up to the front desk.

"Yes, I have an appointment to have some tests run on my daughter." Mom shifted me to her other side so she could reach into her purse and pull out some cards that she pushed across the desk.

The woman took the proffered cards and began typing away at her computer. I loved the sound of clicking keys; whenever Mom was working at home, she would bring her laptop into my room and the constant *click-click-click* never failed to lull me to sleep. But not today. Instead of feeling calmed, each subsequent *click* seemed to hit a nervous place inside of me, ratcheting up my feeling of unease.

Soon enough, the older woman was handing the cards back across the counter. "Yes, of course Mrs. Oritt. If you'll just have a seat, we'll call you back in a second."

Mom thanked her, turned, and carried me into a big room full of ugly chairs (most of them empty), with a TV set in one corner playing a cartoon. No sooner had we sat down than a nurse, younger than Mom and with long, light brown hair, came out through a door marked **Staff Only** and came right over to us.

"Mrs. Oritt?" She asked politely.

We both looked up at her. Mom nodded.

"My name is Jessica Gardner, I'm the RN in charge today. I've been briefed on your situation and I just want you to know that I will be here through each step of testing today, and can answer any and all questions you have." Jessica delivered all of this in a warm voice, with a smile, and I trusted her instinctively.

Mom seemed to trust her as well, standing and holding out her hand. "Thank you Jessica, that is most appreciated. Please, call me Kristi." They shook hands, and some of my nervousness evaporated.

Jessica turned to me, white teeth flashing as her smile deepened. "And this must be Annie! Nurses and doctors here still tell stories about you! You made quite an impact on the staff here."

I smiled back at her, a little shyly. "Thank you," I said, struggling to enunciate as clearly as possible. It still grated on me that the rest of the world saw me as a baby, when I knew deep down that I was so much more. "When all of the tests are done, may I please have a lollipop?"

Mom and Jessica both laughed.

"Girl," Jessica said, reaching into one voluminous pocket and whipping out a sucker like it was a magic trick. "You can have one right now!" Yes, I liked Jessica. I stuck the sucker into my mouth as Mom followed Jessica through the **Staff Only** door and deeper into the hospital.

9

That day seemed to last a lifetime, and it was only with Mom and Jessica by my side that I was able to make it through it without a single tantrum.

I was hustled through room after room, surrounded by what seemed a small army of other people in white coats. I was poked and prodded. They took my temperature. They took my blood. They checked my blood pressure. I was put into a machine that made a weird humming noise and told not to move. I had wires attached to my chest so they could look at my heart on a computer. They took *more* blood!

Through it all, Jessica kept up a constant stream of questions to my mom, writing down the answers on a clipboard that held dozens of different papers. What was my weight. Had anything unusual happened since they had adopted me (that question had a looong answer). What were my sleeping habits. My eating habits. My bathroom habits! It was humiliating!

By the time the day was finally done, I felt like I had gone 12 rounds with Muhammad Ali (I didn't understand exactly what this meant, but I had heard Alex say it before, and going from his tone it seemed to apply to my situation). After Jessica had given me another lollipop, and told my mom that they would be in touch once the results came back, Mom carried me out of the hospital and back out into the world. It was freezing, and the snow had started back up again. After the closed in, sterile world of the hospital, the cold air on my cheeks was heaven. I was asleep before Mom finished buckling me into my seat.

"...nerve wracking." Mom was saying. I slowly blinked open my eyes and looked around. I was in my crib, two blankets deep. I felt like I was back in my birth mother's womb. Mom and Dad were standing above me.

When they saw I was awake, they smiled down at me. I smiled back, closed my eyes, and drifted off again, content.

10

Jeff brought two glasses of red wine into the living room, handed one to Kristi, and sat down next to her on the couch.

"Annie was, for lack of a better word, *perfect*, the whole time," Kristi said, taking a sip and settling back. The fire was roaring in the fireplace, and she felt the tension of the day starting to ease. "I mean, the grace and solemnity that girl portrayed, even as they were running a full scale assault of tests on her. It was simply unreal."

Jeff nodded, staring into the fire. "She's something...new. We've known that for a while now, but to see how she's been growing in such leaps and bounds. I think she's more of an adult than Jacob is, these days."

Kristi giggled into her wine. "Good lord, you're right. Maybe we should ask Annie to help Jacob with his college homework."

Jeff snorted. "Couldn't make it any worse than it is now. Hell, at least the homework would get worked on."

Kristi reached up a hand and brushed a few errant strands of hair behind her ear, face turning serious once more. "Do you know what the worst part of the hospital was? How do you tell a nurse 'No really, my daughter is perfect, but could you try to find something wrong, anyway?'"

"Nobody is that perfect," Jeff replied, shaking his head wearily. "I don't know what I'd rather have happen: that all the tests come back negative, once more leaving us in the dark as to what the true nature of our child is, or that something comes back positive, which would at least give us some kind of an answer."

Kristi fell silent, wine glass suddenly forgotten.

Minutes later, an eternity later, Jeff broke the silence. "Whatever happens, we'll face it together. As a family."

11

Less than a week later, Kristi and Jeff were back at the hospital. This time Annie had been left at home, to play games with Jacob and Maddy. Alex had gotten on a plane back to Miami the day before.

Jessica was sitting across the desk from them. The three of them were in Jessica's office, sparsely decorated but homey all the same. A few pictures of her family sat next to Jessica's computer, and a single oil painting of a forest landscape graced the wall behind her.

Jessica pulled out a tan folder stuffed thickly with papers and set it on the desk in front of her, then folded her hands over it. "Every single test came back negative."

Jeff and Kristi let out a collective breath of relief.

"That's the short answer," Jessica went on, looking from one to the other with a penetrating gaze. "The long answer begins with the fact that from all outward appearances, and inward, for that matter, your adopted daughter is nothing short of a medical marvel. We ran every single test we could think of. Echocardiogram, to check her heart. White blood cell count. Blood cultures. Head ultrasound. EKG. EEG. We tested her platelets. Arterial blood gas. Capillary blood gas. EVERYTHING. And she is, beyond any shadow of a doubt, perfect in every. Single. Way. More than perfect! The speed at which she's growing, physically *and* mentally." Jessica shook her head in consternation. "This just doesn't happen. Never has happened, in all of medical history. And because of this, because we don't have a single precedent to go on, we also have no idea how to predict what will happen in her future.

Will she continue to grow and develop at an accelerated rate until she hits puberty at age four, and then slow down to match the rest of us? Will she continue to develop beyond the natural borders and limitations of humanity? We have no idea. None. I could almost wish we *had* found something, if only so we had something concrete to work with."

Jeff and Kristi shared a look.

"That had crossed our minds, as well," Jeff said quietly.

Jessica sat back in her chair, expression unreadable, studying them both. After a second she sighed. "The only definitive thing we *did* find was in her stem cells. And what we found was remarkable. Beyond her powerhouse of a thymus gland, that we discovered during initial testing after her birth here, Annie *also* continues to produce embryonic stem cells, and at an accelerated rate. What's remarkable about this is that Annie is not, in fact, an embryo. She is an infant girl who should by all rights be about to enter junior high school. And her body is still rapidly producing embryonic stem cells. Let me ask you this: in the time that you've had Annie, has she ever been sick?"

Kristi shook her head. "Never. Not even a little head cold. Not even the *sniffles*."

"I didn't think so. What about injuries? Babies, infants, as soon as they start crawling, they start running into things. Getting little scratches, bumps, bruises. Have you ever noticed a bruise that stuck around long enough to go through the healing process of changing colors?"

"No," Jeff answered this time. "She's always so careful. I don't think she's had a single accident."

"Let me tell you what I think," Jessica said, leaning forward in her chair again. "I think that if she *did* experience a little accident or injury, I think she would wake up the next day without a mark on her. *That* is how remarkable her stem cell development is. When you brought Annie in for testing, and we drew blood, the skin closed back up almost before we could get the needle out. You both know that during initial NICU testing last year, we renamed her blood type AZ, because of the accelerated, chimeric T cells that her thymus gland was pumping into her bloodstream. What we didn't know then, because testing wouldn't at that time have shown anything abnormal, is that her embryonic stem cells had somehow been affected, as well." Jessica looked down, and seemed suddenly to remember the tan folder. She pushed it across the table. "These charts represent Annie's updated medical history. My official recommendation to you is that you bring her in every few months so that we can track her progress. My *un*official recommendation is that you keep this under wraps as long as you possibly can, unless you want to be on the cover of every medical journal in the world, and maybe US magazine as well. If this gets out, the medical world will never, ever leave you alone. Your daughter is going to shake the world."

12

That was what my life was to become for the next four years. Every three months, Mom or Dad or both would take me to Primary Children's, and I would go through a repeat of every test they could think of to run on me. And every single time, the results were the same.
Normal.
Perfect.
Unexplainable.
Every time we went, it was nurse Jessica who took care of me. She became something of a favorite aunt, a cherished extended member of my family. I became less and less nervous with each visit to the hospital, because I knew that Jessica would be there standing as a bulwark between that cold, sterile world, and fragile, little me.
Yes, I was still little. At least on the outside. My brain seemed much too large for my body when I thought about it, but outwardly I continued to look as I should (or rather, as society said that I should). This was something of a surprise, because nurse Jessica at first hypothesized that considering how my body was functioning on the inside, it should show with accelerated growth on the outside. But thankfully, that is something that never came to pass. And as I met others outside of my family unit (friends of my siblings, for example, who came over to dinner once in a while, or people from the OUTSIDE WORLD when Mom or Dad would take me with them on errands) I began to realize how very important it was that all of my changes were only happening on the inside. How would Mom or Dad explain to a friend how I was growing too fast? At least with my growing happening on the inside, I learned how to control what I showed the OUTSIDE WORLD.

That was how I began to think of it. I had my INSIDE WORLD, which consisted of my family, and nurse Jessica, and other hospital people who by necessity needed to be kept 'in the know'. With my INSIDE WORLD, I was allowed to be exactly who I was. I could speak as much as I wanted, and use words with as many syllables as I pleased (I recently learned the word MISAPPROPRIATION; I loved saying it just to feel the syllables rolling off of my tongue).

But with the OUTSIDE WORLD, I must show an intellect (or lack thereof, considering my young age) that matches what the OUTSIDE WORLD expected. I learned (much to my own disgust) how to make baby sounds. Though it made me writhe inside, I perfected the smile of a simpleton while allowing things like "Goo goo" and "Ga ga" to escape my mouth. What a joke this life seemed at times!

But what made it all worth it, at the end of the day, was the utter and complete acceptance of my adopted family (yes, I learned early on the meaning of the word ADOPTED; no, it didn't bother me one whit). My adopted family didn't care that my brain was growing at hitherto unknown speeds. Maddy didn't care that I was helping her with her math homework instead of Dad. Jacob didn't care that I could beat him in chess before I turned 3. And Alex didn't care that I now knew more about the globe than he did, though he did point out every so often that he was the one to start me on my obsession of understanding the world around me.

Was my life hard? Absolutely.

But it was perfect, too.

13

When I turned 5, on an absolutely frigid New Years Day, 2008, I received gifts that no normal 5 year old would even dream of asking for. I had learned through the use of media (TV, mostly; even though it seemed fairly boring most of the time, I still recognized how useful it was in showing me what the OUTSIDE WORLD expected from each gender at each age) that 5 year old girls asked for things like dolls, and clothes, and shiny things. I had zero interest in these stereotypical objects.

What I continued to crave above all else was knowledge. I had by this time memorized what our world looks like: peoples, cultures, languages. Things that define us as we make our way through the world as an unruly mass of individuals that are overcrowding this planet. All thanks to an offhand comment from Alex years ago about how far away Florida is from Utah.

Thanks to Jacob, I had developed an interest in outer space. I had devoured books on our solar system and the planets within its boundaries. I learned about the difference between planets and stars, and how incredibly lucky we were to even have a planet that was habitable for human life. I was fascinated with the idea that the universe *just kept going*. Forever. It made me feel infinitesimally small, while at the same time, as precious and unique as a single snowflake in a blizzard. Suffice to say, Neal Degrasse Tyson became my role model.

But I wanted so much more. I didn't just want to know about different peoples, I wanted to know the governing rules behind them. The reasons for why we do the things we do. The reasons why there are so many things we *can't* do. And so I was beyond delighted when I unwrapped Dad's gift to reveal a book that seemed to weigh as much as I did, titled The Court and The World. Dad said that if I actually enjoying this page-turning thriller (delivered in quite the sarcastic but smiling voice) then I was welcome to help myself to his own personal law library. I was ecstatic, and all for ending my party right then and there so I could start reading.

From my other family members came books no less exciting in their own way.

Biographies from Mom.

Histories from Maddy.

Alternative energy solutions (non fiction, of course) from Alex.

And from Jacob, the self proclaimed comic book nerd, a historically accurate account of World War 2 and the Nazi labor camps, as told from the perspective of mice and cats, in graphic novel form. Jacob went on to explain that while he supported my quest for knowledge, it was also important to have 'fun' hobbies as well, and he hoped that he could bring me around to the wide world of superheroes. I promised I'd consider it.

It was one of the last perfect moments in my INSIDE WORLD. Because, you see, the OUTSIDE WORLD was about to come knocking.

2008 was the year I started kindergarten.

14

From my nearly obsessive study of current media, I knew that most children tend to feel scared about starting school. They worry about leaving the comforting embrace of their parents, and the familiar rooms of their homes. They panic over the day to day schedule of their lives being turned upside down and inside out. But I would be willing to give my last tooth (only my first set; I wasn't willing to part with my adult teeth once they started coming in) that I was the only child there at my brand new kindergarten (appropriately named Kids Kampus) who was afraid that I wouldn't act childish enough in front of my new peers, and the adult teachers.

My fear wasn't wholly my own. I knew that Mom and Dad were as nervous as a couple of cats in a room full of rocking chairs. Sure, they tried to comfort me and tell me that everything would be fine, and that they were just a phone call away should anything go awry, but I could see the truth in the way the skin around their eyes tightened with suppressed worry, and in the way their eyes flicked to one another and back to me when they thought I wasn't paying attention.

But that's part of my curse. I'm always paying attention. As my brain continues to move faster and faster, I find myself unable to 'switch off'. I don't have the gift of childish ignorance. Today is one day that I really wish I did.

On that fateful morning (August 28th, to be exact) Mom helped me get dressed in my new school clothes, and off we went to Kids Kampus for me to begin my formal education. Which in of itself was a joke; my education began the day I was brought home to my new family. But I couldn't very well start applying to colleges just yet.

I will say this about Kids Kampus: the place was built to put kids at ease. As we pulled up to the front of the school, I was immediately charmed by the sprawling connected buildings with a sign that read Kids Kampus in a fair imitation of a child's loose and lazy writing. If you're familiar with the variety of fonts available on Microsoft Word, picture Comic Sans and you won't be far off.

In front of the main building was a perfectly cultivated little park. Tall, leafy trees (oak, unless I missed my guess), white picnic tables, white benches, and even a big jungle gym, complete with a swirling slide in a friendly mix of white, blue, and red. While butterflies still rolled around in my stomach, the sight of such a school at least lessened the violence with which they were crashing into each other.

Mom parked and we disembarked into the loosely organized chaos of the first day of school. Kids running around and screaming, parents cajoling and hugging and reassuring their kids, teachers reassuring the parents.

I loved it.

Up until this point, I had only really had friendly interactions with my family (and the hospital staff, of course). This wasn't the fault of my parents whatsoever. I was the one who had never really had any interest in making friends my own age, because I always assumed that due to the uniqueness of my mind, I wouldn't have anything in common with other children. Well, there's one thing that transcends intelligence: playtime!

By the time Mom had found my new teacher and introduced herself, I had already gone down the slide three times and met another girl whom I later discovered was in my classroom. Her name was Beckie, and we became immediate confidantes with the ease and innocence of children who have barely begun to interact with the world.

Beckie and I were the exact same size, but different in every other way. I was fair skinned to the point where Mom said that I tended to glow when the light hit me just right, and Beckie was so perfectly dark skinned that she seemed to shimmer like onyx. I had long, white-blonde hair that was always pulling loose from my ponytails and wisping around my face; Beckie had kinky, curly black hair that framed her ever-smiling face in a tight cap. My eyes were bright blue, while hers were dark coals that burned mischievously.

Best of all, in the first few minutes of conversation with her, I could already tell that she was smart like me! Well, maybe not *exactly* like me, but close enough to make me feel less like an outsider.

On our last mad rush down the swirly slide (our last for that moment, only because both of our moms were calling our names and a bell was ringing somewhere) Beckie took the final turn with a little too much exuberance and ended up bouncing off of the end of the slide and going down on her knees on the wood chips at the bottom. I was right behind her and rolled off to one side so I wouldn't crash into her. When we both came to a stop, arms and legs akimbo, I was fine (as always). Beckie, however, had gotten a little scrape on her right knee that started oozing blood immediately.

Beckie climbed up to her feet, brown eyes already bright with unshed tears, although she was trying to hold them back and look strong in front of me. I looked around for our moms but saw that they had their heads together and were smiling, probably talking about how cute we looked, or some such casual conversation. I looked back at Beckie and smiled reassuringly, wanting to help but not knowing how (just because I'm overly intelligent doesn't mean I've got my doctorate).

"Don't worry," I offered confidently. "It doesn't look so bad."

With an instinct I didn't understand, I leaned down and touched the palm of my hand to her scraped knee. As I touched her injury, I felt something like static electricity that seemed to pass through me and into her. I looked up at her again, and her eyes were wide.

We both looked down as I pulled my hand away.

The skin knitted back together before our astonished eyes.

15

The first half of the day sped by and I barely remember anything that happened. Our new teacher spent most of the time talking about what school would be like, what kind of activities we would get to take advantage of, and then gave us a tour of the building. It was all very nice and pleasant, but I couldn't keep my mind on it for more than a second at a time.

I knew Beckie was in the same place, mentally, that I was. As luck would have it, we got seated next to each other, and more than once I would glance over at her to catch her staring at me. Not with fear, thankfully. I don't think I could have taken that. More with wonder. And she kept furtively scratching at her knee, although I knew that there was nothing there to scratch. I can only assume she was feeling some kind of phantom itch, like I imagine an amputee might experience.

At long last, lunch arrived! Beckie and I grabbed the bag lunches our moms had made for us and trooped into the cafeteria with the rest of our class, where we immediately sequestered ourselves at a table in one corner of the big, colorful room that was filled with yellow tables and yelling children.

"What did you do?" Beckie asked, voice brimming with curiosity, the moment we sat down. "You fixed me!"

I shrugged, too excited to feel uncomfortable. "I don't know. I've never been hurt myself, and I think I just kind of...gave...that to you."

She cocked her head to the side, rolling that idea around. "Really? You've never gotten hurt?"

I shook my head.

"Have you ever been sick?"

I shook my head again.

Another long beat. And then "Does that mean I'll never get hurt again?"

Now that was an interesting idea. "I...I don't know. Maybe?"

With a serious expression that defied her young age, she nodded immediately, decisively. "Ok. I won't tell anyone. This can be our secret!"

We both smiled, and then tore into our sandwiches. I felt more hungry than usual and, judging from the way Beckie worked her way through her lunch, so did she. Something to think about, later.

Another thought that flickered through my mind like quicksilver, there and then gone, was a simple one: was this my purpose? To heal?

Interesting.

Later on, after Mom had picked me up and I was telling her all about my day, and my new friend, I felt a little guilty about holding back on that moment on the playground. But I decided that it was more important to keep this a secret.

Besides, what seemed most important in that moment was that I had successfully navigated through this new world of school, and not a single person (excepting Beckie, of course) suspected for a second that I was anything more than I seemed. I knew how to speak like a normal 5 year old, I interacted well with the other kids, and the teachers loved me for being so 'mature for my age'. Not just important to me, but important to Mom and Dad, too. The more I changed, the easier it became for me to read people's facial expressions, and Mom and Dad were both bursting with relief.

What none of us knew at the time, but would learn all too soon, was that I had already set something in motion when I healed Beckie. Something that I wouldn't be able to take back, no matter how much I might wish I could in the years to come. The world would change, had already experienced the first change in what would become a wildfire.

I was the catalyst.

16

While Annie was recounting to her mom the fun (and safe) time she'd had on her first day at school, Beckie was doing the same at her house. She was sitting at the dinner table, surrounded by her mom, dad, and two older sisters, both of whom were in middle school and as such accounted themselves full of worldly wisdom and light years ahead of their baby sister. Kendra was in 8th grade, Iris was in 7th grade, and both of them had been suffering from a mild head cold that was making the rounds at their middle school. Iris, who was 12 (and forever resentful that she was younger than Kendra by just a single year) had been hit the hardest, and while she felt well enough to be joining the family at the dinner table, she did so with a handy box of tissues to keep her personal grossness (her words) at a minimum.

Beckie, who just that morning had felt the warning tickle at the back of her throat that heralded the arrival of her own sickness, now felt better than ever. She, too, cherished the miraculous secret that she shared with her new friend Annie, and didn't share it with her family. Besides, she reasoned, it's not like they would believe her, anyway. Grownups never did.

Beckie's mother, Trini, was beaming with pride at her youngest daughter as she recounted her day, as her father, Steven, walked around the table, placing a plate of pan-seared chicken on a bed of rice and broccoli in front of each member of his family.

"...and then the teacher said that we would have arts and crafts every single day!" Beckie finished in a rush. Her passion, for the last month, had been painting, ever since Trini had shown her an episode of Bob Ross on Netflix.

"That's wonderful!" Trini gushed. Trini was an artist herself, and had always hoped to pass her passion down to one of her daughters. It had been for naught with Kendra and Iris, who were both much more interested in whatever the boys at their school were doing, but Trini hoped to nurture Beckie's interest and have another painter in the family.

Beckie, who hadn't paused to take a full breath since she had started telling everyone about her new school and friends, realized how thirsty she was. Not paying attention to the layout of the table, she reached for the water glass to her right, lifted it with both hands, and gulped down nearly half of it before Iris noticed and grabbed it back.

"That's MY water, Beckie, and I don't want your germs. Yours is on the left. Geez." Iris took a drink from the reclaimed glass before setting it down on the other side of her plate, away from Beckie. She wouldn't notice any effect until the next day, but as the water that had been contaminated by Beckie's 'germs' slid down her throat, the new thing that was inside of Beckie attacked the disease that was lining her esophagus, destroying the diseased cells and rapidly replacing them with healthy ones. By the time Iris woke up the next morning, she would feel perfectly healthy again.

Beckie, in response to Iris snatching away the water glass, simply rolled her eyes, grabbed the water glass to her left, and resumed drinking. Dinner went on like nothing out of the ordinary had happened. After all, the three girls were always sniping at each other for something or other. They were at that age where everything seemed to turn into at least a little bit of a fight. Trini and Steven just hoped they'd grow out of it one day.

17

The next day, Kendra got to stay home from school because her head cold had taken a turn for the worse. With a fever of 103 degrees, the only place Trini was willing to take her oldest daughter was an Urgent Care clinic to make sure Kendra didn't have something more serious. Iris, however, was back in perfect health, and off she went to Bryant Middle School.

In her homeroom class before the bell rang, Iris gave her best friend Alana a hug of commiseration. Alana had the sniffles, and was worried about getting as sick as so many other kids (and teachers) were that week. They hugged exuberantly, as children do, cheek to cheek. As they separated, Alana reached up and swiped a bare forearm across her face to wipe her running nose.

By second period, Alana felt perfectly healthy, and thought nothing of it. With the short attention span of pre-teens, she forgot that she had even been feeling a little sick. Later that night, Alana's mom gave her a kiss as she tucked her into bed. Alana's mother, too, had been feeling the sniffles, as minor diseases such as head colds and the flu tended to ravage families whole.

The following day, Alana's mother had to call in sick, as her sniffles had progressed to a raw throat and a pounding headache.

18

By the time October rolled in, there wasn't a single sick child to be found at Kids Kampus.

Or Bryant Middle School.

Or any of the neighboring elementary and middle schools where children from Bryant and Kids Kampus had other friends that they interacted with regularly.

19

December of 2008 found the entirety of Salt Lake City without a single child under the age of 15 that displayed symptoms of any kind of sickness. The only children calling in sick to their schools were kids that had faked illness to get out of school, and had parents gullible enough to believe it.

In point of fact, not a single of those sickness-free children had any injuries to complain of, either.

20

On January 1st, 2009, when Annie turned 6, another girl who lived on the other side of Salt Lake City turned 15, and puberty came knocking.

The girl's name was Bella.

She was sickness-free. Injury-free. Practically perfect in every way. As healthy as any parent could wish for their child.

Bella died.

Part 2: The Trial (The Year 2018)

1

IN THE THIRD JUDICIAL DISTRICT COURT

CALVIN MICHAELS, et al.
    Defendants
    Vs
STATE OF UTAH
    Plaintiffs

        CASE NUMBER:
        COB34-24601

        June 1, 2018

2

    This was the beginning of what would become the biggest trial the world had ever seen. The defendant, Calvin Michaels, was the biological father of little Orphan Annie, adopted by the Oritt family and raised with love and care until the age of 15, when she died as mysteriously as the rest of those children afflicted by what had come to be called the Angel Virus.

    Calvin Michaels was not only Annie and Grace's biological father, he was also the doctor who delivered the twin girls before vanishing into the night with Grace and leaving Annie behind. But most importantly, Calvin Michaels had admitted to being the geneticist behind the world changing modification of his twin daughters while they were still in the womb. His prenatal DNA altering work on his twins brought about the scourge that was the Angel Virus, making him personally responsible for the annihilation of nearly a quarter of the population.

    On the planet.

    Before Annie (known throughout the trial as Patient Zero), the world population stood at around 7.25 billion people, with population growth trending upward at a faster and faster rate with each passing year. Many people, especially those in the scientific community, speculated that the Earth would pass it's global tipping point by the year 2045, if not sooner.

    Roughly 42% of that 7.25 billion were considered to be in the Youth category (those under the age of 25). 25% (give or take a percentage point) were in the Adolescent category (those under the age of 15). Calvin Michaels, through his daughter, Patient Zero, decimated that category.

    Dr. Michaels, in the beginning of 2018, turned himself in and admitted to everything, saying only that he demanded a fair trial in order to explain himself in front of a jury of his peers, before accepting the foregone conclusion of such a trial. Given the nature of his willing arrest, an initial appearance and arraignment in court was pushed to the side, and his case went straight to trial by jury.

    Jeffrey Oritt, adoptive father of Annie and state attorney general of Utah, volunteered to be the plaintiff's attorney (in this case it was thought best that the CDC would be labeled as the plaintiff, since their organization was the first to discover the Angel Virus for what it was and what it represented).

The first witness called to bear testimony was Dr. Jackson Telford, lead genetic researcher for the CDC and the first of many medical personnel to look into and study the Angel Virus, searching desperately for a cure that wouldn't be found.

June 1st, 2018, the first day of the trial, dawned bright and sunny, not a cloud to be seen in the azure sky above Salt Lake City. The sun was almost mocking as it sat perched above the green and brown Wasatch Mountains to the east of the city, as a day like today should, by all rights, be overcast and gloomy, to set the tone for the macabre scene about to take place.

The trial was set to unfold at the Third Judicial District Court, an imperious white marble building located in the heart of downtown Salt Lake City. Due to the nature of the trial, it would be closed to the public, as one might assume, for the safety of the defendant until sentence could be passed. That didn't mean the courtroom wasn't filled from corner to corner, with medical professionals, reporters, witnesses waiting to be called, and representatives from the Department of Justice.

Everything started off like any other trial. The plaintiff for the State of Utah (which was the CDC as represented by its director, Richard Matheson) entered the courtroom with prosecuting attorney Jeffrey Oritt. Then the defendant, Calvin Michaels, with his state appointed defense attorney Gabriel Conklin.

The minute Jeff laid eyes upon Calvin, his hands twitched of their own volition, wanting to wrap around the man's throat and squeeze until there was no more need for this sham of a trial. Jeff restrained himself from leaping over the plaintiff's box and doing just that, but barely.

The judge presiding over the case, the Honorable Judge Erikson, then called in the twelve men and women of the jury. They entered and seated themselves one by one.

The trial began.

3

Jeffrey rose to his feet with dignity even as a fire smoldered within his breast. He was dressed in a smart, three piece dark blue suit, with a blue striped tie. Annie had given him that tie for his birthday last year, and he thought it fitting to be wearing it today.

As prosecuting attorney, it was Jeff who would give the opening statement, which he had worked on long and hard in order to keep all emotion out of it. He approached the jury, took a deep breath, and began the process of sending the defendant to a justly deserved death.

"Good morning, my name is Jeff Oritt, and it is my honor and privilege to represent the Centers for Disease Control and Prevention and the state of Utah and serve as a prosecutor on this most important case. In the year 2002, the defendant in this matter admitted to what he has described as gene alteration on his then-pregnant wife. Said wife was pregnant with twins, and the gene altering allegedly changed the genetic makeup of one of the twin girls. The defendant's wife passed away shortly after childbirth. One of the twins was born on the verge of death herself, until it was discovered by the defendant, who was also the doctor who birthed the girls, that her life could be saved via a blood transfusion from the healthy twin.

"The transfusion worked, and the sickly twin recovered at a pace the medical team called 'miraculous'. This should be a story with a happy ending. It's not. The defendant, again by his own admission, then absconded with one of the twins, neither of whom had been seen until the defendant came forward of his own free will to admit to his role in the pandemic of the Angel Virus that has decimated our global population.

"The defendant claims that he engineered the Angel Virus himself, turning his own daughter into Patient Zero. He is responsible for the premeditated murder of 25% of the global population. 1.8 billion people, *children*, are dead."

At these words there was a combined gasp of shock from the jury box. The members of the jury had been picked because they didn't have any children who had been affected by the Angel Virus, and would therefore be somewhat more impartial in the trial. The jurors knew of the horror of the Angel Virus, but it was hard nonetheless to wrap your mind around that number. 1.8 *billion*. And the man who claimed responsibility sat not 20 feet away from them.

Jeff turned and looked at the defendant, sitting calmly next to his attorney at the defendant's table on the other side of the aisle, and had to push down another surge of rage. He turned back to the jury box and continued.

"At the conclusion of the case, and after you have heard all the evidence, we are confident that you will return a verdict of guilty."

The defense attorney, at the request of the defendant, declined to make an opening statement.

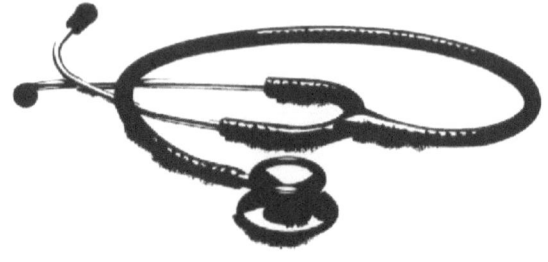

Part 3: A Curse (The Year 2009)

1

    That first death on January 1st, 2009, didn't elicit a panic. Didn't draw any kind of response at all. People die every day, right? Yes, this one was a medical mystery. Yes, Bella was completely healthy. Yes, the autopsy turned up nothing unusual whatsoever. But it was just one more death in a world of constant biological turnover. The parents were grief-stricken and confused, but that's where it ended.
    For the time being.

2

    In their second semester at Kids Kampus, Annie and Beckie were thick as thieves. From that very first day when Annie had inexplicably healed Beckie, that secret had bonded them together. As the months passed, and Beckie's intelligence began to grow faster than the other children around them, Annie was thrilled. Here at last was someone else like her! Someone to share her journey! Yes, she had her family, and her family knew what was happening (to the extent that any of them really knew or understood), but it wasn't the same as having a friend the same age who was going through the same thing.

Her family, likewise, was excited not only that Annie was navigating the Outside World with such alacrity, but that she had made a real friend! And when Beckie was over at the Oritt's house for a playdate and began to show the same signs of higher intelligence as their adopted daughter, well, it was an easy thing to turn a blind eye to, as all of the Oritts had become somewhat inured to Annie's mature behavior already. Seeing that same maturity in Beckie, the other Oritts assumed that Annie was just having a positive effect on her new friend.

If they only knew.

3

Beckie's life, unfortunately, became harder in ways that she couldn't have foreseen. It was so easy for her to spend time at the Oritt's, because they already understood something of what Annie was, and so they naturally passed along that understanding to Beckie when she spent time over at their house. But it was much more difficult with her own family.

Beckie's family was wonderful, from an outsider's perspective. Her mother and father, Trini and Steven, had a loving marriage, and were very caring to their three children. Her older sisters were, well, they were ok. They were both in middle school, which meant that they both tended to act a little imperious and snooty around her, assuming they knew so much more of the world than she did. After all, they were teenagers! At least, Kendra was. She had turned 13 a few months ago. Iris wouldn't turn 13 until late summer this year, but she acted like she was closer to 20 than 13. And with Beckie being *so far below* them at age 6, they sometimes treated her like she was still in diapers.

Then Annie had changed her. And Beckie had passed along that change to her sisters, yes, but considering they were a lot closer to maturity than Beckie was, the change to her sisters was more minimal.

All her parents seemed to notice was that both Kendra and Iris were getting more A's than C's in school, and they were overjoyed! They attributed it to the two girls finally buckling down and studying more. Kendra and Iris attributed it, arrogantly, to natural intelligence coming with their burgeoning maturity.

Beckie *felt* her changes a lot more keenly. She was becoming increasingly bored at Kids Kampus, with their emphasis on basic arts, student interaction, and an overabundance of playtime. Like Annie had once expressed to her family at a much younger age, Beckie wanted to *learn*! Really learn about the world around her, not just about which crayons she should use during art 'class'.

At first, Beckie had been excited about reading and writing. But then her reading skills had skyrocketed above the baby books that all the other kids were stuck on. And her handwriting looked more adult and professional than most of the teachers at the school.

One day in late January, before school started, Beckie pulled Annie aside at the colorful coat rack where the other kids were milling around en masse.

"I'm scared," Beckie announced without preamble.

Annie's eyes widened. "About what? Did something happen?"

"*We* are happening!" Beckie hissed urgently. "We don't belong here anymore! My handwriting is better than most of the adults here, but I still have to practice my ABC's almost every day. My reading level is at *least* equal to the adults here as well, and probably above some of them. I stole a copy of Mrs. Johnson's *US Weekly* just to have something 'mature' to read, and I didn't get more than five pages in before I gave it back in disgust. Do you know the stupid things that grown ups occupy their time with?"

"Yeah," Annie replied with a grimace. "I've spent my fair share of time flipping through all the magazines at the hospital when I go there for my regular testing, and it's pretty bad."

"Are we just going to have to continue faking it throughout the rest of our childhood? Because I honestly don't know if I can do that. When can we tell people that we're child prodigies and start skipping up through the grades?"

Annie looked around at all the children running around and playing like only young, carefree children can. "Look at them," she said, gesturing at the shameless mayhem surrounding the two changed girls. "What do you see?"

Beckie glanced over her shoulder, giving their classmates a cursory once over. "Kids. I see kids without a care in the world and barely a brain in their respective heads."

Annie leaned in. "*Really* look at them. Look at them as individuals, not as a group."

Beckie sighed, but she turned around and studied the other children. And she finally saw what Annie was trying to show her.

Taken as a whole, the dozens of kids in front of her looked like a pile of barely organized chaos. But looking at them individually, Beckie picked out a boy standing off to the side with his head buried in a *Time* magazine, undoubtedly stolen from his parents. A pair of girls near the drinking fountain were purposefully standing apart from the other kids, with identical looks of consternation on their plump, cherubic faces as they surveyed the other children, much as Annie and Beckie were doing. And another boy was at the chalkboard just outside their classroom door writing out math formulas. Not 2 + 2, but actual formulas. Beckie looked closer and realized it was the Pythagorean Theorem.

She gasped as the realization hit home.

"Yes," Annie said softly. "We're not the only ones changing. It's spreading. I can feel it inside me, almost as if I'm connected to them."

Beckie turned back to Annie as a new realization rocked her. "My sisters. They haven't gotten sick since you changed me."

Annie nodded. "They have it now, too. So when you ask me how long we're going to have to continue the charade of acting like we're 6 year olds, instead of adults with fully matured and, dare I say, *above* average intelligence? No, I don't think we'll have to continue that much longer."

Beckie smiled. The smile faded quickly. "So then...what happens next?"

Annie shook her head slowly. "I don't know. But it will be big."

4

In February of 2009, another two dozen perfect teenagers turned 15 and died inexplicably. People started to talk. Hospitals began to dig deeper, looking for answers to a possible new disease that didn't leave a trace on the body. Panic hadn't yet begun, but it was edging closer, like a predator stalking its prey.

5

In March of 2009, the as yet unnamed virus spread into the neighboring states of Colorado, Wyoming, and Nevada, as well as several regions of Mexico, from kids going on family vacations over Spring Break.

6

On a Friday in early May, with less than a month to go before summer vacation began, Annie finally came to the conclusion that she needed to tell her parents what was going on. At first, when it had just been her and Beckie, she thought it wise to keep this secret. But now all of Kids Kampus had been changed, to one degree or another. Some kids manifested a new maturity more rapidly than others, but anyone with their eyes open could see that their school didn't look like a school for toddlers anymore. It looked like a senior class of tiny, waddling high schoolers preparing to enter college.
And for those kids like Beckie who had been changed at the onset, they looked like they were nearly ready to defend dissertations.
The one thing that had stopped any big reveal (yet) to the outside world was quite simple: adults, with predetermined views on what the world *should* look like, tend to see just that. So while more and more teens around the tri-state area were turning 15 and dying for no reason, the general public hadn't gotten wind of it. It was still a case by case situation due to geographical region and relative distance between families that were losing children, rather than an epidemic that would inevitably lead to global panic.
The other factor that played into Annie's decision to tell her parents was this: she watched the news. Every day. Sometimes twice. Jeff and Kristi had given her a small TV to keep in her room when they saw that she was interested in channels like Animal Planet and the Discovery Channel, rather than being obsessed with cartoons like regular children.
These days, when Annie turned on the late night news when the rest of the family had gone to bed, she began seeing sound bytes being dropped almost casually in between stories of heroic firemen

and politics updates. Sound bytes related to 'mysterious deaths' whose natures were 'unknown', with 'investigations ongoing'.

Annie was of course intelligent enough to read between the lines. The instant she heard one anchorman say something about the fatality in question being a medical mystery due to lack of illness or reason, she knew.

She *knew*.

Annie didn't know exactly how she knew, but she did, beyond a shadow of a doubt. The kids that were dying had been changed, and while she wasn't able to put all the pieces together, still she realized that it was *her* change that had done this. At the very least, it was *her* change that had become the catalyst that had led to these mysterious deaths.

She had to roll the dice and tell her parents, because (and this last part was the most important to her) maybe then she could become part of the solution, instead of the problem.

The problem that was somehow killing people and leaving no trace behind.

7

"Mom? Dad?" Annie walked into her parents bedroom on the second floor of their house.

It was 8 in the evening, and Jeff and Kristi were both lying in bed. Kristi was reading a murder mystery that had just come out, while Jeff was trying to make some progress through a stack of magazines that had been ignored for a few weeks due to a monster of a Stephen King book that had until recently been occupying his attention.

Jeff looked over at Annie and smiled. "What's up, hon?"

Annie walked around their bed and pulled herself up into the big recliner next to their TV. "I have to tell you something. Something that happened at school."

Jeff and Kristi instantly wore matching expressions of concern.

"What happened?" Kristi asked. "Is it about you? Has someone said something, or noticed anything?"

Annie looked down at the floor, suddenly ashamed that she hadn't told them right away, right after she had changed Beckie.

"Well, none of the teachers have noticed or said anything, but it *is* about me. See, at the beginning of school, when I met Beckie..."

The whole story came out. Speaking slowly at first, but with increasing speed, Annie told them of how she had inadvertently healed Beckie without even realizing what she was doing, and how Beckie had begun to mentally grow at the same rate she did. How Annie and Beckie, through contact with other children at Kids Kampus, had spread that change, like the flu or a cold, passing it along from child to child until every single one of them at the school was exhibiting the same change in behavior and mental aptitude.

And yet, not a single one of the adults. Only the kids.

"...and I've been watching the news and hearing about teenagers dying mysteriously, and it got me thinking, if I changed Beckie, and then the change spread throughout our school, then it stands to reason that those kids are going to their respective homes and spreading it to their siblings, to their friends. Whatever is inside of me seems to only be able to be passed to other children, but do you know how many children are in this city? In this country? In the whole world?" Annie was crying silently, terrified of the implications of what was happening.

But she was more terrified of what her parents would think of her.

Thankfully the latter fear was mollified right away. Kristi got out of bed, scooped Annie up in her arms, and held her close against her chest.

"Annie, there is nothing wrong with you," Kristi said soothingly, rocking Annie back and forth. "And you are *not* responsible for anyone dying! You know people die every day, right?"

Annie nodded, head buried against Kristi's shoulder.

"Sometimes doctors don't understand right away why a person has died," Jeff jumped in. "But that doesn't mean that there is any kind of super flu going around, and it *certainly* doesn't mean that you're the cause of it! If you are spreading what you have inside of you to the other kids at Kids Kampus, that's not a bad thing. It's a *wonderful* thing, honey. This world needs more intelligence and maturity, and it sounds like you are blessing them with it. Now, if you really are worried about it, we can schedule an appointment at Primary Children's and ask them some questions. Would that help put your mind at ease?"

Annie nodded again, feeling a weight lifting off of her tiny shoulders.

"Would you also like us to talk to Beckie's parents? Maybe they could bring her into Primary Children's as well, see if you two share the same wonderful gift."

Annie finally looked up at her parents, unclenching her fists from Kristi's sweater.

Kristi smiled down at her. "We will make some calls first thing in the morning and put this whole thing to bed. But first, I'm putting YOU to bed!" Kristi spun Annie around and then raced out of the bedroom and down the hall, making airplane noises.

Jeff closed his eyes and felt an icy tendril of fear snake its way up his spine.

Dear god he thought. *What if Annie's right?*

8

The death toll had risen to over 500, and the CDC was about to get its first phone call.

9

The following morning, shortly before a hospital in Santa Monica, CA made a hesitant call to the CDC (less of a call to arms and more of a check in about the strange deaths that were mounting around the country, and whether or not the CDC had any information to share on that score), Jeff and Kristi were placing their own call to Primary Children's hospital. As luck would have it, their favorite nurse had just come on shift and was immediately handed the phone from the charge nurse at the front desk of the NICU.

"Hey there!" Jessica's voice was cheery and laden with caffeine. "How are you guys? Is everything ok? I don't think you have another appointment scheduled for another week or two."

"Everything is fine, at least on the surface," Jeff answered after a brief pause. Kristi stood at his shoulder. Gone were the smiles that they had been wearing the night before to ease Annie's mind as she unburdened herself of her secret. After Kristi had put

Annie to bed, she and Jeff had stayed up and gone over Annie's incredible story again and again, trying to put the pieces together and figure out what it could mean. Trying to figure out the repercussions. Trying to convince themselves it couldn't, just *couldn't*, be related to the mysterious deaths happening all over.

There was a longer pause on Jessica's end. When she spoke, all traces of good humor had vanished as the professional nurse in her took over. "Did something happen? Do you need to bring Annie in?"

"If you have a free appointment in your schedule today, we *would* like to bring her in," Jeff answered the latter question first. "As to something happening, that's what we are trying to figure out."

Jeff heard the phone shifting hands on the other end of the line, and then the sound of keys being tapped at a rapid fire pace.

"How about you bring her up in about an hour? Does that work?"

Jeff mouthed *An hour* to his wife, who nodded. "That would be perfect. There *is* one more thing, though, that I wanted to let you know in advance. Whatever it is that is inside of Annie, causing her maturity, her mental growth, the whole shebang...Annie thinks that she somehow passed that on to another student, a friend of hers at her preschool." He refrained from mentioning the entire scenario that Annie had painted, that somehow the *entire school* was now maturing at a speed hitherto unheard of. "Is that even possible?"

Another pause. Then "Is there any chance you can bring this friend in as well? The only way to ascertain if Annie is somehow contagious in some unknown way would be to test the friend."

"Hang on just a sec." Jeff put his hand over the receiver and leaned over to Kristi. "Jessica wants us to bring in Beckie as well so they can run tests on both of them."

Kristi frowned. "How do we justify to Beckie's parents that we want to take her to the hospital?"

Jeff's forehead creased as he quickly thought it over. "Today's Saturday. We could have Annie invite her over for a playdate, then say we forgot about a doctor's appointment for Annie and just bring her along?" He put the phone back up to his ear. "I think we might be able to manage it, but I don't know what testing you would be able to do without getting the permission of the other girl's parents."

Jessica was obviously prepared for this. "We don't need to do any specific testing today, I think from what you're describing I could just speak with the other girl and see what happens. If it seems like she really is like Annie, it should be pretty obvious, and then we can figure out the next step from there."

Kristi, who had her ear right up next to the receiver by this point to catch the other side of the phone conversation, nodded.

"Yes, all right, I think we can manage that," Jeff responded. "We'll see you in about an hour." Hanging up the phone, he reached out and pulled Kristi in for a brief hug. "Ok," he said with a sigh. "Let's go talk to Annie. At least we'll know one way or another, right?"

Five minutes later Annie was on the phone with Beckie, inviting her over for a playdate.

10

"You have reached the Centers for Disease Control and Prevention, how may I direct your call?" The receptionist sounded bored and tired.

"Good afternoon, my name is Dr. Stephen Smith, I'm a neurologist at Kaiser Permanente in Santa Monica, CA," the tall, salt-and-pepper haired man in scrubs replied haltingly from across the country. "To be completely honest with you, I'm not sure who I should ask to be directed to. We are dealing with a series of unexplainable deaths here, and by here I mean across California. I suppose I was just calling to see if there have been any other reports on mysterious illnesses and deaths, and whether the CDC has a line on what's going on."

"Please hold."

Dr. Smith heard a click, and then his ear was filled with the on hold muzak that he had come to despise. He sighed and ran a hand through his hair which, while it was now more salt than pepper, at least it was still full, despite his 56 years of age.

Coming in to work earlier today, Dr. Smith had never thought that he would be ending his day by calling the CDC. As a neurologist, he had never had any contact with the disease control center, as he was a specialist of the mind. But over the course of his shift (which had started at midnight, and required five cups of coffee to get through) he had gone over a total of eleven different charts, all for fifteen year olds from around the state. Each one of them now deceased. Each one of them unexplained.

Only one of the victims (*If victims is even the right word for it*, he thought) was in their own hospital. Around 5:30, after reviewing the last chart, Dr. Smith had gone down to the hospital morgue in the basement to have a look at the body. At the time, he hadn't felt any sense of foreboding. Yes, the charts were all a bit odd. How could they not be, when there was no explanation for the deaths? And yet he was a man of medicine, and there was always an answer. One just needed to look close enough to find it. He had believed that throughout his entire distinguished career, and it had won him an award or three over the years.

And so, as he had made his way from his office on the fifth floor to the elevators and down to the morgue, he had felt confident that if he could just get a closer look at the body and not just the charts, then he would find his answer.

The music cut off abruptly, putting an end to his reverie, but not to his disquiet. "Hello?" The answering voice belonged to a pleasant, if slightly harried, woman on the other end of the line. "This is the CDC, Diseases and Conditions department. The receptionist said you were looking into a possible outbreak of something?"

"That's...not exactly it," Dr. Smith replied, shaking his head in frustration. "I'm a neurologist and my hospital is currently looking into a series of deaths that we simply can't explain. I'm the resident in my department and they called me in to review charts and look for an answer. The problem is, I can't seem to find one." He knew he was starting to ramble a bit but he couldn't stop himself. "For the last several hours I've gone over eleven charts and each one of them is the same. Teenagers, age 15, perfect health, no illness, injury, or reason for death. Dead anyway. We have one body currently in our morgue, and I just finished a post-op examination. There is nothing wrong with the body whatsoever. It is a complete and utter medical mystery." Dr. Smith realized his voice was rising and took a deep breath to reign himself in. When there was no immediate response, he went on. "I've never worked alongside, or even had contact with, the CDC. But in this situation, it seemed rational to reach out." (*Is anything rational about this?* A little voice in the back of his mind asked. He pushed the voice away.)

The silence on the other end went on so long that Dr. Smith thought the call might have disconnected. Finally, the woman sighed. "You're the first hospital to reach out to us, Dr. Smith, but that doesn't mean we haven't been paying attention to the news. We have people here with the express responsibility of keeping their finger on the pulse of the world, so to speak. And I can tell you, not without a little trepidation and yes, even fear, that it's not just happening in California. To date, we have a potential five hundred linked cases, in four different countries."

"*What?!*" Dr. Smith practically exploded. "Five HUNDRED?! How in the absolute hell has this not made national news?! Is anything being done about the situation? Why-"

"Look," the woman, whose name he didn't even know, interrupted. "The problem at hand here is that we have zero answers, zero *leads*, and even the link between cases is still circumstantial at this point in time. Like you yourself just said a moment ago, you read the charts, you looked at a body, *there is nothing repeat nothing wrong with them*. So why hasn't this gone national? Because we don't want to start a panic. Because we don't want to say to the country and the world 'Hide your kids, there's an invisible boogeyman and he may or may not decide that all the 15 year olds of the world are fair game'. Now I don't mean to be glib about this, I really don't, but I hope you can appreciate what we are trying to figure out here. Is it a superflu? Something airborne? A colossal coincidence? If you have any ideas, we'd love to hear them."

Dr. Smith slumped back in his chair, all the fire draining out of him at once as the severity of the situation settled around his shoulders like a great, immovable object. "No," he whispered. "I have no idea."

She, whatever her name was, sighed again. "Neither do we. But I *can* promise you this: we are aware of the situation, and we are doing everything within our power to find answers."

Dr. Smith was nodding, somehow feeling reassured even though he hadn't gotten a single answer. If anything, he had more questions than before he had picked up the phone.

"I appreciate you calling in," the nameless woman went on. "And if you discover anything new, please don't hesitate to share it with us. But please, *please* try and keep this to yourself as much as you possibly can. I'm not asking you to cover anything up. I'm simply asking for your discretion. Because believe me, when this comes out, and it *will*, one way or another, there will be a panic. Unless we can figure it out first, and present humanity with an answer."

Fear suddenly gripped Dr. Smith with a cold hand. "Are you saying this is an international emergency?"

"I'm saying that this is going to get a lot worse before it gets better. If you're a praying man, I would start now."

The line went dead.

11

Dr. Samantha Hanson, Sam to her friends, hung up the phone and turned to her friend and colleague, Dr. Bob Stone. "Cat's out of the bag," she said with tired resignation. "Start the clock."

12

As a bewildered Dr. Stephen Smith was putting down his phone and leaning back in his chair, wondering what in the world he was supposed to do now, Kristi, Jeff, Annie and Beckie were walking through the front entrance of Primary Children's Hospital in Salt Lake City.

As Jeff and Kristi had surmised, it had been no problem at all to get Beckie over to their house on the pretense of a playdate with Annie. And once Beckie was at their house, Jeff and Kristi had immediately seen what Annie had been trying to tell them the night before, what they hadn't seen because they hadn't *wanted* to see. But the blinders were off, and they were both kicking themselves for not noticing it sooner.

Beckie could have been Annie's intellectual twin.

It wasn't just in the language Beckie used (for example, saying *realistically speaking* instead of *prob'ly*, which would have been par for the course for a normal 6 year old), but it was in how Beckie carried herself. Like a mature adult stuffed into a prepubescent body. It brought to mind a bizarre twist of Benjamin Button's fate.

Once Jeff and Kristi admitted to themselves that Annie was in all probability right in her supposition that she had somehow passed her gift along to Beckie, they were forced to consider the far reaching implications that Annie had tried to get them to understand the night before: it hadn't stopped with Beckie. If Annie was some kind of 'patient zero' with this gift, and if Beckie was a carrier now as well, and if they had passed this along (they both refused to use a word like *infected*, although it was scarily close to the truth of the matter)...well, suffice to say it was too many *if's*.

One more *if* they were forced to consider: what if Annie was right about the connection to the mysterious spate of deaths around the country?

"Yes, how can I help you?" The charge nurse in blue scrubs at the front desk was someone the Oritts hadn't met before.

Jeff took a half step forward and tried to force a smile onto his face. "Yes, we have an appointment to see Jessica? The last name is Oritt."

The nurse, squat and with iron gray hair pulled back into a severe bun, dropped her eyes to her computer and dutifully searched her database. A moment later she was confirming their appointment and asking them to take a seat, it would be just a minute if they didn't mind.

They didn't, and they sat. Annie and Beckie wore almost comically adult expressions of concern on their faces, matching that of the elder Oritts.

Annie was thankful to be there, thankful to have worked up the courage to tell her adopted parents her secret and so share the burden that had been weighing her down. She was still nervous, still scared, but it was alleviated now that she had brought her family in.

She glanced over at Beckie, who was sitting there staring out at the waiting room without really seeing it, and Annie suddenly felt a pang of guilt flash through her. Annie had done this to her friend, and it didn't matter that she hadn't done it on purpose; it was still her fault. And with teens dying all around her, the only thing she could think about is that the same fate awaited her and-

"Hey guys! How's everyone doing?" Jessica's bright, chipper voice interrupted the dark pit that Annie's thoughts were circling.

The relief on Jeff and Kristi's faces was unmistakable. Here was someone who could help, someone who might have answers! More than that, here was someone they could count on for discretion, which was all important in their current predicament.

Jeff was the first on his feet, offering Jessica his hand. "Thank you so much for seeing us on such short notice. As soon as we heard about...you know...we wanted to look into it as soon as possible."

Jessica shook his hand, and then Kristi's, still smiling. "That's why I'm here, right? I promise you, we are going to figure

this thing out. You made the right call, bringing Annie up for a little visit. And you must be Beckie!"

Beckie jumped a little, as if goosed, showing a glimpse into the child that she by all appearances should still be. Then the adult inside of her looked up at Jessica with her too-wise eyes and nodded. "Yes, I'm Beckie. Very pleased to meet you, nurse. Annie has spoken very highly of you."

In that one moment, Jessica knew, just as Jeff and Kristi had known: Beckie was changed. She didn't need to run a single test to see that with her own eyes. But just looking was one thing: she needed proof. And to do that, she was going to have to step off of the straight and narrow path of ethical medical care for a brief moment, because this was bigger than all of them.

Still keeping that smile on her face, Jessica reached out and shook the little hand that Beckie proffered. "The pleasure is all mine, Beckie. Now, I'm not going to patronize you: you know why you're here?"

Beckie nodded.

"And you understand that I would like to run a few tests to see if, on the cellular level, you and Annie match up more than medical science could possibly explain?"

Another nod.

"I have to ask, do your parents know about any of this?"

Beckie shook her head solemnly. "I've been very careful to keep up the act while at home. When my folks look at me, they see a normal 6 year old girl who is enjoying normal preschool. I color, I do puzzles, I read the preschool level books that they get for me. Then, when they go to bed, I read the books that I actually find interesting. I recently finished *Catcher in the Rye*, was less than impressed, and I have *To Kill A Mockingbird* on deck." Beckie paused, and when she next spoke there was an undercurrent of fear in her voice. "I've also changed both of my older sisters. They are in middle school. My oldest sister is almost 15."

This statement was met with a stunned silence that no one knew how to break. Jeff and Kristi immediately thought about the night before, and Annie telling them that everything came down to *her*, and that the kids they were hearing about on the news, the ones that were dying mysteriously, they were all 15 when it happened…

To her credit, Jessica snapped right back into nurse mode after filing away this revelation, and knelt down so she could look Beckie in the eyes without looking *down* at her. "I am going to do everything in my power to get answers. I've been watching the news the same as everyone else, and if there's a way to figure out what is going on with you, and with Annie, and with everyone else, we will figure it out here. Do you trust me?"

Beckie searched Jessica's eyes for a long moment, then nodded once, decisively. "Yes."

Jessica stood back up, reaching out one hand for Beckie and the other for Annie. "Then let's go see what we see."

13

That day was just another day at the hospital for Annie and her folks, but it was a brand new experience for Beckie. After being led down an endless green corridor with a jarring floor pattern of red and yellow cross-hatched linoleum tiles, the two girls were led into a large examination room with two paper covered beds with the backs raised. While Jeff and Kristi stood off to one side and watched, Annie and Beckie were directed to sit up on the side by side beds.

Jessica started with the usual battery of non-invasive tests: blood pressure, temperature, reflex check (with the little rubber hammer tapped lightly on each knee; both girls passed with flying colors). Next, Jessica explained, would come the blood tests and saliva swab. But first, she just wanted to have a quick word with Annie's folks, would that be alright?

Annie and Beckie assured her that would be fine. Jessica gave each girl a bright red lollipop, then crossed the wide room over to where Jeff and Kristi had been following along attentively and silently.

Jessica got right to the point. "You both obviously know that what we're doing here isn't exactly legal. Beckie is a minor and I'm sure I can assume that her parents have no idea she's here?"

"They think the girls are just having a normal Saturday playdate," Kristi answered with resignation.

"I thought so. That being said, this is the first time in my career that I'm willing to risk coloring outside the lines, so to speak. If this situation really is what it looks like on the surface, then it goes *way* beyond running a few discrete blood tests and checking out some genetic markers. However, I'm still going to be trying my damndest to cover my own ass in this. What I propose is this: I'll run on Beckie the same kind of tests we've been running on Annie for the last 6 years. Blood, saliva, the works. I'll label the tests as if they both came from Annie at different times, mostly because I'm confident that the tests will show that these two girls are almost eerily similar at a genetic level; call it gut instinct. I mean, *look* at them. It's almost supernatural. And if these two girls are passing this along like Annie says they are? The implications are world changing. So yeah, I think me bending the rules a little bit is a drop of water in the ocean."

Jeff sighed. "That's reasonable, and more than we have any right to expect, let alone ask for."

Jessica gave him a piercing look. "You know I'm not just doing this for your family, no matter how much I've come to care about Annie."

"We know. Still, we're thankful."

"You can thank me once I actually figure this thing out. Which I'm not nearly as confident about as I let on to Beckie earlier. This...this is beyond western medicine. And even if we do find out exactly what's going on, it doesn't mean we'll be able to do anything to stop it."

14

Two hours later, the four of them were on their way back to the Oritt's house. The mood in the car was hesitantly hopeful. Hopeful because each of them felt good about having done *something*, but hesitant because they still didn't know if it would make a bit of difference.

Right before they left, Jessica had promised them that she would be in touch the minute they got any results back, which should be sooner rather than later. Due to the nature of the situation, Jessica had put a high priority on each test she had sent off.

She had also reminded them to take the bandaid off of Beckie's arm before her parents came to get her, unless they wanted to explain why they had taken Beckie to get her blood drawn at the hospital without their permission.

Jeff had dryly assured her that yes, they would remember to do that.

And so they went back to the Oritt's house and pretended to have a normal Saturday. Board games in the living room. Juice for the girls. A *large* glass of red wine for the adults. Then a big spaghetti dinner, complete with garlic bread and a salad that both girls ignored in favor of the tastier options (and who were they to worry about cholesterol and calories, anyway?). For dessert, a chunk of dark chocolate for everyone from a bar they kept in the freezer.

Then 8 o'clock rolled around, and Beckie's parents arrived to take her home. Jeff and Kristi weren't surprised to see Beckie put on the same mask of childhood that Annie used anytime they left the house, nor were they surprised to see Beckie's parents buy it hook, line and sinker.

After all, who suspects a 6 year old of being anything other than a 6 year old?

15

As soon as the Oritt clan departed (*plus Beckie, who was now an inductee into that clan at the very least* Jessica thought to herself) the confident smile slipped right off her face and crashed down to the floor. She raised a shaking hand up to her forehead where a real bitcher of a headache was starting to come on.

"This is bad," she whispered to herself. "This is so, so bad."

One look at Beckie, even before that sweet little girl had opened her mouth, and Jessica had known. She had been a nurse for long enough that her instincts were honed and, more often than not, correct. And Beckie had the same eyes, the same *look*, that Annie had. Wisdom looked out of those eyes, wisdom and knowledge that had no business being in the eyes of a child.

Annie had changed Beckie. Jessica didn't need to see the test results to know that. And if Annie was capable of changing kids into what she was...Jessica ran the numbers in her mind and groaned. Her knees suddenly felt weak, and she leaned back against the wall, trying desperately not to slump all the way down to the floor.

If Annie could pass along her gift, or whatever you want to call it, then odds were she had changed her entire preschool. And if those kids then went home and passed it along to siblings, to friends...and was it just children? *It must be*, Jessica continued to reason, trying to think past the headache taking root in the center of her brain. *If Annie could change adults, then I would be different, the Oritt parents would be different, it would be spreading even faster than it already appears to be.*

Jessica shook her head, which immediately caused her headache to spike.

First aspirin, she thought, pushing herself away from the wall and walking down the hallway toward her office. *Then...what? Try to figure out if this is a brand new pandemic? A new generation of superkids start to take over the world, then die when they turn 15! Because if the two events are linked...*

Jessica came to a sudden stop in the middle of the hallway. A doctor who had been walking behind her stifled a curse as he dodged nimbly to the side, narrowly avoiding running into her back. Jessica didn't even notice.

If they're linked, then we are going to lose a massive percentage of the global population unless we can do something about it. It suddenly became imperative that Jessica get the results of those tests back. She started walking again. In seconds she was running.

16

Sam Hanson of the CDC was sitting in her office that Saturday, running simulations on her computer. It wouldn't have surprised her to know that right at that very moment, a nurse in Salt Lake City, UT was doing similar simulations in her head, and coming up with very similar answers.

Very little surprised Sam anymore, now that the world was potentially facing an unstoppable crisis.

The petite brunette had just finished her most recent sim, taking into consideration the most current data they had available, which now amounted to over a thousand unresolved deaths that ranged across both Americas, as well as Bermuda, Jamaica, and England. Her computer showed a graph with a stark red line that started on a near horizontal path at the bottom left of the screen before taking a sharp turn upwards before it disappeared off the top of the graph.

Suffice to say, it wasn't good news.

A knock on the door, and then her colleague Bob Stone was pushing his large bald head into her office.

Sam swiveled around to face him, taking in his clean cut appearance: carefully pressed button down white Oxford shirt, black slacks, black tie, black wingtip shoes. *He may as well work for the*

Men in Black, Sam thought ruefully, looking down at her own outfit for the day: oversized Cornell University sweatshirt and black leggings. *Hardly the picture of a respected CDC doctor.* Well, it would have to do. Besides, it was Saturday. Neither of them were even supposed to be working that day.

"What's up, Bob?" Sam asked tiredly.

Bob crossed her office and dropped a manila folder in front of her. "Our sniffers just got a ping on something that I thought would interest you. Remember the girl from Utah, the one that we've been looking into as a possible patient zero? Well, strike the 'possible' out of that sentence."

Sam's eyes widened, and she snatched at the folder, opening it up to see a blow up picture of a cute little girl with white blonde hair next to a medical chart. She ignored the pic for the time being, focusing instead on the information provided in detail on the chart.

Medical background, birth, adopted family, testing history- "My god," Sam muttered. She looked up at Bob, who was smiling humorlessly. "These genetic markers are identical to every post-mortem we've gotten to date. They're perfect. She's the first live subject we've gotten these results on."

Bob nodded. "That's not even the most interesting part. Look at the most recent testing."

Sam looked back at the page, scanning down to the bottom. "There aren't results yet," she answered, confused. "This just says 'Annie Oritt blood tests 1 and 2, check for comparison of genetic markers'."

"Exactly. Why would they run back to back blood tests from the same patient, looking for a comparison of genetic data? It makes zero sense. Which means that what they're really doing-"

"Is comparing Annie with another subject to see if the genetic markers match up," Sam finished. "Which means Annie's family believes she is passing it on to another child, and the nurse is in on it, running tests on the sly."

Bob tapped his nose with one hand and pointed at Sam with the other. "Got it in one. This is it, Sam, I can feel it. Annie is our patient zero. Whatever is going on with these so-called 'perfect' teens dying for no reason, Annie is at the root of it all. And furthermore, she's *adopted*. How much you want to bet that plays a part in this? We need to find her birth parents."

Sam set the manila folder aside and looked up at Bob with ice in her eyes. "We need more than that. We need Annie. Here. Whatever it takes."

Part 4: The Trial Con't (The Year 2018)

1

After a brief recess in which the jurors were allowed to review the information that the prosecuting attorney had presented them with during his opening statement, the trial got back under way. While it was true that the jurors had been selected because of their assumed impartiality in the trial, it could be rightly assumed that there was at least a little bias considering the nature of what they were judging. Particularly because each of the 12 men and women in the jury box was well aware that the defendant had already admitted guilt. During the recess, several of them had voiced their confusion as to why they were even *having* a trial.

Be that as it may, they were here, and they had a job to do.

Following opening statements (well, opening *statement*, singular) it was time for the prosecuting attorney to call his first witness. Mr. Oritt called to the stand his medical expert, Dr. Jackson Telford, the geneticist who had run point for the CDC in this case. Dr. Telford was brought in, sworn in, and invited to take his seat at the witness stand.

Dr. Telford was taller than average, slender in build, and, despite being in his 60's, still sported a full head of silver hair. With his faded blue eyes, lined forehead and cheeks, and sun darkened skin, he looked more like an aging cowboy than a medical professional who spent his days in a lab with his eyes pressed up against a microscope.

Jeff briefly reviewed his notes before he rose and walked to stand in front of Dr. Telford. The courtroom was so quiet you could have heard a pin drop.

"Dr. Telford," Jeff began, speaking in a calm, measured tone that hid the anger burning deep within. "You are the CDC geneticist who has been running the lab working on the Angel Virus, is that correct?"

"Yes."

"Can you tell us the exact nature of the Angel Virus?"

Dr. Telford cleared his throat. "I believe that the only person who can explain the Angel Virus in its entirety is sitting at that table over there." He nodded in the direction of the defendant, who had crossed his arms over his chest and leaned back in his chair. "But I can explain what we have discovered. The Angel Virus is, at its core, a metabolism booster of unheard of potential. As the human body ages, all of the systems begin to slow down. Our metabolism slows. We don't have as much energy as we did when we were younger. It takes us longer to heal from injury. Vision goes, hearing goes, etc, etc. Eventually, due to organic entropy, we die. But the Angel Virus somehow shoves every bodily function into a perfectly balanced overdrive. Healing happens almost instantaneously. Infection and disease never have a chance to even get a foothold within the body. Synapses within the brain fire faster over time, not slower, which is why the Angels, as people have named them, were so unbelievably intelligent, especially at the end. But the trade off is, as we all know, death around the age of 15. We still don't know the *why* behind the early age of death; is it random? Pre-programmed? Connected to puberty? We don't know, not for sure. But we did manage to figure out the why behind the early death in a more general sense." Dr. Telford paused to take a sip of water. Every single juror was leaning forward in his or her seat, rivetted. "Think of the average human being as a candle. We burn for an average amount of time, generally somewhere in the neighborhood of 70 to 90 years, and then we burn out. But with these supercharged Angels, they are less like a candle and more like a firework exploding in the sky: huge, brilliant, *blinding*, and then gone." Dr. Telford snapped his fingers to illustrate his point, and one of the jurors jumped in his chair.

Jeff nodded, having already been briefed on Dr. Telford's diagnosis. "And how was this Angel Virus passed on?"

"That was the most diabolic part." Dr. Telford leaned forward, faded blue eyes blazing. "Due to the specific genetic manipulation of proteins within this 'virus', Patient Zero was able to pass it along the same way the common cold or flu is passed along: bodily fluid, a sneeze, a simple cough, and the genetic code was out there in the world for another child to breathe in or ingest. Given the overall uncleanliness of children and their propensity to play rough, skin their knees, shins, hands, and then interact with their friends and classmates, well, it comes as no surprise that the virus spread as rapidly as it did."

Jeff closed his eyes for a moment, thinking of Annie and Beckie, and the visit to nurse Jessica that seemed like a million years ago. Back when they thought it was a blessing, not a curse. Not a *virus*.

He forced himself to open his eyes and get back to the job at hand. He wasn't just here to get justice for Annie, but for every child that had succumbed to this pandemic. "As studies have shown, it appears that the Adolescent category of the world has essentially been decimated; those still under the age of 15 are, for the most part, being kept in quarantine, but there don't appear to be any more carriers still living, especially after the aptly named 'hell on earth' of the last two years. If there are no more carriers, do we still need to worry about the survival of the virus in any kind of dormant phase?"

Dr. Telford let out a long breath. "That is the one piece of good news I have to offer. My team and I, through our extensive research, have found that the Angel Virus *must* have a carrier to live inside: in our atmosphere it deteriorates almost immediately. No living carrier, no more virus."

"No further questions," Jeff said, giving Dr. Telford a nod before turning and heading back to his seat.

Judge Erikson looked over at the defendant, Dr. Calvin Michaels, and his state appointed attorney, Gabriel Conklin. "Your witness."

Dr. Michaels and Gabriel put their heads together for a minute, conferring quietly. Then Gabriel, short at 5'7" but with a puffed up chest that made him appear an inch or two taller, rose from his seat and made his way over to the witness stand.

Jeff watched him walk, trying to keep a scowl off of his face. Jeff had faced Gabriel in court numerous times in the past and had a general disdain for the man. For one, Gabriel enjoyed taking on the cases that other lawyers didn't want. He seemed to thrive on the losers, always looking for sneaky ways to get his clients off on technicalities of one kind or another. The man was a slimebag. But he was a *skilled* slimebag, and that made him dangerous.

The puffed up rooster of a lawyer stopped in front of the witness stand and stared at Dr. Telford for a few moments before beginning his cross examination. If his intense scrutiny was meant to put Dr. Telford on edge, it didn't work. Dr. Telford even cracked a brief smile at the little man's posturing.

Gabriel frowned, then launched in. "Dr. Telford, how long have you been working for the CDC?"

"23 years."

"And for how long have you been running the genetics lab?"

"For the last decade."

Gabriel nodded. "Have you ever come across a virus like this before?"

"Well," Dr. Telford shrugged. "Essentially, all viruses share similarities of one kind or-"

"That wasn't the question," Gabriel interrupted. "Have you ever come across a virus of the same nature as the Angel Virus in the past?"

Now it was Dr. Telford's turn to frown. "No."

Gabriel spread his arms wide as if to say *Aha!* "Then how can you claim to be a medical expert on the exact nature of the Angel Virus?"

Dr. Telford bristled visibly. "I am a medical expert in the fields of genetics and virology, and as such am giving my expert analysis of what my team and I have discovered, after *extensive* research."

"Even so, this is something new, is it not? Which means it's possible you and/or your team might have missed something, or gotten something wrong?"

"Objection," Jeff interjected. "Badgering the witness."

"Sustained," the judge replied. "Back it off, counselor."

Gabriel held his hands up, conceding the point. "I'll rephrase. How can you be sure that your analysis of the Angel Virus is correct?"

"Just because we haven't seen this kind of virus in its entirety before, we *have* seen the individual parts. We've seen the mechanism that causes the spread of the virus. We've studied the proteins, the individual strands. We've taken apart the puzzle, analyzed it, and put it back together. Through studying the parts, we now understand the whole. That is why I *know* that our analysis of the virus is correct."

"And yet, you recently admitted to the prosecuting attorney that you don't fully understand why the Angels died at the age of 15."

"Correct. Although, as I *also* stated, we know why they died young."

Gabriel pushed his attack. "Not good enough, doctor. You said that you understand the whole, and then you back pedal and say you only understand *most* of the whole, *most* of the puzzle pieces. But most doesn't mean all. Which throws into question your entire analysis!"

"Objection!" Jeff said again, this time rising to his feet, anger bubbling just under the surface of his projected calm.

"Sustained," the judge said loudly. "Is there a question in that tirade, counselor?"

Gabriel glanced back at Jeff, looking smug and decidedly victorious. "No further questions, your honor."

"Then we will have a 10 minute recess before moving on to the next witness." The judge brought his gavel down, and Jeff dropped back down into his seat with a barely stifled curse. Despite his sustained objection, he knew that Gabriel had still managed to get into the jury's heads with that last parting shot. He only hoped that the truth would ring louder than the bullshit.

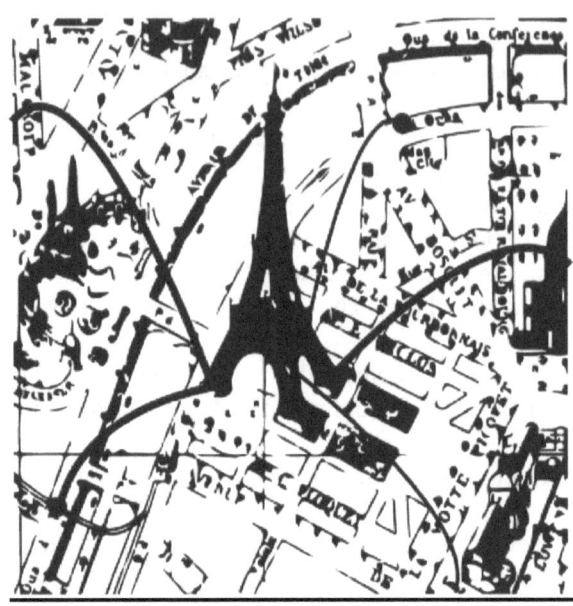

Part 5: An Epidemic (The Year 2009)

1

    Kristi and Jeff had taken Annie and Beckie into Primary Children's on Saturday for tests to be run. It was now Monday. Annie and Beckie were back at Kids Kampus, pretending (with the rest of their class, who were all by now *way* too intelligent to enjoy preschool) to be engrossed with If You Give A Moose A Muffin. One little enterprising boy in the back of the classroom had snuck his moms Kindle to school and was making his way through War and Peace.

    Meanwhile, Jeff and Kristi were back at Primary Children's talking with Jessica in her office. Jeff had just finished telling Jessica everything that Annie had told them about her worries over the nature of her genetic anomalies, and her fearful predictions for the future. The mood was somber, with a note of panic lurking just under the surface.

    Jessica took a deep breath. "First and foremost, the test results show what you two already have guessed: Beckie has what Annie has. Looking at their samples side by side, they look nearly identical. The good news is, that makes my little deception with the tests (running both of them under Annie's name) completely believable. The bad news is that I've matched up these test results with other samples from other hospitals that I've been able to get access to, samples from some of the mysterious deaths that the news has been going on about recently. I'm not going to sugarcoat it, there are similarities. Annie's worry about there being a connection may be right."

Kristi's face fell. "What does that mean? Is our daughter going to die when she turns 15? Is this a death sentence?" Jeff reached over and put his hand on hers. She clenched it tightly, like a drowning sailor clutching at a thrown lifeline.

Jessica shook her head. "I have no idea. All I have to go on are the samples I've studied, the test results, and the news. There is no hard and fast solution as to why these kids are dying. On the surface, every single thing about your daughter, and Beckie, too, for that matter, is perfect."

"So what do we do now?" Jeff finally asked, eyes naked with concern.

Jessica looked down, unable to bear the desperation in his gaze. "I'm sorry, I just don't know."

The silence that fell in that little office was deafening.

2

As Jessica was going over the test results of the child who would soon be called Patient Zero, Drs. Sam Hanson and Bob Stone were in a conference with their head of genetics and virology at the CDC, Dr. Jackson Telford.

"You're asking me if I condone bringing this young girl here, by force if necessary, so we can study her? My answer is *absolutely not*. Are you kidding? Are we a police state, or a fascist regime, to go around kidnapping people, children, in the middle of the night to satisfy our own agenda?!" Jackson's faded blue eyes smoldered under bushy, steel gray eyebrows.

Sam sighed, and not for the first time. "How is this not getting through your head? We have on our hands a potential *genetic pandemic*. If we can stop a global outbreak by studying Patient Zero, does the end not justify the means? It's the most simple mathematical calculation in the world! Sacrifice one, save millions. *Billions!*"

Jackson burst out of his chair. "She's a 6 year old child! I refuse, *refuse*, to be part of any kind of abduction plot! This is patently insane." He turned to Bob, who had yet to contribute anything to their 'discussion'. "What about you? This jive ok with you, too, Bob?"

Bob, bald head gleaming slightly from the harsh overhead lights, shrugged. "If you have other ideas, we'd love to hear them. But essentially, I agree with Sam. In theory, at least. Did you not hear the part about this potentially turning global?"

"Oh, I heard it," Jackson replied angrily, pacing back and forth in front of them. "So here's a thought: just send me and a team to Utah! I can run initial testing of my own at this Primary Children's hospital, which will also give me access to all of the data they've already compiled on Annie. On *Annie*, not on *Patient Zero*. Jesus, I know doctors are supposed to be detached from the patient, but this girl is 6 and she has a name, so maybe we should try using it, huh?"

Sam and Bob shared a long look.

"Ok," Sam said.

Jackson stopped in his tracks. "Ok?"

"Yeah," Bob said. "It's a good idea. Get your team together, make a plan, and we'll send you to Utah to investigate."

Jackson dropped heavily into his chair. "O...ok. Sounds good."

Sam held up a finger in warning. "But you keep your eyes on the prize. Patient Zero...*Annie*...might have the answer to all of this. Remember your perspective. The CDC is looking out for the best interests of the world, not just the individual."

"Of course," Jackson agreed, keeping a smile on his face and getting back up to his feet. "You'll have the names of those on my team and an outline of our game plan by the end of the day." He turned and headed towards the door, wanting to go while the going was good. As he let the door swing shut behind him, he allowed the smile to disappear. "Sociopaths," Jackson muttered under his breath, pulling out his phone and starting the first of a series of texts he needed to send out as quickly as possible.

3

Back in the office, Sam and Bob continued the conference *mano a mano*.

"We could still bring her here, with or without Jackson's cooperation," Bob offered. From the bland expression on his face, he might as well have been discussing the weather. *Gonna be a cold one today. Maybe we should kidnap a child.*

"No," Sam shook her head, turning to her computer and booting it up. "Jackson was right about the whole 'police state' thing. It's too soon to push our forceful arm out too far. It might be necessary in time, especially if we're right about the call for quarantine that will be coming down the pike, but there is no need to start setting up leper colonies before the general public begs us to. And trust me, they will. Sending Jackson to Utah may be, at the end of the day, like locking the barn door after the horse has already escaped. Right now we aren't trying to stop Humpty Dumpty from falling, we're trying to put him back together before anyone notices that he fell to begin with."

Bob smiled humorlessly. "Any more similes or analogies you have on tap, or should we move on?"

"Smart ass," Sam shot back. "You know I'm right."

Bob sighed. "I know. That's what scares me."

4

One month later.
June 7th, 2009.

For many students, it was the first day of summer. The death toll had risen to nearly two thousand, but since there was still no reason as to the *why*, it had yet to elicit a panic. Whether this was due to how the various news stations and papers were reporting (with vague language and a slew of differing opinions) or because humanity has shown itself over the years to be remarkably skilled at keeping its collective head in the sand remains unclear. What is clear is this. By the end of June 7th, the Angel Virus would make landfall in Europe for the first time.

If the CDC had ever had a snowball's chance in hell at figuring out a way to stop this, that chance would vanish over the horizon with the setting sun.

The pandemic was here, and an oceans worth of tears would be shed before this butcher's bill was paid.

5

"Daddy, come *on!*" Colton, an overly energetic little whipcord of a ten year old, yanked at his dad's hand, trying to get him to move faster.

Colton and his father, Keaton, were on their way to see the Eiffel Tower. It was a beautiful sunny day in Gay Paree, and what better way to kick off summer vacation than in another country?

The day before, right after the bell had rung signaling the end of 5th grade, Keaton had driven to Boulder Elementary to pick up his only child, with whom he shared custody with his ex-wife. Said ex-wife, a somewhat shrewish but passably reasonable woman who had left him for a fitness instructor ten years younger and fifty pounds lighter than he, had allowed this 'male bonding' trip (most likely due to the guilt she still felt over the divorce, but hey, he would take it).

Keaton and Colton had gone straight from Boulder Elementary to the airport, to jump on a puddle hopper from Boulder to Denver, and then on to Paris, France. The flight was grueling and boring, with a fair amount of turbulence that made Keaton's hands clench on the armrests hard enough to dimple the pleather pads. Colton, bright eyed and bushy tailed throughout the entire 9 hour flight, didn't voice a single protest, for which Keaton was thankful.

In fact, Keaton had mused as he tried and failed to read a new mystery he had picked up at the Denver airport as they waited for the main leg of their journey to begin, *little Colt hasn't complained much at all lately. When did that start?*

Colton, going into 5th grade the year previous, had been a fairly typical pre-teen boy: that is to say, he found something to gripe about at every turn, including trying to turn every little cough into a reason to stay home sick from school.

Then, right around Christmas vacation, the grumping and groaning had simply ceased to be. As had his tendency to get a mild cough at the drop of a hat, whether real or feigned.

Well, if Colton wanted to grow up a little earlier than most, then that was just fine and dandy. Keaton meant to capitalize on this little father-son trip to France, and maybe open his son's eyes a bit to how cool his old dad could be. Keaton needed all the help he could get if he didn't want his son turning to that young jackass of a fitness instructor for advice instead of his own father.

And so here they were, on their way to see one of the greatest sights in the world, the Eiffel Tower. As Colton pulled and dragged his dad down the Avenue Pierre Loti, Keaton felt amazed anew at the changes in his son. Colton being more energetic and less prone to complaining was only the tip of the iceberg. Keaton couldn't quite put his finger on it, but Colton almost seemed more...

Mature? Keaton thought, glancing up and up as the Eiffel Tower reared its beautiful head 1063 feet above them. *No, not mature, although he is. But it's more than that. He seems...older. Especially when he looks at me. I'd swear that there was someone my age looking out of his peepers. It would be creepy if it didn't feel natural at the same time. I wonder if this is something that happens to all kids as they start to grow up?*

As Colton was Keaton's only kid, and not having any nieces or nephews either, the single father had no frame of reference, no way to compare. So, like so many other parents in too many other places right at that very moment, Keaton kept his blinders comfortably in place.

Despite the popularity of the attraction, Keaton and Colton only had to wait in the ticket line for five minutes, then another ten minutes in the line to get in the east entrance (which had the shortest line). Colton, with his newfound boundless energy, had been all for taking the 704 stairs to the second floor, but Keaton (or rather, Keaton's beer belly) had to disagree. The father and son ended up crammed into the little elevator that ran smoothly up the middle of the tower, surrounded on all sides by other parents and other kids.

Four of those kids were under the age of 15.

Colton, who was sweating lightly from his physical exertion, bumped up against each one of them.

Bodily fluids that less than a year ago had been harmless were transmitted to each one, and absorbed first into the skin, and from there into the bloodstream.

Two of the other kids were from New York.
One was from Ireland.
The fourth was from South Africa.

Each of the four children, each of the four new *Angels*, came into contact with yet other children before returning to their respective home countries.

The Angel Virus, as yet unnamed (though that would soon change) had sped right past the point of no return in perfect silence.

6

"Dr. Jackson Telford to see nurse Jessica Gardner?" The tall, blue eyed man asked the charge nurse at the front desk of Primary Children's hospital.

The charge nurse, a young and not-yet-disillusioned brunette fresh out of school, smiled brightly up at him. "Just one second, I'll page her. If you'd like to have a seat?" She gestured with a perfectly manicured hand at the waiting room behind him.

"Yes, thank you." Dr. Telford walked over and dropped heavily down into one of the padded chairs, glancing over at the others already waiting for their turn. A handful of moms with a double handful of kids, no surprise there.

What *was* surprising, Dr. Telford noticed as he looked closer, is that not a single one of the children was in any way misbehaving. Not a sniffle, not a complaint, not even any loud talking. Every one of the kids was perfectly mannered. Four boys were playing with blocks in one corner of the large, square room. Another, a little girl with blonde pigtails, was sitting cross legged on the thin carpet, reading a comic book.

Dr. Telford felt a shiver snake its way up his spine, though he couldn't explain why. There was just something...*off*... about kids who were perfectly mannered. It wasn't natural. Kids were *supposed* to act out, at least a little. Dr. Telford, who didn't have any children of his own, had always just assumed it was hardwired into you at that age, and then eventually most people grew out of it. Not all, by any means, but most, sure.

"Dr. Telford?" Nurse Gardner, he presumed, as the tall blonde in scrubs approached him.

He rose to his feet smoothly and held out a hand. "Jackson, please. Thank you for agreeing to meet with me."

"If you're Jackson, then I'm Jessica," she said with a smile. "And when the CDC sends someone out from the East Coast for a meeting, you don't turn them down. Shall we go back to my office?"

"Please," he replied, following her as she turned and walked briskly down the broad hallway to the right of the front desk. A pair of double doors opened quietly as they approached, and then closed behind them.

A minute later they were both seated in a small but comfortably furnished office. Jessica's nursing degrees hung on the wall behind her. Each of the other three walls held a single painting, all watercolors.

"Can I get you coffee? Water?" Jessica asked politely. The smile, however, was gone, Jackson noticed.

"No, but thank you. Is it safe to assume you know why I'm here?"

"Annie." It came out as a flat statement, not a question.

Jackson cleared his throat. "Yes, Annie Oritt. The CDC is currently investigating a new and potentially dangerous infectious disease-"

"You could have requested all of our medical records as they pertain to your case," Jessica interrupted. "We would have complied, and sent you everything we had, and offered whatever assistance was requested. But instead *you* came to *us*. Which means you don't just want medical records, do you?"

Jackson looked down at his hands, then back up at her. Jessica's eyes were blazing at him, angry and hot. "You have to understand how serious the situation is," he said quietly. "People are dying. We don't know why. But the people above my pay grade are reasonably certain that it started with Annie."

"I know," Jessica shot back. "I've known ever since I met with Annie and one of her friends and ran tests on the two of them, confirming the similarities between the two."

Jackson cocked his head at her. "Then I confess I don't understand why you seem upset. We're on the same team here."

"Are we? Really? Because before you arrived I had various correspondence from 'the people above your pay grade', and I get the distinct impression that all your people care about are numbers and statistics, rather than the value of the individual human life. Annie, whom your bosses so heartlessly referred to as 'Patient Zero', is just a little girl, for Heaven's sake. So why don't you tell me, *honestly*, exactly what you want." Jessica leaned back in her chair and crossed her arms tightly across her chest.

Jackson took a deep breath. "I...that is to say, my superiors...want Annie. They want her in quarantine, first of all, though I already told them that setting up a quarantine would be like locking the barn door after the horse has already escaped. Following that, my superiors want more invasive testing done. They believe that if we can pinpoint the exact blueprint of whatever it is that Annie has, then we can figure out a way to counteract it. To cure it."

"Quarantine."

A nod. "Yes."

"For a minor. For a *6 year old*."

Another nod. "Yes."

"And then invasive testing...you say invasive, but what you mean is painful, am I right? Bone marrow. Biopsies from each organ. Blood work *ad nauseum*. Right?"

Jackson ran his hands through his silver hair in frustration. "You're a medical professional, Jessica. How can you not understand that we are trying to stop a global pandemic, here? It's simple math! We are trying to save *countless* six year olds, not just one!"

Jessica stabbed a finger at him, and he flinched back as if struck. "That girl has a name. Annie. She was born in this hospital. She is here all the time for regular check ups. There isn't a single doctor or nurse here that doesn't know and care for her. Yes, I care about the rest of the world. But Annie is like a daughter to me, and I won't have you lock her away in a box and run tests on her day in and day out!"

"I'm truly sorry," Jackson said, reaching into his jacket pocket and pulling out a piece of paper that he laid on the desk between them. "If it helps, you don't actually have a choice in the matter."

Jessica snatched the paper up and read through it rapidly. Her eyes were as wide as dinner plates by the time she finished. "You got a court order?" She whispered. "This shouldn't even be possible without the parents at least being *contacted*, let alone given consideration in the decision making process!"

"The court was made to understand the unique and time sensitive nature of the situation," Jackson explained, leaning back as though worried Jessica might actually leap over the desk and wrap her hands around his throat. The look in her eyes said he might not be too off track. "Believe me, we will do everything in our power to make this as smooth as possible. We aren't monsters, Jessica. We just want to get to the bottom of this and find a solution. Don't you want that, too?"

"Not like this," she answered, all of the anger draining out of her as she sagged back into her chair. "Not like this."

7

After having Jessica sign a standard Non Disclosure Agreement, Dr. Jackson Telford and his team got to work. Luckily for them, Primary Children's already had a quarantine area set up in the NICU, generally used for infants born early or with some kind of immune deficiency, who needed to be separated from the other children until their immune systems were up to speed and could begin to interact with others. Jackson and his team took over the space, bringing in their own computers, testing equipment, and tools, all of the very best that the CDC had to offer. They were finished in a matter of hours.

That was the easy part.

Getting Annie would prove to be one of the hardest things Jackson ever had to do in this lifetime.

8

June 14th, 2009.
10 a.m.

Jeff and Kristi had just gotten home from their morning exercise class. Jacob and Maddy were in the living room with Annie, playing Monopoly and laughing. Well, Maddy and Annie were laughing. Jacob was groaning melodramatically as his two younger sisters teamed up and worked toward taking all of his money and, therefore, his pride.

It wasn't the first time, either.

"Park Place *again?*" Jeff heard Jacob grump as he made his way upstairs to shower off the mornings exertions. As he shut the bathroom door, he thought he heard someone knocking downstairs.

Kristi, water bottle in hand, was the one who opened the front door to reveal a pair of older, white haired men in dark suits with serious looks on their faces. The taller one, whom Kristi took to be the leader of the pair, looked like a grizzled old cowboy straight out of the Wild West: he was tall, skinny but with the bearing of an iron core of strength, and his skin appeared to have been stretched and tanned under a desert sun. His eyes, the color of faded blue jeans, looked at her with something like sympathy.

Despite the chill raising goosebumps on her arms, Kristi managed a calm "Yes? Can I help you?"

"Is this the Oritt household?" The old cowboy asked. His voice was smooth and pleasant, but it held an undercurrent of something that put Kristi on guard.

"It is. And you are?"

"My name is Dr. Jackson Telford, and we are with the Centers for Disease Control and Prevention. We're here to-"

"The CDC," Kristi interrupted. A ball of ice formed in her stomach. "You're here about Annie."

"Yes, ma'am," Jackson confirmed, nodding his head. "May we come in?"

"Give me just one second." And with that, Kristi shut the door in their faces.

Jacob, curious as always, had left the Monopoly game (he was losing, badly, and was more interested in the goings on at the front door) and poked his head around the entryway. "Who was that?" He asked innocently.

"Jacob, take your sisters upstairs, and tell your father to please come down. He may already be in the shower. Tell him it's important."

Seeing the look on his mom's face, Jacob didn't question her, for which Kristi was thankful. He immediately gathered up his two little sisters and herded them, quite skillfully, up the stairs and out of sight. A moment later she heard him knocking on the upstairs bathroom door.

Kristi took a deep breath, held it in, released it, trying to calm her pounding heart. Deep down she had wondered if something like this might happen. Especially after last weekend, when Annie had told them her secret, and her worries about a possible connection between her and the deaths happening around the country.

And in her heart, hadn't she always known Annie was something different? Not just special, but *DIFFERENT*. Something new. Something, yes, a little bit scary? Yes. She had.

The knocking started back up just as Jeff, wet but clothed in a Stephen King t-shirt and a pair of running shorts, came down the stairs, taking them two at a time.

72

"I said give me a second!" Kristi snapped loudly at the front door. The knocking cut off abruptly.

"What's going on?" Jeff asked as he rounded the staircase and trotted up to her.

"The CDC is here," Kristi explained *sotto voce*. "They said they're here about Annie and they want to come in."

Jeff snapped into lawyer mode in the blink of an eye. "They can only come in if we give them permission to come in," he said, expression hardening. "We'll keep this on the front porch."

Kristi turned back to the door and opened it to reveal to Jeff the two men from the CDC. The tall one, Jackson, opened his mouth to speak, but Kristi held up a hand to forestall him. "You may not come in. We will speak to you on the front porch."

Jackson shut his mouth and nodded, still wearing that same expression of sympathy on his face. Kristi irrationally wanted to slap that hangdog look right off of him.

But she held her temper in check, and she and Jeff stepped outside, shutting the door behind them. It wasn't yet noon but the temperature was already on the rise, and she took grim satisfaction in seeing the two men beginning to sweat in their suits.

Jeff took the lead. "What can we do for you Mr…?"

"Dr. Jackson Telford," the tall one extended a hand, which Jeff shook

"Roland Mulaney," the shorter one said, speaking for the first time.

"No Dr. in front of your name?" Jeff asked as he shook his hand.

Roland shook his head. His hair was white and long, and reached halfway down his back in a loose ponytail. "Just a Masters for me. I'm the head lab tech in Dr. Telford's department."

Jeff turned back to Jackson. "And what exactly is your department, Dr. Telford?"

"Genetics and Virology. My two bosses have put the wheels into motion that brought me and my lab team here, first to Primary Childrens, and now to your doorstep."

"You've already been to Primary Childrens? Then you've spoken with nurse Gardner." It wasn't a question.

Jackson answered it anyway. "Yes, we have. I must say, I was very impressed with her. Not just as a nurse, but as a friend to your family. She was fiercely protective of you and yours."

Jeff raised his eyebrows. "For what reason would she have need to be protective?"

Jackson cleared his throat uncomfortably. "My bosses have obtained a warrant to place your adopted daughter, Annie, into protective quarantine until such a time as we can determine the full extent of her genetic makeup and what, if any, communicable disease she has been spreading."

Silence dropped, sudden and overwhelming, over Jeff and Kristi, so stunned were they by this turn of events.

What felt like an eternity later, Kristi finally managed to find her voice. "You've come here to take our daughter."

"Yes," Jackson answered, voice barely louder than a whisper. His face was red from the shame at what he was being forced to do.

"You actually obtained a court order for this." Jeff's voice was as hard as steel.

"Yes."

"Give it to me."

Jackson reached into his jacket pocket with a sense of *deja vu*, remembering the same moment when he handed this same document to nurse Gardner. He held it out with a hand that had the tiniest shake to it, and Jeff snatched it away.

Less than a minute later, Jeff was looking up in stunned disbelief. "How in the hell did you get a judge to agree to this?"

Jackson glanced at his partner Roland, then back to Jeff. "My superiors were able to get the judge to understand the severity and uniqueness of the situation." The feeling of *deja vu* got stronger, like a maddening itch on that one place on your back that you can almost, but not quite, reach. "You have to understand, this isn't about Annie. It's about the whole world."

"Spare me," Jeff snapped. "This is our daughter you're talking about. How dare you stand there calm as you please and tell us you're just going to walk in and snatch-"

"I'll go with them," a young voice interjected.

In the heat of the moment, none of the four adults had noticed the front door opening behind them. Annie stood there, feet half in and half out of the doorway. Her childlike face was somber and somehow *old*, so much older than her years.

Kristi went down on one knee in front of her. "Annie, how much of this did you hear?"

Annie shrugged, a gesture that was somehow old and young at the same time. "Just the end, but I was able to put together the back story from the little bit I caught. These men want to figure out what's inside of me. This has to do with the mysterious deaths. I knew it did. I knew *I* did."

Jackson was staring at her as if encountering something he'd never seen before. "What did you know?" He asked, immediately picking up on her *different*-ness after taking one look at her eyes.

Annie looked up at him, and he almost took a step back. Lord, the weight in that gaze! "I knew I was connected to the people dying." She answered calmly. Matter of factly. "I started making people different, like me. I thought they were better. I thought *I* was better. But I'm not, am I?" She asked it with such innocence that Jackson wanted to weep.

"That's what we want to find out," Jackson said softly.

Jeff took a step toward Annie and knelt down on her other side. "Are you sure you understand what this means, kiddo?" He strove to speak normally, but Annie could feel the undercurrent of fear in his voice. "They want to take you to the hospital and keep you there. We don't know how long that might be." He looked over his shoulder, eyes flinty. "You don't know, do you? How long this will take?"

Jackson looked down again. "No. We don't."

Annie reached out both hands, putting one on Kristi's shoulder and the other on Jeff's. Her smile was radiant and lit up her face. "It's ok. Really. I think I knew that this would come to pass. When I made the connection...I want to know what's going on. I don't want people to die because of me. I couldn't live with that."

Jeff pushed down the tears that threatened at the corners of her eyes, but Kristi felt no such compunction to hold back. She grabbed Annie and pulled her into an embrace as the first tear fell.

Jeff slowly got up to his feet and turned to face the men from the CDC. "You have a court order. Furthermore, *and more importantly*, you have my daughter's acquiescence. But nowhere on this piece of paper does it say we are to be kept out of the loop. Therefore you *will* keep us apprised of your testing every step of the way. Do you understand? And, quarantine or no quarantine, we want access to her. I think it's safe to say that if we could have caught whatever it is she has, we would have by now."

Jackson was already nodding before Jeff had finished. "Of course, we agree to all of that! And please, I truly hope you understand how sorry I am about this entire situation. We really aren't the bad guys here. And," Jackson reached into a back pocket and pulled out a business card that he handed over to Jeff. "Please feel free to contact me *at any time*. I mean that. That's my personal cell, and email. Also, we will be working hand in hand with nurse Gardner, due to her personal experience and expertise. I hope that helps."

Jeff stared at him long and hard. "It helps," he said after a moment. Then, turning his back on Jackson and Roland, Jeff dropped down to where Kristi was still clutching Annie to her and wrapped his long arms around both of them.

By this point, Jacob and Maddy were crowding the doorway behind Annie, confusion written all over their faces. They didn't yet understand why their parents were on their knees holding Annie as if they were going to lose her.

They would both understand soon enough.

9

"For the record, I would like to point out, *again*, that this is not only wrong but also completely unnecessary. The virus is out there! Turn on the news, any station at all, and within five to ten minutes you will at least get a sound byte on a new 'mysterious' death." Jackson was standing outside the retrofitted quarantine room that Annie had been occupying for the last week and a half. He had his cell phone clutched in a white knuckled grip, pressed hard against his ear.

"Your point is taken, and on the record once more." Dr. Sam Hanson, still working out of her main office across the country, sounded tired and frustrated. "Believe it or not, I have superiors that I have to answer to, who are passing down the orders that I then pass along to you. Do you think I wanted that girl removed from her family and placed in quarantine just for the fun of it? Wake up, Telford. We know it's too late. MY boss knows it's too late. Even the president, in his infinite wisdom, understands that it's *too late*. But we still have to go through the motions, don't we? Do you understand that or not?"

Jackson sighed and ran a hand through his hair for the hundredth time that day. "Yes, I understand. Have you been getting my updates, with the sample results attached?"

Sam's voice perked up a bit at the change of subject, happy as always to get away from the whole *You're the bad guy, not me* schtick that Jackson had adopted of late. "Yes I have, and I've been going over them with Bob extensively. This virus, deadliness aside, is *fascinating*. I've never seen anything like this before in all my years at the CDC."

"Neither have I," Jackson replied, staring through the glass at the young/old girl napping on the bed they had brought in and set up for her. Despite her evident maturity, she still slept with a teddy bear that had been a gift from her parents when she was 3. "The virus, just like whatever host it resides in, is perfection personified. It resists whatever we try to do to it. I've tried multiple ways of damaging it, breaking apart its protein chains, heating it, cooling it, everything. And it just bounces right back. The only thing that destroys it is destroying the entire genetic sample. Kill the sample, kill the virus." Annie stirred in her sleep, and it sent another pang of guilt through Jackson.

There was a brief pause on the other end of the line. When Sam spoke, her voice had changed again. Jackson could detect a quiver of unease threading through her calm tone. "Like I said, Bob and I have reviewed everything you've sent us, particularly the strength of the virus when it is inside a host. We've also been discussing possible ramifications for humanity. You recall before you left for Utah when Bob and I were initially set on bringing Annie to us?"

"Yeah..."

"What you don't know is that after you left, we continued brainstorming possible...situations...that might become necessary in time to enact. One such possible outcome is mass quarantine. In going over your most recent data, Bob and I have come to the conclusion that mass quarantine is more than just a potential outcome, it may in fact be the *only* outcome that will stop humanity from spinning out of control."

Jackson felt his jaw drop. It took a moment before he could get his mind wrapped around what Sam was really saying. "Leper colonies," he finally gasped out, trying to work saliva back into his suddenly dry mouth. "That's what you're talking about. Leper colonies for a new Age. Segregating the infected children and what, just waiting for them to die so the planet can get on with its day to day routine?"

"Dammit, Jackson, do you still think that we actually *want* any of this to come to pass?! Open up your eyes, you're a doctor for hell's sake! The virus will bounce back from everything except complete destruction! PUT THAT INTO CONTEXT. When this news spreads, *and it will*, you know it will, how do you think people will react? What will parents do when they realize that their children could be given a virus that will kill them dead in a matter of years, and that said virus is passed along as easily as the common cold? Is it outside the realm of possibility to imagine parents taking up arms to ensure the survival of their children?"

Jackson opened his mouth to respond, but Sam steamrolled right over him.

"Maybe not in America, at least not at first, but what about other countries? Brazil? Mexico? Various countries in Africa where they still utilize child soldiers *to this day*?! This virus isn't just about the virus itself, not anymore. It's about how people are going to react to it. So tell me, *doctor*, exactly how should we proceed?"

During this whole tirade, Jackson hadn't been able to tear his eyes away from Annie. From, God help him for thinking this, *Patient Zero*. He finally understood.

Jackson hung up the phone without replying, sat down at the nearest table, dropped his head down onto his arms, and started to cry.

10

When Jackson finally got himself under control (during which his phone rang three times; he ignored it as if by not answering he could avoid taking part in any more of this madhouse situation) he raised his head.

Annie was standing on the other side of the glass, staring at him with concern.

Jackson jolted up and out of his chair, rendered temporarily speechless with surprise.

"You just had a phone call," she said. Her voice was relayed to him through the speaker system they had set up, as the quarantine room was soundproof among other things. "A bad one. I can tell from your face. It's about me, but not just about me. It's about what's going to happen next, isn't it?"

Despite working with Annie and getting to know her over the past week and a half, Jackson still found himself dumbfounded not just by her intelligence, but by her nearly superhuman powers of deduction. She was like a tiny little Sherlock, always on the case, sniffing out answers.

Not quite trusting his voice, Jackson simply nodded.

Annie, still clutching the teddy bear in her thin arms, cocked her head at him. "You are holding onto so much guilt over this. Over me. But it's ok. I've known for longer than you how this might play out, and I'm ok. If anyone should feel the guilt of the world riding on their shoulders, it's me. You know that, don't you?"

Jackson nodded again, unable to break the ancient gaze holding his.

"I didn't ask for this, whatever it is, inside of me. I have a feeling that my birth father is out there watching this play out. If anyone *deserves* to have guilt washing through them, it's him. But he isn't here. We are. So tell me about your phone call. Your bosses want to institute quarantine on a large scale, correct?"

"Yes." His voice was rough and low.

Annie's unblinking eyes held him as surely as a fly in amber. "You know it's already too late for that, and so do your bosses. But global quarantine still shows the world that you have your hands on the steering wheel, as it were. Better to be seen doing something if it means avoiding worldwide panic."

"How do you just...know things? As much as I'm coming to understand this virus, the speed of your comprehension is-"

"Eerie?" Annie finished his sentence with a smile. "I'm not quite sure myself as to why I, and all the others out there with this virus, can do what we do. You say you understand the virus, but you mean you understand what you see happening under a microscope. Being inside my own mind, all I can surmise is that my synapses are faster, or maybe I just have more of them. Either way, I believe I am able to think faster than most people on this planet. I wouldn't say that makes me a prodigy, but I can absorb and dissect information at a rapid pace. Furthermore, in regards to my own situation within this glass room, it's only natural that the next step would be to put every infected child in a similar room. But you also understand the inherent problem in this solution, don't you?"

Jackson pulled his chair over to the glass wall and sat down, putting them on the same eye level. Somehow it didn't seem appropriate that he should be the one looking down at her. "Yes. The problem is, how can you tell who is infected, and who isn't? Especially once we put mass quarantine into effect, and kids get scared. You've been carrying this inside of you for your entire life, and yet your condition has only now come to light. Over the last six years of your life, you have passed this on to an unknown, but probably quite a large, number of other children. How many of them have gone unnoticed?"

"Most of them," Annie answered.

"Precisely," Jackson felt his blood pressure returning to a normal range now that he was back in his element, speaking clinically instead of emotionally. "The one and only reason the virus has finally come into the public arena is because people, teenagers, began to die for no reason. Given the carefree way that children interact with each other, as opposed to adults, this thing is past the tipping point of control."

"Correct," Annie said. "And your bosses know that, I'm sure. But they can't sit back and do nothing. Mass quarantine is as good a stopgap solution as any. Because if they do nothing, and humanity panics, then blood will be shed."

Jackson gulped and ran a hand through his silver mane. "Don't you worry that blood will be shed no matter what happens?"

"Of course," Annie replied matter of factly. "But if you do something instead of nothing, if you give humanity something to hope for, then maybe you can avoid the worst case scenario. Mass hysteria. Panic. Killing. Me and mine aren't long for this world, and you already know that. At this point, we simply hope the world can pick itself back up when we're gone and figure out a way to heal.

"Otherwise, you may as well put us all down right now."

11

Over the past week and a half of government forced quarantine, at least one of Annie's family members, and often the entire clan (minus Alex, who was now 31 and living in New Orleans, Louisiana) came to see her. Kristi and Jeff particularly made an effort to come by in the morning, or the evening, or both, and they always brought a gift. One day it was a slice of the coffee cake that both Oritts were well known for baking. Another day it was the globe that Annie prized so much. Suffice to say, her wonderful adoptive family was making every effort to turn her hermetically sealed hospital room into a cozy bedroom with all of the perks that Annie had become accustomed to.

Annie, for her part, continued to try to make her family understand that she didn't blame the CDC, particularly Dr. Telford, for what was happening. It seemed that Annie's comprehension of the world around her, and her acceptance, had surpassed that of even her parents. When questioned further about this, Annie could only surmise that due to her rapidly functioning mind, she was leaving part of her emotional state behind her. So while Jeff and Kristi were still extremely agitated and emotional over the turn that events had taken, Annie could see the logic in her quarantined state. Why get emotional over something that was logical in nature?

Apparently, most humans allowed emotion to triumph over logic.

And it was in that moment that Annie saw herself becoming something more than human. Or at least something apart. The thought didn't scare her.

It was only logical.

That didn't mean that she didn't experience warmth and joy inside of her every time she saw her family. Quite the opposite, in point of fact. Seeing her family was always the highlight of her day.

As the days passed, Annie began to pick up trends in the subjects that her family members were willing to speak about, and subjects that they avoided. Jeff tended to stick to the facts of the situation, meeting her in the arena of logic as they calmly discussed what was happening in the world currently, and what Annie predicted for the future.

Kristi tended to be more nurturing, making sure that Annie was being properly taken care of, and that she didn't want for anything (which she didn't). Kristi never seemed completely convinced, but Annie understood her perspective. For example, when her mom invariably asked if she was sure she had everything she needed, Annie's inevitable response was "Seeing you here is everything I need." This mollified both of her parents every time, and in this way, the time passed peacefully enough, despite the regular blood tests, biopsies, and scans.

In fact, there was only one day that brought a little confusion and uncertainty into Annie's mind. It was her 8th day of 'captivity', and the day before she and Dr. Telford had their talk about the future of the human race, and the plan for mass quarantine.

On that fateful evening, around 7 p.m. (right after a hearty dinner of spaghetti and meatballs, yum!) it was Maddy alone who came to see her. Maddy was 18-going-on-19, and was in her first year of college at the University of Utah. Maddy, Annie already knew, was becoming quite the young genius herself, and not for the same reason Annie was.

Which is exactly where the conversation took a turn.

After Maddy arrived and took a seat right up close to the glass wall of Annie's 'cage' (as the family tried *not* to refer to it as, but Annie could always see it in their eyes) she opened up their little familial palaver with the usual niceties.

"How's everything going today?" The ever popular opening line, inviting casual conversation while avoiding what was really going on.

Annie smiled, and it lit up her face. "You know I'm doing ok. But I'm always happy to see my big sister! I love your hair, by the way. You should wear it loose all the time!"

Maddy blushed with pleasure at the compliment. From a very young age, Maddy had had gorgeous wavy red hair, the color of a perfect sunrise. No matter where she went, she drew compliments like flowers drew bees. "Thank you! I actually have a date later, so I spent a little extra time on it."

"A date!" Annie burst out. Regardless of her relative young age, she well understood dating, and the kind of love that can be provided by someone not in your family unit. She had learned all about it from The Notebook. "Who with? Where did you meet him? What's his name? Tell me everything!"

"Slow down!" Maddy said with a laugh. "His name is John, and he's in Pre-Law at the University of Utah. We met in my economy class."

"Is he a fox?" This was a phrase Annie had recently picked up while watching trashy TV in her hospital room in between her various examinations. She had decided she needed more pop culture understanding to fit in.

Maddy laughed again. "Total fox! And he's tall, too!" This had always been important to Maddy, who stood just shy of six feet herself.

Annie clapped her hands and bounced up and down in her chair. "Good for you! Come back tomorrow and tell me how it goes!"

Maddy promised she would, and then her smile slowly faltered and fell. Annie, watching closely, knew they had come around to the reason that Maddy had come to see her solo.

Maddy blinked a few times and cleared her throat. "Um..." A pause. "Can I ask you something that I've been thinking about lately?" Her voice, usually so expressive, had gone monotone.

Annie nodded and smiled reassuringly. "Of course. We're sisters; you know you can ask me anything."

Despite Annie's attempt at reassurance, Maddy looked more uncomfortable than before. Annie felt the first stirrings of concern, deep in her chest. Annie, who was always so perceptive, was suddenly afraid of whatever Maddy was about to say.

Maddy cleared her throat again. Shifted a little to the left in her chair. Then back to the right. Then, all at once and in a rush, "Why wasn't I infected, too?"

A long pause.

Annie's eyes widened.

She...she had never thought about that.

Not once.

And she had been thinking of little else these days.

But Annie had never once considered why, if she was able to pass along whatever was inside of her to other children of a certain age, why had she never passed it along to Maddy? Yes, Maddy was brilliant, but it was the brilliance of a natural prodigy, not an *un*natural prodigy, which was undeniably what Annie was. And while Maddy did have an excellent immune system (due to her strenuous exercise regime and healthy eating habits), she *did* still get sick. Occasionally she dealt with a minor injury or two. She had even, just last year, had minor heart surgery to have a stent put in, due to a very slight genetic defect in one of her coronary arteries. Not to mention the overwhelming evidence against her having what Annie had: Maddy was *still alive*. Had Annie infected her, Maddy would have been dead for at least three years now.

She wasn't. Here she was in front of Annie, vibrant and full of life.

And yet.

When Annie was born, and then shortly thereafter adopted by the Oritt family, Maddy had only been 12. That leaves a *three year* gap when Annie could have, *should* have, inadvertently infected her. The two sisters had played together, wrestled together, shared straws and utensils.

And yet.

Annie realized she had been holding her breath, and let it out in a long *whoooooosh* that briefly fogged up the glass in front of her.

"Yeah," Maddy said, in response to Annie's facial expression. "My feeling exactly."

What Annie said next were three little words that hadn't crossed her lips in over two years. "I don't understand."

Maddy's shoulders slumped. "Neither do I. Don't get me wrong, I'm grateful, because by all reports I should be...you know..." She trailed off uncertainly.

"I know. I'm grateful, too. But...it doesn't make sense. By my calculations, every prepubescent person I've come into contact with has gotten what I have. I can't even say with certainty that it started with my friend Beckie. I just know that she was the first one that I was able to observe as the change began. But before Kids Kampus? How many others did I pass this along to without even realizing what was happening? A handful? Dozens? All I know is that according to the news, this...*thing*...is international. Did you hear about South Africa?"

Maddy nodded. "The first death, in Johannesburg, was reported yesterday. It's all people are talking about."

Annie abruptly stood up and started pacing back and forth. Her mind was racing. "If I didn't pass it along to you, is there a reason why? Do you have some kind of natural immunity? Are there others that I've been in contact with who never got it, either?"

Catching movement out of the corner of her eye, Annie turned back to face Maddy, who was also on her feet and shaking her head frantically.

"What?"

"*That* is why I came alone today! I haven't spoken of this to mom and dad, and I guarantee it hasn't crossed their minds. I don't want anyone else to make this connection except for you, me, and Jessica. I already called her and told her that I want to have a private meeting tomorrow afternoon when I finish my classes for the day. My plan is to ask her to *discreetly* take a sample and just see what she sees. If I have something new, or different, or whatever, inside of *me*, I want to be able to deal with it by myself before I decide what to do next. With the panic that is obviously gnawing at the collective consciousness of humanity right now, I couldn't handle being thrown into the mix. I'm so sorry, I don't mean to sound callous, but I'm a little freaked out about this whole thing. Please tell me you understand." Maddy's voice was pleading, and she was actually wringing her hands without realizing it.

Annie held up her own hands and placed them on the glass. Maddy put hers up as well, the closest they could come to touching with the glass barrier between them. "Of *course* I understand. I don't want them to stick you in a cage next to me, not if it can be avoided. Just promise me you'll keep me in the loop?"

Maddy smiled gratefully. "Of course I will! You'll know everything the minute that I do. I just...I had to come talk to you first."

"Hey, we're sisters, regardless of parentage. Nothing is going to change that!"

Maddy's smile widened, and she offered Annie a fist bump against the glass, which Annie returned with a giggle.

"Now get out of here and go on your date! I'm going to want an update on that, too, and it better be a good one!"

That brought on a laugh, natural and filled with good humor. "You got it. Love you, Annie!"

"I love you, too."

And in a whirlwind of blazing red hair, Maddy was gone.

12

July 1st, 2009.

The virus had spread silently across South Africa, and had recently crossed the border into Namibia and Botswana. The current death toll for the continent still stood at less than 100, which meant that panic hadn't set in.

Yet.

But.

People wondered.

Speculated.

Parents in Johannesburg, not exactly knowing what they were looking for, began talking about keeping their kids home from school when the upcoming fall semester began, at least until this thing blew itself out. Because it would, of course.

Wouldn't it?

13

July 2nd, 2009.
The virus had spread from Paris into all of the outlying provinces. As the sun set on an uneasy populace, the virus crossed the border into Spain.

14

July 3rd, 2009.
The president of Russia, avidly keeping up with every new report and beginning to believe that something more sinister, something that just might be *man made* and not an *act of God* was at work, began to consider closing down his country's borders.

15

July 4th, 2009.
America's Independence Day. A day, nationwide, of celebration with friends, family, neighbors. A day of block parties, concerts, drinking, camaraderie without reservation.
Before the last of the days fireworks faded from the sky, the virus would be in every single state.

Part 6: The Trial Con't (The Year 2018)

1

"Your Honor," Jeff intoned with dignity and gravitas as court was announced back in session. "I'd like to call to the stand nurse Jessica Gardner."

The defense had been given advance access to the witnesses that the prosecution would be calling, just as Jeff had gotten the names of the defense witnesses, and so both the defense attorney Gabrial and the defendant himself knew that Jessica would be called next. Even so, Jeff thought he noticed Dr. Michaels squirm just a little bit in his seat. Something about Jessica being there that made Dr. Michaels uncomfortable in a personal way? Definitely worth keeping an eye on.

After Jessica had been sworn in, Jeff took his place before the witness stand and relaxed his stiff attitude by a notch or two. After all, here was a friend, and an ally, not just an expert witness to give testimony. He noticed she was wearing a fairly severe pantsuit, which he hoped would add weight and formality to her words.

"Jessica," Jeff began with the barest of nods, given in thanks for her willing participation. "You're a nurse at Primary Children's hospital, correct?"

Jessica nodded. "Yes. I've been working there since 1999, first as a certified nursing assistant and more recently as an advanced practice registered nurse, or APRN."

Jeff clasped his hands behind his back, feeling confident. Jessica was there not only as another medical expert, but also to help humanize the situation. She was the most important character witness he had. "And what department do you work in within the hospital?"

"NICU, or neonatal intensive care unit. I've been there for my entire career." Jessica maintained a formal pose, hands held carefully in her lap, so as not to betray the slight shake that had started the moment she walked into the courtroom. Just like Jeff, a primal part of her longed to throw herself, fists first, at the man sitting behind the defendants table.

"So you were working there in 2003 when Patient Zero was born?"

Jessica's eyes flashed, even though Jeff had prepared her for the course he was going to take. "Yes, I was there when *Annie* was born, though I wasn't actually present for the birth."

"Of course, thank you for the correction. Up until 2003, had you ever had any contact with the defendant, Dr. Calvin Michaels?"

Jessica looked over at the defendant for the first time since she entered the room, and her fists clenched tightly in her lap. "No. As I said, I work in the NICU, not in delivery or genetics, which I believe *was* the specialty of Dr. Michaels." The emphasis she placed on *was* may have been slight, but it was there for everyone to pick up on. The defense attorney scowled but kept silent.

"What can you tell us of your initial contact with Annie?"

Jessica turned back to face Jeff. "After her birth, she was immediately brought to my department and placed on life support. She had abnormal stem cells and many of her internal organs weren't fully formed, which we believe was due at least in part to her stem cells. To be honest, none of us thought that she would last the night. And then, miracle of miracles, we find out that Annie had a twin sister who was born an hour after Annie was brought to us. The twin was apparently the very picture of health, and we immediately decided to try a blood transfusion."

Jeff held up a hand, palm up. "And then?"

"Like I said, it was a miracle. Annie healed in every single way before the sun rose the next morning. Her organs continued developing until everything was fully formed and fully functioning. Her stem cells began multiplying not just at a normal rate but at a rate previously uncharted. And her thymus gland was the biggest change of all."

Jeff cleared his throat. "For the sake of the court, could you clarify what the thymus gland does?"

"Of course," Jessica nodded. Getting caught up in her explanation, she forgot that the general layman doesn't know the intricacies of the human body. "The thymus gland is the body's producer of T-lymphocytes, or T cells for short, which are a type of white blood cell that protects the body from specific threats, such as viruses and infections. The thymus gland is unique in that it's only active in the human body until puberty. However, by that point it has already produced all of the T cells that a healthy human will require for their lifetime."

"Thank you," Jeff said, waving a hand for her to continue. "You were saying that Annie's thymus gland was the biggest change?"

"Correct. Annie's thymus gland appeared supercharged after the blood transfusion from the twin, producing T cells so rapidly that it's really no surprise that Annie could instantly fight off anything that tried to get a foothold in her body."

Jeff turned from Jessica and ran his eyes over the judge and then the members of the jury to emphasize his point. "So we had a sickly infant who was at death's door, and then suddenly a miracle arrives in the form of a twin sister, who provides a blood transfusion that doesn't just save the sickly twin, but turns her into a disease fighting machine. It's nearly supernatural." Jeff turned back to Jessica. "Final question: where did the miracle twin go?"

There were a few audible gasps from the members of the jury who hadn't even considered the twin angle.

Jessica, fully prepared for the question, had her answer ready. "No one knows. After the twin was brought in for the transfusion, the entire NICU staff on duty, as well as a few doctors and nurses from other departments, were caught up in Annie's healing process. The word miraculous seems to be an understatement. Your word choice of 'supernatural' more closely describes what we were seeing happen right before our very eyes.

By the time someone thought to inquire after the healthy twin, or the man who delivered her, both were gone."

Jeff allowed a moment of silence so that fact would sink in before he spun on one heel and walked back to the prosecutors desk. "Your witness."

2

The defense attorney, Gabriel, approached the witness stand where Jessica still sat with her hands clenched in her lap.

"Gabriel is a snake," Jeff had told her when they had been preparing for the trial. *"But he's a very skilled, very dangerous snake. He'll try to get you riled up and emotional, so as to take away your credibility in the eyes of the jurors. The good news is that you're not being brought in as my medical expert, you're being put on the stand as a* character *witness, and as someone who was there and witnessed the beginning of this all. Gabriel will try to get under your skin, but there's not much he can say or do to tarnish your testimony, because of the personal nature of your statement. So keep calm, answer whatever he throws at you, and please try not to punch him in the face."*

This last statement had gotten a laugh out of Jessica at the time, but she wasn't feeling very humorous now. In fact, staring at Gabriel's weasel-ish features as he approached the witness stand, with his pointed chin, overbite, and greasy hair, she found that she really *did* want to punch him in the face.

Easy Jess, she told herself sternly. *You've handled bigger jerks than this guy. Just breathe.*

"Miss Gardner-"

"Mrs." Jess interrupted automatically.

Gabriel blinked, momentarily thrown off track. Jess mentally gave herself a point. "Excuse me?"

"It's *Mrs.* Gardner." She delivered this in a calm, quiet voice, like a teacher correcting an elementary student.

Gabriel cleared his throat. "Yes. Well. *Mrs.* Gardner. You said that before receiving Patient Zero-"

"Annie," Jessica interrupted again. *Point.* She was enjoying this.

Gabriel narrowed his eyes at her in an obvious challenge. "Call her whatever you like, Annie or Patient Zero, but the facts before the court are that she is the one to first be diagnosed with the Angel Virus and in turn spread it across the world. My point is, before *Annie* was delivered to your department at the hospital, you had no interaction whatsoever with my client, Dr. Calvin Michaels."

"No."

""You've never assisted with birth?"

"No."

"Never been brought in to work with genetics?"

"No."

"So you admit that genetics is in no way, shape or form part of your medical expertise?"

"Objection," Jeff said with quiet force from his seat behind the prosecutors desk.

The judge turned to face him. "On what grounds, counselor?"

Jeff raised a hand towards Jessica. "Relevance, Your Honor. Nurse Gardner was not brought in as a medical expert, therefore whether she has any knowledge of genetics isn't relevant to this case."

The judge turned back to face Gabriel and Jessica, peering at them both in turn over his thick, horn rimmed glasses. "Overruled. As nurse Gardner is an expert in her specific medical field, I'll allow this line of questioning." Those stern eyes looked directly at Gabriel and narrowed. "But watch yourself, counselor."

Gabriel nodded to the judge before looking back to Jessica. "Your answer, nurse?"

Jessica tried not to grind her teeth and just barely succeeded. "No, genetics is not my area of expertise. As I stated before, I've been a NICU nurse for my whole career."

Gabriel waved a hand as if to dismiss the importance of her statement. As he did, Jessica noticed that he wore three large, shiny rings on his right hand, each capped with a different colored stone. The word 'gaudy' didn't begin to describe them. "So by your own admission, you didn't know my client from Adam before the events of the birth and subsequent blood transfusion that saved *Patient Zero*. So you have no way of knowing what did or didn't transpire to cause one twin to be sickly and the other to be healthy. All you have to go on is your own eyewitness account of *Patient Zero* as she went from a sickly state to a healthy one, albeit more rapidly than usual, before she went on to infect the world with her virus." Gabriel leaned in close enough to Jessica that she could smell stale tobacco on his breath. "Better for the world if Patient Zero had died that night."

Jessica slapped him across the face hard enough to spin him half around and nearly sent him to the floor. The whole courtroom erupted in noise. Despite repeatedly banging his gavel and bellowing for order, it took over five minutes to restore peace to the proceedings, at which point the judge ordered another recess, this time for an hour.

3

"I shouldn't have slapped him," Jessica said. It was 20 minutes later and she was sitting with Jeff in a private room down the hall from their courtroom.

Jeff shook his head and let out a rueful chuckle. "Honestly Jess, if you hadn't I probably would have, and then at the very least I would have had to recuse myself, assuming the judge didn't just throw the whole case out. As it is, your testimony stays on the record, and your slap might have even won us a few points with some of the jurors."

Jessica threw her hands up. "I just don't understand this whole process! The man *confessed*. He confessed to everything and yet still he asks for his day in court? He's like a dime store supervillain who wants a chance to have a lengthy monologue before the hero comes along and foils his grand plans!" She sighed, and her voice dropped almost to a whisper. "Except his grand plans came to pass. There's nothing left to foil."

Jeff rose to his feet and placed a hand on Jessica's shoulder. "We can still see that justice is done," he said firmly. "And you've helped with that. Let me do the rest and, god willing, we'll never have to see that man's face again."

Jessica looked up, her expression void of any emotion. "Does Utah have the death penalty?"

"Damn right we do."

Part 7: A Pandemic (The Year 2009)

1

July 5th, 2009.
The global death toll was still unknown, because not every country had been as willing as the U.S., UK, and South Africa to admit out loud to the world what this was. A pandemic. A plague the likes of which had never been seen before (outside of mainstream fiction, that is). And could you really blame the countries that were still desperately trying to play this down in order to avoid mass panic and hysteria?

The numbers that *were* available were alarming enough. The U.S. stood at just over 300,000 confirmed deaths.

The UK, smaller than the US geographically and *much* smaller in terms of population, had risen to 50,000 confirmed deaths, and many more that were still under investigation.

South Africa was still in the process of data gathering, but they had admitted publicly that they weren't far behind the UK, especially due to the relatively young median age of their country.

In their manic fear, the religious fanatics around the US began to whisper that this was the coming of the foretold apocalypse, and the dying children represented *The Rapture*. The children were dying because they were in fact being saved! Lifted up to heaven! Obviously only the children were being saved because they were the only ones who were still pure. They hadn't yet grown into maturity and been corrupted by the three headed demon that was Government, Media, and Temptation.

The religious fanatics gave a name to these 'saved' children. Angels.

This new name was picked up and embraced by the wider, secular communities around them, adding a word to emphasize not the *saving* of the children, but the scythe of the reaper that was falling faster and faster around the world.

The Angel Virus.

The CDC still had absolutely no idea what to do next.

2

July 6th, 2009.
10 a.m.

Kristi had just pulled into the nearly full parking lot at Primary Children's hospital. Today she was there not just to see Annie, but to sit down with Jessica. On the phone the night before, Jessica had asked Kristi to come in for a private meeting to go over recent events at the hospital. Despite the feigned calm in Jessica's voice, Kristi could hear the underlying tension, and it transmitted through the phone line like a static shock.

"Of course I can come in. What time?" Kristi asked.

"I'm working the night shift and then I'll be sticking around tomorrow morning for a while, to catch up on the paperwork that has been drowning me of late. Is 10 a.m. ok?" Jessica responded, striving to keep the exhaustion and fear out of her voice.

"I'll be there."

And now, 10 a.m. on the dot, Kristi found herself nearly unable to get out of her car. Her heart was full of dread. Jessica was the one person in the entire hospital that she trusted to give her the straight truth, but suddenly she didn't know if she could handle it. Annie had been here under quarantine for just over two weeks, and yet it felt like months had passed.

Just over two weeks, each day spent feeling on edge, nerves raw, each night tossing and turning and desperately trying to sleep and being denied time and time again. Kristi and Jeff felt like they were slowly losing their minds with the *not knowing* of the situation.

But could finding out new information from Jessica make things better?

Or so very much worse?

Finally, heaving a deep sigh of resignation, Kristi forced herself out of her Subaru. A fierce desert sun boiled above her in a cloudless sky, causing beads of sweat to instantly swell across her forehead. Kristi put her head down and quickly stepped across the softened tar of the parking lot, moving by instinct between parked cars that she didn't really see.

A brief moment later and Kristi was walking through the double doors that automatically opened before her, bringing the relief of cool air conditioning. And the swell of a multitude of voices, ebbing and flowing across her senses as she approached the nurses desk, ignoring the long line of parents and children who were awaiting their turn with doctors and nurses who didn't have answers for them.

The harried looking nurses behind the front desk were both older, career nurses that Kristi had interacted with in the past. Both were tall and statuesque, with identical silver gray hair pulled back in severe buns. Most people, upon first meeting Betty and Dolores, thought they were sisters, though they weren't.

Dolores noticed Kristi approaching and gave her a brief nod. "Jessica will be right out. Feel free to take a seat. If you can find one." And with that, Dolores turned back to the woman in front of her who was clutching a silent, solemn-looking toddler to her breast and had a wild look in her eyes.

The toddler caught Kristi's eye just before she turned away and nodded. Kristi shivered. Despite having watched Annie grow up and becoming used to and even inured to her unnatural maturity and wisdom, it was still a shock seeing that same gravitas in another child.

Jessica saved her from having to find a place to sit in the overflowing waiting room, popping out of one of the doors that led deeper into the hospital and flagging Kristi down.

Seconds later the two friends were walking down a stark, beige hallway that seemed almost eerily silent after the noise of the waiting room.

"Thank you so much for coming to see me this morning!" Jessica said at once, turning to Kristi as they walked side by side and reaching up to brush a few errant strands of hair behind one ear. It seemed an effort in futility, as much of Jessica's ponytail had pulled itself free over the course of however many hours she had just worked in a row.

Kristi, arms held tight across her chest and a purse hanging by her side, nodded and attempted a smile. "You know we all appreciate having you here, and supporting us throughout this crazy time."

They reached the end of the corridor and turned into Jessica's office. "Believe me, I've been doing everything I can to stay on top of this thing, and to keep my ear to the ground with the CDC people," she said as they both sat. "Calling it a crazy time is a bit of an understatement now that word has gotten out to the public. Have you heard the recent posted death tolls?"

Kristi nodded uncomfortably. "It's all that's on the news right now. Everything else has vanished from the media. Little surprise, of course."

Jessica sat forward, face grim. "There will be a new development on the reporting of the Angel Virus soon enough. I just spoke with the main CDC guy here, Jackson. You remember meeting him? Well, it turns out he's actually a decent guy, and over the course of his time here we've had the chance to speak a few times. I get the sense that he's not happy with the approach the CDC is taking on this, and managed to get stationed here, working with Annie, so he could be on the frontlines trying to figure out a solution before more drastic steps are taken. But as you know, despite the fact that we're starting to understand the structure of this virus, we still don't have any idea how to stop it."

Kristi's hands tightened on the armrests of the chair. "What are you saying?"

"I'm saying that Annie's quarantine here was always meant to be a test run by the CDC, to see if it could be a viable containment option. Worldwide."

"You've got to be joking," Kristi said softly. "That's...it's not...it's impossible. With how far the virus has already spread, you would have to quarantine the entire prepubescent population of the *world*."

"Which is roughly 26%." Jessica shook her head, and suddenly the exhaustion she had been trying to hold back rushed through her all at once. "Jackson showed me the statistics that he's run. Our current global population is 6.8 billion with a B. Population of ages 0 through 15 is just under 2 billion. And the best the CDC, and by that I mean our government, can come up with is mass. Fucking. Containment. Excuse my cursing."

Kristi let out a humorless laugh. "I'd say now is as good a time as any for cursing, Jess."

Jessica looked up, and Kristi could see all at once how much she'd been holding onto. "That's just the point. There isn't a single good option available to them. Jackson said the president is getting hourly briefs from the CDC, and his entire cabinet has been scrambling. The CDC doesn't have a cure, a vaccine, nothing. But our fearless leader in the White House knows that the common people need *something*."

Sudden white hot rage bloomed inside of Kristi. "So that's it," she spat out, not at Jessica, but at the situation Jessica was laying out in front of her. "Keep your kids home safe, unless they've been infected, in which case the government, the *world* will come knocking to snatch them up from right under your nose, regardless of how young they are, and lock them up until they die? And then what?"

"And then we don't lose 2 billion kids in the next decade and a half," Jessica responded quietly.

The anger drained away as quickly as it had come. Kristi shut her eyes as if to block out the situation by sheer will power. "Annie's going to die like the rest of them?" It was almost said as a statement, but Jessica treated it as a question.

"Annie is only 6. We still have nearly a decade before she hits puberty, assuming it doesn't happen early. I believe that we *will* be able to figure something out. The biggest positive in this whole god-forsaken situation is that eventually, every government on the planet will come together and pool their resources to come up with a solution. Nothing brings people together like shared trauma, and this is the mack daddy of them all." Jessica paused, and then rushed forward. "And that's not the only reason I asked you to come in. Maddy came in to see me the other day, asking about the virus."

Kristi's eyes shot open and bored into Jessica's with frightful intensity. "What?"

Jessica immediately held up her hands, either in placation or in defense. "Maddy's fine, I promise. The reason she came in was because she wanted me to run some tests to make sure that she didn't have the virus, which of *course* she doesn't. Maddy is, as far as we know, too old to contract the Angel Virus. She's too old *now*."

Jessica's point sank home immediately, and Kristi rocked back in her chair as if she'd been slapped. "Maddy was 12 when we got Annie. But she never got the virus. How have we never seen this before? We've never even *considered* it."

"Of course you didn't," Jessica said quietly. "None of us did, not even Annie, because the situation has only escalated fairly recently. It was Maddy herself who finally thought about it. She came in to speak with Annie first, to see if she might have light to shed on the situation, which of course Annie didn't. That's when Maddy came to see me. I did a couple of tests on the sly, with Jackson's help, and the results were exactly as expected. Maddy's clean."

Kristi let out a breath she didn't realize she'd been holding. "How? If every other kid who has *ever* come into contact with Annie has gotten this thing, why not Maddy? Is there something special about her, some antibody that no one else has?"

Jessica was shaking her head before Kristi finished getting the question out. "That's exactly what we wondered, but as of yet we haven't found anything that would suggest Maddy having some kind of unique immunity. And believe me, Jackson and I have gone over the blood tests with a fine tooth comb. If Maddy had a magical immunity, that would be a game changer."

The implication behind that statement wasn't lost on Kristi. "The world would never leave Maddy alone if they realized that she alone didn't contract the Angel Virus. Even if there was never any recorded proof or reason why, she wouldn't have a single day's peace."

Jessica turned and reached over to her file cabinet. A thin manila folder was sitting on top. Jessica plucked it off of the cabinet and handed it across to Kristi. "This is the data we got from Maddy's tests. As soon as we printed off these results, Jackson and I both deleted the information from our computers. We didn't want anyone trying to make a miracle cure out of a hope and a dream."

Kristi accepted the folder and opened it on her lap. In it were three different pages showing different colored graphs and numbers. "All of this simply shows that Maddy is just like anyone else?"

Jessica nodded. "So far as we know, yes. No magical antibodies, nothing but another enigmatic piece in this whole damn puzzle. But here's the direction my mind has been churning. All of the statistics and numbers that have been released thus far have said that kids under 15 have been contracting this virus at a 100% infection rate, after coming into contact with another so-called Angel. And then, at age 15, instant death. But where did the magic number 15 come from? From the information that Jackson has been able to share with me, I've seen a few hospital reports that don't say 15, they say *teenager*, or *pubescent*. I don't have proof, yet, but I'm beginning to wonder if it's not the age that's important, but the act of reaching puberty. In which case, with Maddy-"

"-she might not have contracted the virus because she hit puberty early. That's what you're saying?"

Jessica nodded. "Again, at this point it's just conjecture, but it makes sense. After all, everyone's body is different. Kids don't hit puberty at the exact same time. Maddy might have escaped this thing by sheer luck of genetics. But the media has latched onto the number 15, and if anyone has hard proof otherwise, like the CDC, they are keeping mum on the matter."

Kristi looked up. "What exactly do we do with this information?"

"For now? Keep digging."

3

July 10th, 2009.

An emergency UN summit was held in Washington D.C. Before the day was out, it had been unanimously decided to shut down the borders of every country for the time being, until an answer to this disease was found.

If there was an answer.

It was already too late, of course, but it at least had a calming effect on the general populace, as people were able to take comfort in their leaders doing *something*.

4

While many people worldwide sank deeper into panic and despair, particularly those with children of their own, there were others who embraced life in the midst of the Angel pandemic. It was now well known that if you were an Angel, you had only until your 15th birthday before inevitably succumbing to the doomsday clock inside of you. Therefore, surviving your 15th birthday became a cause for riotous celebration. Parties were thrown. Parents, teary eyed with joy, allowed their kids to drink, even if it was just a glass of champagne to toast the long life they had ahead of them.

Of course, being just 15, many of these kids had no head for alcohol, and no understanding of limiting their libations.

In Austin, Texas, a brand new 15 year old, flush with vitality, found his father's moonshine, drank it all with two of his friends, and then 'borrowed' the family truck and promptly wrapped it around a telephone poll downtown, instantly killing all three of them.

In Los Angeles, a week later, a girl turned 15 and immediately went out to celebrate with her older sister. The sister took the two of them to a pool party. The girl, who had never touched a drop before that night, polished off a six pack of wine coolers. She was found floating face down in the pool the next morning.

In New York, a boy who had just turned 15 smoked weed that had been laced with meth. Wandering downtown, mind reeling, he stepped off the curb. In front of a bus.

These kids, victims of their own misperceived immortality, were dubbed Devils by the media, and quickly became a grisly subset of the Angel Virus.

And thus the fear spread like a living thing from household to household, country to country.

5

August 1st, 2009.
"It won't be long now," Annie said softly.
It was late morning and she was still in her pajamas, red and black plaid, with her hair pulled back in a loose ponytail. She sat in a chair in her little apartment, as she thought of it, looking through the glass wall at Jessica, who was seated opposite her. Jessica had dark circles under her eyes, and her eyelids drooped. It was obvious to even the most casual observer that she hadn't been sleeping.

Jessica had just told her about the outpouring of news across every media about the Devils that were killing themselves with their own birthday parties. The hysteria following in its wake was nearly as loud as the panic over the Angel Virus.

"What won't be long?" Jessica asked with a frown.

"Quarantine. Leper colonies, as Dr. Telford is wont to say. It was going to happen anyway, but with this? The Angels will be blamed for the so-called 'Devils' as surely as the sun sets in the west."

Jessica was shaking her head before Annie finished. "No way. How can they? This is completely separate, an illogical response to-"

Annie raised a hand, much like a child in class, and Jessica trailed off. "All the public will see is more death. That's it. Even the name for these poor souls, Devils, is connected to us, to the Angels. We're all connected. And so kids will be gathered up and separated, to make the rest of the world feel safe. Safer, at least. Think about women who are pregnant right now. Doesn't it make sense that they would be leading the charge for quarantine, to make sure their unborn children will be born into a safe world?"

Jessica threw her hands up. "No! None of this makes sense! Jackson said that you and he already talked this through. How will people know who is an Angel and who isn't? Yes, we have rudimentary testing set up now that we know to look for supercharged T cells and an abnormal thymus gland, but we absolutely don't have the means or the equipment to test every single child in the world in a short enough period of time to tell exactly who needs to be quarantined and who doesn't."

Annie's mouth quirked up in a mirthless smile. "Eventually we will all be gathered up, I think. Here in America it might be a slower process, because we can at least start testing, and give peace of mind to a percentage of parents. But think about countries that don't have the infrastructure in place that the United States does. When people get scared, their baser instincts emerge. It's why mob mentality is so terrifying. Children will be gathered up, separated, segregated, treated like walking time bombs. Which, in a way, we are. I haven't run the statistics, but if you ask Dr. Telford, I'm sure he'll give you a very scary number about the number of children that we can predict have already been infected. With every passing day, it spreads faster and faster, despite parents keeping their kids home in self imposed quarantine. And now the day when a new school year *should* be starting is fast approaching us. I think that will drive the issue home, honestly. By the end of this year, you will see quarantine camps popping up all around the globe. And next year? Suffice to say, this will get worse."

Jessica's shoulders slumped. "Is it really so hopeless?"

Annie shrugged. "I know Dr. Telford and his team are working as hard as they can to find a cure. I'm sure other teams in other countries are working just as diligently. I commend their efforts, I really do, and I'm just as willing to hold out hope that they'll discover something. But humanity is scared, feeling cornered, and when an animal is backed into a corner, it is irrational and at its most dangerous. In all honesty, I feel safer in here than I do out there."

6

August 2nd, 2009.

"Mr. President?"

The most powerful man in the free world looked up from his desk in the oval office. "Yes?" He had just been going over his brief from the recent UN summit, preparing for his upcoming phone call with the British Prime Minister.

Arnold, his chief of staff, walked in with a folder in his hand, which he set down on the desk in front of the president. "The CDC just sent over the latest numbers. It's...sir, it's worrying. Their earlier predictions were off by almost a magnitude of 10."

The president froze with his hand outstretched to take the folder and he looked up at Arnold sharply. "What about a cure? Any developments?"

Arnold shook his head. "They've included what they've discovered so far about the nature of the Angel Virus, but have made zero headway in developing a way to combat it. It's bad, sir."

The president sighed. He had two children of his own, a son and a daughter, but both were in their 20's and therefore out of the danger zone. But that knowledge did little to ease his mind when he had to consider the welfare of his country, and the world. "Did they offer secondary solutions, as I requested?"

Arnold nodded. "Yes sir. The final page. They apologized for not having more, and said they are available day and night if you have any further questions."

The president thanked Arnold and dismissed him before pulling the manila folder towards him and opening it with a feeling of dread settling into the pit of his stomach. He flipped past the first several pages of graphs and went straight to the final page, which was simply headed 'Solutions'. It was two paragraphs, double spaced. The first paragraph outlined a plan for mass quarantine. The second explained why it wouldn't work, but that at this point in time it was all they had.

7

August 10th, 2009.
The President of the United States of America gave an emergency address that evening, announcing that all professional sporting events would be cancelled indefinitely. All sports stadiums would be undergoing speedy renovations to turn them into quarantine zones for all infected children, with medical tents set up outside in order to test any child under 15. All parents were required by law to bring their children in for testing. Any child who tested positive would be remitted to government care in the quarantine zone until such a time as a cure could be found. Furthermore, the president promised that each government worldwide was sparing no expense in their study of this disease so that a cure could be found as soon as possible. Parents would, of course, have access to their children at any time. The president ended his address by thanking everyone for their cooperation in this unprecedented emergency, and would keep everyone updated as soon as new information became available.

8

Annie watched the emergency address from her room in the hospital. When it ended, she turned the tv off and lay back in her bed, feeling a chill sweep over her. "And so it begins," she whispered to herself. Sleep would be a long time coming that night.

9

A short distance away, Beckie sat with her sisters and parents in front of the tv as the president closed his address. Beckie, Kendra and Iris all sat on the carpet in front of the couch, legs crossed and hands folded neatly in their laps. Not one of their faces showed a glimmer of surprise.

Steven exhaled heavily and shut off the tv. Trini turned to him, fear writ plain in the tightened lines of her face. Steven, staring down at his three daughters, knew the truth that lay before him.

Beckie felt his eyes on her head and was the first to turn and meet his gaze. "Yes, daddy. We have to go get tested and get quarantined. It makes sense." Iris and Kendra nodded agreement without turning around.

Being a little bit older and closer to the cusp of 15 when infected, Iris and Kendra hadn't experienced as rapid a change as Beckie had, but both still knew the logic and wisdom of Beckie's statement. They were all three of them self aware in a way they never had been before. They were infected. Angels. Being quarantined was the logical course. The intelligent solution.

Trini's head whipped around, eyes wild as they met the ageless gaze staring up at her. "NO! There is nothing wrong with you! This whole situation is...is.."

Steven placed a gentle hand on his wife's shoulder. "We've known they were different for months, dear. And we've known they were Angels since we learned about the outbreak."

Trini turned her feral, fearful stare on Steven. "Not all of them," she whispered. "Not all my girls. Beckie, maybe, but not Iris and Kendra. Not my girls!" Tears began to slip unnoticed down her cheeks.

Steven shrugged in resignation. "Maybe not," he said, unwilling to take that last vestige of hope away from Trini. "But you heard the president. We still have to go and get them tested, just to make sure."

Trini was on her feet and whirling out of the living room before Steven could stop her. Later that night, after everyone was asleep, Trini was manically awake, drinking coffee and trying to figure out how she could get her girls away from all of this madness.

She wasn't the only parent trying to get her kids out of quarantine. Not be a long shot.

10

August 29th, 2009.

The Delta Center, home of the Utah Jazz basketball team, had just finished their 'speedy renovations' and set up medical testing tents outside the perimeter to start the first wave of Angel testing and subsequent quarantine.

Among the medical professionals that day were Jessica Gardner and Jackson Telford, the eyes and ears of the CDC who could witness first hand what the process would look like. The Delta Center was the first such quarantine arena being opened in the United States, a test run for the rest if all went well.

"Why are we going to be the first?" Jessica asked Jackson the week before. "The Delta Center isn't the biggest arena in the states by a long shot, and isn't big enough to hold all of the prepubescent kids in the city even if all of the parents do *show up with their kids. Why not start with the Superdome, an arena that already has experience and infrastructure in place to accommodate an emergency of this magnitude?"*

Jackson held up his hands in a helpless gesture of acceptance. "Because of us, Jess. Because of me, and you, and Annie. This is where it all started, even if the general public doesn't know it. You and I are the ones who figured out what to look for when testing for this. We now know that with a simple blood panel test, we can isolate the T cells and check fairly quickly to see if they are supercharged or not. What we don't know is how the general public is going to react."

Jessica's eyes widened in incredulity. "Are you kidding? Of course we know. Anger. Fear. Probably riots. It's going to be a shitshow."

"You're probably right. But it's still better, in the opinion of the CDC AND the White House, to start with a sample group and determine if different measures would need to be established when we go country-wide. Also, you're right about the Delta Center not being able to hold everyone. We already have different teams in place preparing college arenas and community centers. Believe me, everyone is scrambling as fast as they can on this."

Jessica tried to work a little moisture into a mouth suddenly gone dry as she got around to the question she had been afraid to ask. "What about Annie? Is she going to go to one of these quarantine centers?"

"Absolutely not!" Jackson shook his head emphatically. "The least we can do is keep her under our protection here. Could you imagine what would happen if it became public knowledge that she is our Patient Zero? Parents would tear her apart."

Jessica nodded. "Ok. I get that. And I appreciate that Annie will get to stay here. But answer me this: what happens today if and when things go to hell?"

"We have the majority of the SLPD at our disposal for crowd control. This is to be as orderly a process as possible, but just in case, we have resources to ensure our safety, as well as the general public. All we can do is pray it won't come to that."

"Pray?" Jessica barked out a humorless laugh. "I don't know if God is listening right now, Jackson."

8 a.m.

The Delta Center, a four story concrete and glass arena that sat majestically in the south end of downtown Salt Lake, could seat 20,000 people and had concessions and bathrooms on every floor. Part of the renovations done included changing the concession stands from grease pits into honest to goodness 'home kitchens' that would be providing healthy meals and snacks throughout the day. Supplies and provisions had been brought in, on the federal dime, and would continue to be provided as long as the crisis lasted. Which meant, in layman's terms, until all of the kids were dead, and the virus with them.

The arena floor had been cleared, cleaned, and built back up with bunk beds that stretched from corner to corner. The jumbotron had been electronically tweaked so that each of the four screens could play different movies or video games. Children would be provided with special headsets that they could use to tune into a specific screen. For those who were of a more literary bend, an entire library had donated their wares. The library had been set up on the top floor of the arena, in two of the big box suites.

Furthermore, teachers would be brought in daily to provide children with an ongoing education. Although the teachers had to wonder: would their services even be appreciated? If all of these kids were reaching new heights of intelligence at the behest of their virus, what education could the teachers provide? But these were speculations shared behind closed doors; the important thing, the teachers decided, was providing structure on a daily basis.

The singular unimportant issue was the first aid stations set up in various locations throughout the arena. These had been intentionally ignored. After all, these kids didn't get sick, didn't get hurt. What need had they of medical attention?

On the outside of the square shaped Delta Center, surrounding the entire perimeter, were white medical tents with a veritable army of personnel to staff them. Doctors, nurses, phlebotomists, and all the necessary equipment needed for the crucial blood panel test, had been set up over the course of the previous week. The medical professionals would rotate between their regular hospitals and the arena in four hour shifts. All except for Jessica and Jackson, who intended to be there until they dropped from exhaustion. Every piece of data that could be gathered might turn out to be crucial to the days to come.

Lastly, outside of the ring of medical tents was a perimeter of a different sort. SLPD, fully armed in riot control gear and crowd control weapons (not that they intended to need it, but better to be prepared) had set up their own perimeter, along with barricades to guide parents and children through a series of different lines that would take them to the testing tents in what they all dearly hoped would be a controlled and orderly fashion. They also had helicopters on standby, but wouldn't call them in unless absolutely necessary.

The Delta Center was officially open for business at 8 a.m.

Two hours later, it seemed that all of their prep, the multitude of testing tents, the army of police and barricades, had been completely unnecessary.

Not a single family had shown up.

11

"How could we not have seen this coming?" Jessica asked Jackson as she sipped on her third cup of coffee of the morning. "Of course parents aren't going to want to bring their kids down to get tested, confirm their fears, and then get ripped away from them."

Jackson, leaning back against a metal railing, ran a hand through his silver mane of hair, faded blue eyes tight with frustration. "I know it. But we simply can't go door to door and force this. At least, not yet." He sighed. "If this doesn't work, I lay even odds that this will devolve into a police state. THEN you'll see panic, and rioting, and parents-" He cut off abruptly, popping up to his feet and staring straight ahead, out past the line of barricades.

Jessica turned to follow his gaze, and gasped.

At the corner of the block, a bus had just pulled up. Dozens of children were calmly getting off the bus and making their way towards the police perimeter. Children sans parents.

"So that's how this is going to work," Jackson murmured, half to himself. "The parents won't follow the president's directive, but the kids, these *brilliant* kids, will come on their own. Because they know."

Jessica turned to him. "They know what?"

"They know what their parents won't accept. That they're going to die anyway, so why take the risk of continuing to pass along the virus? Think about every conversation we've had with Annie. She's accepted the inevitability of this from the beginning. Why would any of the other Angels behave differently?"

A total of 26 children got off of the first bus, made their way to and through the police line, and were directed to specific medical tents, to submit to blood testing with a calm that was downright eerie. But the medical personnel were all professionals, and they got down to testing without hesitation.

Jessica and Jackson, manning a tent with a med tech who would run the portable centrifuge, greeted the first child to be directed to their station, a petite blond girl in overalls who looked to be no older than 7. As soon as she turned her ageless gaze on the two adults, they both knew that testing was unnecessary. She was an Angel.

But they also knew that they needed to follow procedure, and so they sat her down in the chair at the end of the table. Jackson took notes while Jessica made small talk that appeared to put herself at ease more than the girl, drew a vial of blood, and passed it along to the med tech, who promptly ran it through the centrifuge. When the result came back positive, as all there knew that it would, the blond girl gave all three of them a sad little smile and asked if she could have a lollipop. It was this little gesture, a glimpse of childhood through a screen of adult comprehension, that had Jessica tearing up.

Various volunteers were spread out on site to direct children into the Delta Center and see that they were properly set up. Not a single one of the volunteers was themselves a parent.

Over the course of the morning, more and more children showed up, singly, in pairs, in groups. Some came by bus, some by the Trax train that bisected the city and had a stop just outside of the Delta Center, some on foot. All unaccompanied by adults. All were calm, orderly, precise. By the time the first wave had been seen and admitted, every single medical professional knew what Jessica and Jackson had known from the first: no testing was needed. One look in their eyes, and they knew. But they kept up the testing anyway, because that's the job.

"Jackson," Jessica said as their 5th child was led away from their tent and towards the front entrance. "What happens when parents come storming in, demanding their kids back?"

Jackson, arming sweat from his forehead, turned towards her. He'd been wondering that all morning, as well. "I honestly don't know. But it's been two hours now, and we haven't seen any parents. I'm wondering why not?"

As if on cue, a minivan came screaming up to the curb.

"Speak the devil's name, and he shall arrive," Jackson muttered. "Brace yourself, this could get ugly."

The driver's door flew open, and a short, red-faced woman with tears in her eyes jumped out. Without bothering to shut the car door, she hit the sidewalk at a dead run, seemingly blind to the police barricades.

Every one of the officers on duty came to attention, sharing uneasy looks. One of the officers, a young man barely old enough to grow fuzz on his upper lip, took a step towards her as the distraught mother came barrelling in. "Ma'am, please-"

Without a thought, the small woman plowed right into him. Taken by surprise, the young officer went stumbling back and fell over a barricade, going down in what would have been a comical heap if the situation had been different. The mother, with barely a pause, started screaming.

"My daughter! Give me back my daughter! GIVE ME BACK MY CHILD!" Tears were streaming down her face as she struggled with the heavy barricades.

Shaking off their shock at this turn of events, three other officers converged on the woman, trying to restrain her. Despite the mother's small stature, it was like trying to restrain a whirlwind.

"Oh hell!" Jackson barked, watching from their tent. "We've got to contain this!"

He and Jessica rounded their table and hurried over to the screaming woman. In the 30 seconds it took them to cover the short distance between the medical and police perimeters, one of the officers had blood streaming from his nose from a wildly thrown elbow, and another was on the ground cradling his groin and moaning.

Jessica, a half step ahead of Jackson, did the only thing she could think of: she shoved the cops aside and wrapped up the woman in a hug. "I'm sorry!" Jessica whispered fiercely in her ear. "I'm sorry. I'm sorry."

All at once, the tension drained out of the distraught mother, and she collapsed in Jessica's arms, sobbing uncontrollably. "My only child," she wailed. "She's everything I have. Please, you can't take her."

Jessica held her close, apologizing over and over again.

That was when the second car came screaming up to the curb.

And the third.

And the fourth.

Jackson gulped, grabbed Jessica by the arm, and pulled her away from the sobbing woman, who dropped to her knees on the concrete.

Jessica saw the cars pulling up, saw the angry, scared, wide eyed parents getting out and making their way towards the police barricades. She gasped. "Oh my god. It's happening. What do we do?"

Jackson shook his head, pulling her back towards the medical tents. "We keep doing our job, and we let the police do theirs. We have no other options."

12

By the end of that first official day of the quarantine, the Delta Center held close to three hundred Angels.

After the first punch was thrown by an angry father, police began using pepper spray and tear gas.

When a mother with disheveled hair, wailing like a banshee, pulled a revolver out of her purse, the police switched to rubber bullets.

Fourteen police officers were injured, three critically. One officer was dead from a thrown brick.

Close to thirty parents were hospitalized.

Three parents were killed, two fathers from rubber bullets (one took a rubber bullet through the eye; the other got one in the throat and asphyxiated while the fight raged around him) and an elderly grandmother with asthma who choked to death on tear gas.

That was day 1.

13

September 1st, 2009.

5 p.m.

Kristi walked out of the air conditioned Delta Center and into the dry, unforgiving heat of Salt Lake City. Sweat immediately beaded on her forehead, and she absentmindedly reached up an arm to wipe it away, though it was an effort in futility. She hardly noticed. Her mind was still back in the upper level suite where she had spent the day teaching a classroom full of pre-teens about Shakespeare.

Despite their advanced intelligence, there was still so much these kids hadn't personally experienced, and they took to Romeo and Juliet like a starving man takes to a sandwich. Every one of the 30 kids was enthralled by the old English style of writing, the sheer music of Shakespearean literature. It had felt like an advanced university course in the way that the kids dissected the characters and their motivations, asking introspective questions about the ageless feud between Montague and Capulet, and what drove generation after generation to hate each other.

The class discussion also emphasized the dual nature of these Angels. On the one hand, their neurons were firing faster than a classful of PhD candidates, and it showed in their extensive vocabulary and the ease with which they were able to make logical connections that bordered on precognition. However, on the other hand, they were all still children who had, for the most part, only had limited experiences in the world around them to date, and that came out in the questions that they asked about Romeo and Juliet.

One boy, a tow headed 9 year old with piercing gray eyes, raised his hand while Kristi was outlining the very first scene in the play, when the Capulet boys get into a brawl with the Montague boys. He asked point blank why they cared so much.

"For example," the boy had said with a gravity that was spoiled only a touch by his high, squeaking voice. *"One Capulet says to another 'The quarrel is with our masters' and the other responds, seemingly tongue in cheek, 'And us their men!' The Capulets and Montagues alike, specifically the younger generation, are aware of the feud, but know that it is between the older generation. Why then must the hate be carried down through the years? It can't be born into them. It's an obvious case of nurture, as opposed to nature, and therefore can be changed. And yet each family seems to delight in carrying the feud forward into the future. It's needless, and senseless. And both Romeo and Juliet are shamed for trying to bring the families together through their love? It's illogical."*

Kristi had smiled patiently at the boy, and at the other children who were nodding their heads in agreement. *"You're absolutely right,"* she had replied. *"It's illogical. But then, emotions tend not to ask the logical side of the brain for advice."*

They had all looked confused at this, and it had turned into a lengthy conversation of logic versus emotion. A conversation that had, in the end, gone nowhere. Despite their intelligence, the children still had the naivete of youth, and saw through lenses of black and white.

Kristi was reminded of when Annie once asked why the peoples of the world labeled themselves as 'American', and 'Mexican', and 'Canadian', etc, when obviously we should all just be labeled as 'People'. A simple concept, and a beautiful one.

Walking down the empty sidewalk, still lost in thought and oblivious to the sweat now streaming down her face from the baking sunshine, Kristi's mind now turned to the last few days, and how that initial riot had subsided with almost shocking suddenness, and all because of the kids.

It always comes back to the kids, she thought. *And how THEY are comporting themselves, as opposed to the adults, who are supposed to be in charge of things. If not for the Angels, parents and police would still be killing each other.*

As the sun was setting on that first day of quarantine, and the police were desperately trying to keep the growing mob of parents back, the children had begun coming back out of the Delta Center.

Through the tear gas, both parents and police had been oblivious at first, until one of the children, that young blonde girl that Jessica and Jackson had tested and admitted, found a discarded bullhorn and brought the riot to a screeching standstill.

"STOP." One word, in a high, clear soprano amplified by the bullhorn, slammed into the fighting adults with almost physical force. "YOU HAVE TO STOP. PLEASE."

The adults, parents and police alike, separated themselves out like they were the children and had been caught doing something naughty. Which, essentially, they had been.

The other kids gathered silently around the blonde girl. Their eyes stared out, ageless and judging.

"WE MAKE THIS CHOICE FOR OURSELVES. IT IS THE RIGHT THING TO DO, AND DEEP DOWN I THINK YOU KNOW IT. SO PLEASE, JUST STOP."

The mother that Jessica had comforted pushed her way past police officers that made no move to stop her now. She walked right up to the little girl and dropped to her knees in front of her, tears streaming down her face. In the sudden silence of the swiftly falling darkness, every person there could hear her clearly.

"Sophie, please. You're all I have. You don't have to do this."

Sophie smiled sadly at her mother. "Yes I do. We can't go back and change the past, but I, we, can try to save the future. I'll be right here, and you can come see me anytime. But my place is here now."

The mom grabbed Sophie up in a big hug and squeezed her hard. As if by unspoken signal, the other parents ran to their children. It was a scene to melt the hardest heart.

Kristi reached her car, a silver Honda, and dropped into the oven-like interior. She wasted no time in keying the ignition and blasting the AC, though her mind was still drifting in the recent past.

After the parents had been made to see sense by their children, the entire city had followed suit (for the most part; there were still outliers, parents who absconded with their children to vacation homes by lake or canyon). Over the last few days, more and more children arrived at the Delta Center to be quarantined, many driven there by family members. And now that parents were accepting the situation, many were coming forward to volunteer their time as teachers and aides, much like Kristi was doing.

Once the AC had cooled the car and, most importantly, the steering wheel, Kristi eased off the brake and headed east up South Temple Street, though she wouldn't be heading home right away. She had a meeting with Jessica, and then would pop in to fill Annie in on everything that was going on.

Meanwhile, at Primary Children's a few miles away, Jackson was watching through an observation window as one of his team members, a doctor named Heath who specialized in the lymphatic system, was assisting on an autopsy.

The deceased in question was a 15 year old boy who had, just days ago, volunteered to be transferred from the Delta Center to Primary Children's. He was the first of the Salt Lake City quarantined Angels who would turn 15 post-quarantine, and he had explained that he wanted his death to mean something. He wanted Jackson's team to study him and see if they could learn more about the Angel Virus and, specifically, why kids were dying on their 15th birthday.

Jessica walked up to Jackson, joining him at the window. "Anything yet?"

Jackson shook his head without looking away from the autopsy. "No, although we hope to get new data from this. Emphasis on the word 'hope'. All we know so far is that this virus is definitely centered in the thymus gland. But then, we already knew that. The vital piece is figuring out why it kills in such a precise manner, and how we can stop that." He sighed. "In all my years, I have never encountered anything like this. I've seen virulent viruses before, with horrific fatality rates, but nothing that kills on a timeline."

Jessica frowned. "Speaking of fatality rates, what are we going to do once more of the quarantined kids start dying?" She strove to keep her voice steady, but it wavered almost imperceptibly on the word 'dying'. "It's one thing to have successfully instituted the quarantine, but what do we do as time goes on?"

"Cremation. As callous as it sounds, it's the best option, especially as the death rates continue to increase across the country, and the world. I spoke with my superiors at the CDC earlier today, and was informed that other quarantine sites are running smoothly, with more and more opening every day. Did you know that someone got the riot on film? And not just the riot, but the scene with the kids calming down their parents."

"Really?"

"Yes, and it may have prevented a lot more panicking across the board. The video went viral within minutes, and it had a calming effect on the general population, showing the kids taking matters into their own hands. We've had very little pushback with new quarantine sites."

Jessica turned to face Jackson. "You know that will change when quarantine kids start dying."

Jackson sighed again. "I know. That's why it is so vitally important that we figure out how to cure this."

"And if we can't?"

He finally turned to face her, and Jessica was startled by the fear that shone out of his eyes. "Then a few rioting parents may be the least of our worries. This could change the entire face of our planet. Kids won't be the only ones dying."

14

Kristi walked into an empty waiting room and was shocked by the quiet. Just a few days ago, Primary Children's had been bursting at the seams with distraught parents and calm children, but now that the quarantine had gone into effect, Primary Children's had no children in need of treatment.

She walked up to the front desk, where a younger nurse was idly flipping through a magazine. "Hi, I'm here to see Jessica Gardner?"

The nurse tossed the magazine down on the desk and reached for the phone. "I'll page her."

A few short minutes later, Kristi was once again sitting in Jessica's office. She was disheartened immediately by the harried look on Jessica's face, and the blue scrubs that looked slept in.

"How bad is it?" Kristi asked quietly.

"Right now? Better than expected. According to Jackson and the CDC, the other quarantine sites seem to be up and running smoothly. But the worry, of course, is how long the parents will be supportive when kids keep dying if we can't figure out a cure for this thing. And the infection rate is through the roof. Kids who haven't yet been infected are a rarity, considering how long this thing had to spread before we figured out what was going on."

Kristi considered that. "How confident is Jackson that the CDC *can* find a cure?"

Jessica shook her head, blonde ponytail swinging around. "He's hopeful, because he has to be, but I can read the look in his eyes whenever we talk about it. He's scared. The CDC has been studying this for *months*, long before they let on to the rest of us that they were on it, and they have zero answers. Oh, they've isolated the virus. They know how it spreads, they know how it's affecting the kids, and why they are all turning into little geniuses who suddenly can't be hurt, can't get sick. But why the hell are kids dying? How can a virus make a kid invincible and then strike them down like clockwork?" Jessica closed her eyes and took a deep breath. "There is an autopsy going on right now, on a 15 year old who volunteered to be 'examined' immediately following his somehow preordained passing. Jackson is hoping they learn something new."

"Do you think they will?"

Jessica's shoulders slumped. "Honestly? I think if there was something to find, the CDC would have found it by now. Even if they couldn't cure it, I think they would have found something. The very nature of this virus...it's unnatural. Literally. I don't think this is something nature created. I think this virus was built."

Kristi's eyes widened. "You think someone did this on purpose?"

"I can't think of a single reason why someone would be so monstrous as to put this out in the world, but it's the only thing that makes sense to me at this point. Other viruses, other diseases, are by their very nature chaotic. You look at cancer cells, tumors, AIDS, and they all share a common characteristic. They kill without discretion. The Angel Virus kills *with* discretion. It's too specific, too ordered. You want to know what I really think? Annie's birth father, the one who stole away with Annie's twin sister Grace? He was a brilliant geneticist. I think he's the only one who could provide an answer to this. I think he's behind this."

Ten minutes later, Kristi was in Annie's quarantine room, filling her in on everything that was happening at the Delta Center, as well as all that Jessica had told her.

Annie, uncharacteristically, seemed distracted and a little checked out. After Kristi had told her everything, Annie simply nodded in acceptance and abruptly changed the conversation.

"I want to be transferred to the Delta Center."

15

By the end of 2009, every country in the world had quarantine sites up and running. Many ran as smoothly as the Delta Center, with a constant stream of volunteers coming in to help out. Others experienced riots and bloodshed that didn't abate quite so quickly as the first test site. Many people died before the riots were brought under control. In the end, however, people came to understand that until a cure was found, the so-called 'leper colonies' were the best option for containment.

When Annie turned 7 on January 1st, 2010, the global death toll had risen into the millions.

Neither the CDC nor the WHO had come any closer to understanding how to fight it.

16

As 2010 came to a close, the death toll in the US alone had reached 5 million, and a new fear was sweeping the world: parents who had newborns and were terrified that their infants would inadvertently come into contact with an Angel and get infected. People began to trust the quarantine centers a little less. The new infection rate was low, but not nonexistent, as world governments had promised it would be with the advent of the quarantine centers.

That fear led to a growing distrust not only of the world governments, but of your own neighbors. Slowly but surely, people grew distant, withdrawn, and suspicion bloomed around every corner.

17

　　In 2011, kids between the ages of 15 and 18 (those who had survived; they were few and far between) were afraid to be out in public, for fear that they would be mistaken for an Angel. Many such had already been attacked. Several had been killed.
　　Society began to degenerate.

18

　　In 2012, martial law was declared.

Part 8: The Trial Con't (The Year 2018)

1

    When court was called back in session an hour later, Jeff called his next witness, a child psychologist from Virginia who specialized in deep rooted trauma. Jeff hoped to show the court that this Angel Virus wasn't as perfect, pre age 15, as everyone seemed to think. This witness would truly damn Calvin Michaels, if his soul wasn't as black as the deepest pits of hell already.
    "I'd like to call to the stand Dr. Eric Ellington," Jeff intoned into the quiet courtroom.
    Dr. Ellington rose smoothly to his feet and approached the bench to be sworn in. He was a slender, energetic man in his late 60's with a full head of silver hair and a kindly, paternal smile. Like the best psychologists, he exuded an aura of sincerity about him that made you naturally inclined to trust him.
    After he was sworn in, Jeff launched right into his line of questioning.
    "Dr. Ellington, please state your profession for the court."

Dr. Ellington cleared his throat. "I'm a child psychologist. I tend to work with children with post traumatic life experiences."

Jeff nodded. "Could you explain your specialty in layman's terms?"

"Certainly. Deep rooted trauma means it lies far beneath the surface, and most patients who experience such trauma rarely exhibit any symptoms in the conscious mind. Rather, the trauma comes out in body language, i.e. tics, uncontrollable movement, twitching, oral fixation, etc. In adults, this may be exhibited in smoking, or chewing constantly on toothpicks. In children, who are naturally more energetic, it can be harder to spot. Often the subconscious mind shows the scars of the trauma in dreams."

"Thank you. Would you please explain to the court when and why you were brought to work with the Angels during the pandemic?"

Eric laced his hands together and rested them on the stand in front of him. "In late 2011 I was called and asked to fly to Salt Lake and have a series of sessions with a handful of the kids who were quarantined in the Delta Center. As I understand it, the CDC was concerned about the living condition of the kids in various quarantine zones and, since Salt Lake was not only ground zero for the virus but also that the Delta Center was the first quarantine zone opened two years before, it was thought prudent that I should start there. I would have open contact with the CDC, reporting all of my findings on a weekly basis. The Angels were, of course, briefed on the nature of the sessions, and knew that doctor/patient confidentiality would not apply in this unprecedented situation."

Jeff glanced over at Calvin and Gabriel, then back to Eric. "And what exactly did you learn from these sessions?"

"To be perfectly candid, much more than I expected. I have no children of my own, but I had had various sessions with Angels in Virginia before the quarantine went into effect. I saw with my own eyes the exponential intelligence growth, the early development of logical reasoning. Emotional responses in Angels were seemingly pushed into the background as logic and reasoning took over the forefront of their minds. However, while working with the Angels at the Delta Center quarantine zone, I discovered fairly quickly that while their emotions had been pushed back, they hadn't diminished in any capacity."

"What does that mean, exactly?" Jeff asked.

"It means that despite their intelligence, they were just *children*. Children with little real world experience, forced from the homes of their families into quarantine zones. No more world interaction. What experiences they had from that day forward took place within the walls of their respective zones. Their emotional states, when I could catch a glimpse of them, were deeply traumatic. Fear. Uncertainty. And it came out most often in nightmares."

Gabriel, leaning back in his chair at the defense table, snorted and rolled his eyes. Jeff looked over at him sharply before turning back to Eric. "Please go on. What did this information tell you?"

Eric, unperturbed, went on. Every eye of the jury was glued to him. "It told me that as everyone got caught up in the benefits of the Angel Virus, pre age 15, it also dehumanized the children. Many, especially those without kids, saw Angels as little automatons. Walking computers with no emotional state. But those emotions were there, and they were strong. This man," Eric looked over and caught Calvin's eye, staring him down. "Didn't just kill all those kids, he ruined them completely and utterly."

"Objection!" Gabriel barked out.

"Sustained."

Jeff smiled. "No further questions, your honor."

Judge Erikson turned to Gabriel. "Cross examination, counselor?"

Gabriel sneered. "To continue this inane conversation about dreams? No questions, your honor. The witness may be dismissed."

Part 9: Society Stumbling (The Year 2012)

1

Annie was 9 when her parents finally agreed to her request to be transferred to the Delta Center in late January of 2012. Kristi and Jeff had pleaded with her to stay at Primary Children's, but she had stayed firm in her resolve, saying that she didn't want to spend the last years of her life in isolation as well as quarantine.

The day she was transferred, to be escorted by her parents as well as Jacob and Maddy, Annie was transfixed by the world before her. She hadn't seen the open sky in almost three years, and she stood stunned by the beauty of it, family completely forgotten.

The sky was a uniform steel gray, covered over completely with thick clouds. Fat snowflakes fell almost lazily from the glowing silver ceiling above her. The ground under her was hidden by over a foot of snow from the ongoing blizzard.

Before leaving for the Delta Center, Annie immediately started to build a snowman. Laughing, Jacob and Maddy, and then Kristi and Jeff, joined in with a will. It was the most any of the Oritt's had laughed in years, and each of them felt the stress melting away in that perfect family moment.

When they finally climbed into Kristi's Honda an hour later, they left behind a snowman in front of the Primary Children's entrance that was nearly six feet tall, complete with stick arms and pinecone eyes.

2

As Kristi drove the family down recently plowed streets, the tension slowly built in the car until each of them could feel it like an almost physical weight, pressing them down in their seats. It was Annie who finally broke the silence.

"Thank you for understanding, and for doing this."

Maddy reached over and took Annie's hand, giving it a squeeze. "I wouldn't want to be isolated either. And we can still come visit just as often!"

Jacob tried out a laugh, but it sounded forced even to him. "I'm sure it'll be nice to be around other kids again. And mom goes there to teach, so you can be in her class."

Kristi smiled. "We've moved onto The Taming of the Shrew. My class has grown even bigger, about 60 kids now, and they love the dialogue between Petruchio and Kate."

Annie, who had read the entire works of Shakespeare cover to cover several times, quoted from memory: "'Why, how now, Kate! I hope thou art not mad: This is a man, old, wrinkled, faded, wither'd. And not a maiden, as thou say'st he is.'"

Later that night, Annie would think back to that quote and how it ironically applied to the Angels, for while they looked like children, their souls felt old and wrinkled.

Five minutes later, Annie was standing in the courtyard of the Delta Center, hugging each family member in turn, thanking them over and over for their understanding and willingness to allow her to rejoin her own society. Tears were shed, but smiles were plastered onto each face to mask the turmoil of emotions inside. For each family member, be it conscious or subconscious, had thought that keeping Annie completely isolated would somehow isolate her from the terrible ending to come when she turned 15.

3

"Beckie!"

"Annie?!"

The two friends rushed together in the arena foyer just inside the main entrance, hugging and laughing and crying all at once. Emotions that had long since been pushed down came bubbling up to the surface as both were caught up in the joyful reunion.

"Where have you been? I haven't seen you in three years, since Kids Kampus!" Beckie nearly shouted when they finally separated. "You've grown!"

Annie laughed. "So have you!" She looked her friend up and down, running calculations as she compared the Beckie before her with the girl she had seen in 2009. "6 inches?"

Beckie grinned, white teeth gleaming. "6.72! And you?"

"7.19! Last I checked, anyway. So tell me everything! How is life here in the quarantine zone? I've been in isolation at Primary Children's this whole time!"

Beckie's jaw dropped. "Isolation? Why? I thought you were just sent to a different quarantine zone."

Annie glanced around, suddenly conscious of all of the other Angels and adult volunteers walking around. Some of the kids were throwing them curious glances, but they all respected the personal conversation and made no move to approach.

She looked back to Beckie. "I'll fill you in on everything, but is there anywhere we can speak alone, or is the arena too crowded?"

Beckie caught on immediately. "Of course! This place is bursting at the seams, but there are little nooks and crannies everywhere. Follow me!" She reached out and grabbed Annie's hand and plunged into the crowd.

Several minutes later and the two old friends were comfortably seated cross legged on the floor of one of the kitchens in the bowels underneath the main arena floor. There were a few volunteer parents making snacks, but they were listening to music and gave the two Angels no mind.

Annie opened her mouth, but Beckie jumped in. "You first! Fill me in on everything that's happened with you!"

Smiling, Annie acquiesced, and over the course of the next two hours told Beckie everything, starting with that fateful day when Dr. Telford of the CDC showed up on her parents doorstep, subsequently moving into the isolation room at Primary Children's, all of the testing, and being completely removed from the world, but for her TV, parents, and nurse Jessica.

"...and finally I realized that being in isolation was meaningless. I needed to be around you, and the other Angels, to be a *part* of all of this instead of being an outside observer. My family wasn't thrilled about it, but they understood. At least, they understood that they *didn't* understand, but that I needed it."

Beckie nodded. "None of the parents understand." She glanced over at the adults who had been cooking and now were standing around chatting. At first glance they appeared casual and relaxed, but looking closer you could see the tension in the set of their shoulders, the forced quality to their smiles. "Every time an Angel dies, the parents of that particular child stop showing up. But there is always another to take their place, and every time I meet a new mother or father it's always the same. You can see the hope in their eyes that maybe *their* child will be different, and won't succumb to this virus. Or that the CDC or WHO will finally come up with a solution. It's the hope that drives them, and the fear that brings them here day after day to take advantage of what time they have, because deep down they know. They know."

Annie sighed sadly. "What about the other Angels here? How is life in the quarantine zone?"

Beckie shrugged. "The plus side of being surrounded by your peers is that we're all more or less on the same level. We don't have to hide what we are. We have university professors as well as parents who come in and teach classes in everything from quantum theory to music. Thanks to donations, we have instruments of every shape and form, and due to our advanced maturity there is never any fighting over having to share. That's the positive side."

"What's the negative?"

Beckie shrugged again. "We're all just waiting to die."

4

At that moment, on the top floor of the arena in one of the expensive box suites that only the most affluent arena goers could afford, Dr. Eric Ellington was waiting for his next 'patient'.

The suite was large, about the size of a modest one bedroom apartment, and had its own private kitchen, dining room, and bathroom, as well as a glass partition at the far end that afforded one a view of the arena floor and jumbotron.

Eric got to his feet and stretched, walking over to the glass partition and looking out at the thousands of small bodies packed into the seats below him. He saw that of the four screens of the jumbotron, three appeared to be showing different documentaries, while the fourth was being used to play video games. On the stage at the far end of the arena, a dozen Angels wielding a variety of instruments were playing one of Bach's symphonies, and they were performing perfectly.

Eric shook his head in wonder at the sight, then turned as he heard the door open. A tall, skinny 14 year old boy with straight black hair, brown eyes, and a crooked smile peaked around the door. "Dr. Ellington? I'm sorry, I knocked, but you must not have heard me."

Eric waved at him to come in. "Yes, Jonah, I'm sorry, I was wool gathering. And please, call me Eric."

Jonah nodded and came all the way into the room, shutting the door softly behind him. "Thank you. And thank you for being willing to see me today, even though I hadn't previously requested a session."

"Not at all! Please, have a seat. Can I get you anything? Water, juice?" Eric sat down in one of the plush chairs and Jonah seated himself opposite, crossing one leg over the other.

"No, thank you. I actually just finished lunch. May I get right to the point?"

Eric nodded, meeting Jonah's ageless gaze without hesitation. After working with the Angels in the Salt Lake quarantine zone for the last several months, he found himself becoming used to the mature adult eyes looking out of children's faces. "Of course. What would you like to discuss today?"

"I turn 15 next month."

Eric froze, momentarily caught off guard. He recovered smoothly, allowing his training to kick in and lead him. "I see. How are you feeling about that?"

Jonah gave him a blank stare. He uncrossed and recrossed his legs. The pitter patter of his uncut fingernails against the wooden armrest was quietly deafening. Eric saw all of this and filed it away for further consideration. This wasn't the first time he had met with a child who had some kind of nervous tic that they themselves didn't seem aware of.

"It's interesting, actually. During my waking hours here I experience a dual sensation of both acceptance and disassociation. So many Angels have already died. I know that soon it will be my turn. I'm not overly worried about it, as we all know by now the nature of this virus and the timeline that we are all living. Expiration at 15 is preset, and so why spend futile moments worrying about it? I, like my friends here, prefer to spend our time productively. Just last week I mastered the violin, and it has brought me great pleasure."

Eric nodded. "Mmhmm. You said you experience this during your waking hours. Tell me about your sleep cycle."

Jonah's mouth tightened. He noticed the twitch in his right hand and crossed his arms over his chest. "That's it exactly. I was infected shortly before the quarantine centers opened in 2009. At first, I didn't dream at all. Like the rest of us here, I accepted the quarantine center as a logical response to a global crisis. But as my 15th birthday approaches, I find my sleep becoming broken up by increasingly dark and negative dreamscapes. One in particular has become a recurring nightmare, and I find myself waking up in a cold sweat, unable to fall back asleep for quite some time."

Eric held a hand palm up, inviting Jonah to continue when he paused.

Jonah cleared his throat, uncrossed and recrossed his legs again. "In this dream, I'm having a birthday party with my family. I'm sitting at a long, rectangular table. Seated around the table is a different family member; mom, dad, siblings, aunts, uncles. In front of me is a birthday cake, chocolate with strawberries on top, because my mom knows that's always been my favorite. There are 15 candles on the cake. Everyone is smiling, joyful. Even in the dream, we are all cognizant of the Angel Virus, and that my birthday party means I survived. The tone is light and filled with relief. And then…"

A longer pause.

"And then?" Eric said gently.

Jonah looked down. "I blow out the candles. The room goes black for a split second, and then suddenly everyone is on their feet. I look up to my left, at my mother. Her eyes roll back in her head. Her mouth opens, trying to grasp at her final words to me. She falls to her back, dead. I look to my right, at my father, just in time to see him do the same. One by one, they drop. And I'm sitting at a table surrounded by my dead family."

Eric's breath caught.

Jonah looked back up, and his eyes were shiny with unshed tears. "No one understands. We're not Angels, doctor. We're ghosts."

5

As Jonah was walking out of Eric's 'office', Annie was finally turning the conversation back around to Beckie.

"Your turn. Tell me about your life over the last few years! How are your parents handling this? How are your sisters? Are Kendra and Iris here?"

Beckie glanced away. "No, they aren't here. My mom...when the news about the quarantine broke in August three years ago, my mom couldn't take it. She accepted that I was different, but she couldn't believe that Kendra and Iris were Angels, too. The change hadn't affected them at that point as deeply as it affected me, because they were 12 and 13, respectively. Oh, the three of us sisters knew, but mom just couldn't accept it. The same day that dad drove me down here, mom took Kendra and Iris and just drove away..."

6

August 11th, 2009.
Beckie's house.
"Trini, we have to," Steven said patiently for the third time. It was 11:30 p.m., and they had been trying to talk this through for an hour and a half.

"No. No! Take Beckie to that godforsaken quarantine zone if you have to, but Kendra and Iris are fine," Trini said yet again between clenched teeth.

Steven, sitting with forced calm on the bed, watched Trini pace back and forth in front of him. "We have to look at the facts. Even if Kendra and Iris haven't been infected, we still have to take them down for testing. We have to know for sure."

Trini whirled on Steven. "I already know, Steven. I'm their mother, and I know them! They aren't going to take my girls away from me!"

The argument continued until 2 in the morning, when they finally stopped and went to bed out of sheer exhaustion. When Steven woke up the next morning, Trini, Kendra and Iris were gone.

August 12th, 2009.
"It's ok, dad," Beckie said, putting a hand on her father's shoulder as he tried yet again to call Trini on her cell phone. Again, it went straight to voicemail. "We both know that there's only one place they could have gone, to our houseboat on Lake Powell."

Steven dropped his phone and reached up to cover Beckie's hand with his own. "I know, baby. I just...even after we argued for so long last night, I just didn't think she would actually take off. I thought I knew her better than that."

Beckie sat down in a chair at the dining room table across from her dad. "You DO know mom better. But this emergency has changed all of us, not just those of us who have been infected. Mom is a little broken inside. I think a lot of people are. Mom needs space to come to terms with this. Maybe she'll come back, maybe she won't. In the meantime, I need to go to the quarantine zone. Afterward, you can drive down to Lake Powell. But please don't try to change mom's mind; it will only drive you two further apart, and this family needs each other. Just be there for her. But dad?"

Steven looked up, eyes shiny.

"Don't let Kendra and Iris leave the houseboat. If they won't come to my quarantine zone, make them stay in theirs."

An hour later, Steven was on one knee hugging Beckie tightly in front of the Delta Center. All around him were similar scenes. Parents hugging children, tears being shed, and children walking with firm strides to the testing tents and then on into the arena.

"Are you sure you're going to be ok?" Steven asked again.

Beckie tried to put on a brave smile for him. "Of course. I'll be surrounded by my peers here. And furthermore, maybe we can actually accomplish what our president is intending to do: stop this disease in its tracks and save lives."

One more hug, and then Beckie was walking away, into the last home she would ever know.

Steven watched until she disappeared through the front doors then, shoulders set, he turned, walked back to his car, and pointed it south, towards Lake Powell, 6 hours away on the border of Utah and Nevada.

Meanwhile, at Lake Powell, Kendra and Iris were still sleeping soundly in their little room with the bunk beds on the houseboat that was still tied up at the moor with a dozen others, rocking gently up and down on the mild swell. The sun was already well over the horizon, blazing down through a cloudless sky.

Trini was sitting out on the deck in a sleeveless blouse and shorts, chain smoking cigarettes. She had given up the habit years before, but hadn't been able to stop herself from buying a few packs at one of their stops to get gas on the wild drive through the state the night before. She kept running through the events of the last 24 hours: the fight with Steven, going to bed only to wake an hour later with a fully formed plan in mind, getting Kendra and Iris up and rapidly throwing a few things in a bag for them before leaving without a backward glance.

Kendra and Iris, sleepy eyed, hadn't raised a single protest. Perhaps because they saw how dead set on escaping their mother was, or perhaps because their own change hadn't gone as deep yet as Beckie's had; regardless, they had followed Trini's commands without a word and allowed her to shepherd them out of the house and into one of the family cars.

Once in the car, both girls had slept most of the way down, waking up only when Trini had stopped for gas or bathroom breaks, and then again when they arrived with the sun peaking over the horizon. Once in the houseboat, they both went straight to their room and back to sleep.

Trini couldn't sleep even if she tried. Manic energy coursed through her veins, and her mind was spinning like a top. After the third time Steven had tried to call, she had turned her phone off and gone back to smoking.

She knew that Steven would probably be following her down. After all, where else would she have gone? But that was a concern for the future. In the back of her mind, when she allowed herself to think about it, she figured that once Steven was down here he would get on board with her, and would understand that Kendra and Iris couldn't be infected.

They just couldn't be.

When Kendra and Iris awoke a few hours later, they found their mother gone, with a note on the table that simply read 'Out getting supplies. Back soon. Stay put.'

Kendra, at 13 and just a year older than Iris, had already been changed enough to understand the repercussions of what Trini had done. She looked over at her sister. "We can't leave the boat."

Iris nodded in agreement. "This is our quarantine now."

"Are you scared?"

Iris shrugged her thin shoulders. "I feel like I should be, but I'm not. You?"

Kendra shook her head, braids swinging gently around her cherubic face. "Not for myself. But for mom, yes."

"I think mom is a little broken."

Neither sister would be the least bit surprised to know that Beckie had said that very thing to their dad. The three of them were connected on a deeper level than they ever had been before.

Later that afternoon, Steven arrived at Lake Powell. Per Beckie's advice, he didn't try to convince Trini to come home. In fact, they didn't talk about the quarantine at all. Both adults feigned ignorance and disinterest in the last 24 hours and simply pretended they were on a family vacation.

They continued this facade for the next year, and all was peaceful. Until September of 2010, when everything changed.

September 3rd, 2010.

On Kendra's 14th birthday, she asked for, and received, an acoustic guitar. As the infection had continued to work it's miraculous changes in both sisters, Kendra had fallen in love with music, and Iris had become fascinated with marine biology.

Through YouTube instructional videos, Kendra became proficient at the guitar in her first week of playing. By the middle of the month she was playing as though she had been born with a guitar in her hands.

On September 20th, Kendra began posting her own videos on YouTube.

"Mom, you have to listen to this girl, she's incredible!" Jason, a 15 year old who was down vacationing in Lake Powell that

weekend with his parents to celebrate passing the infection window, beckoned his mom over, turning his computer so she could see. "I'm pretty sure she's staying in one of the houseboats on the lake!"

Jason's mom, Sally, prematurely gray and with worry lines already etched into her forehead, dusted the flour off of her hands and walked over from the kitchen to where Jason was sitting at the dining room table. They both watched in silence as Kendra played a song she had written herself, fingers a blur on the strings of her guitar, eyes closed as she let the music flow through her.

At the end of the video Kendra opened her eyes and smiled at the camera. Sally gasped when she saw Kendra's eyes for the first time. She had seen eyes like that before.

That night, after Jason had gone to bed, Sally sat down with her husband Tom.

"There's a family down at the lake, and they're harboring an Angel."

The next day, Trini and Steven awoke to find a note taped to the railing of their houseboat.

With a feeling of dread, Steven grabbed the note and unfolded it, revealing four words.

WE KNOW. GET OUT.

January 2012.

Night was falling outside on a city that looked like a snow globe.

"What happened next?" Annie asked quietly.

"Dad tried to get mom to leave, but she wouldn't. I think she knew that if they left Lake Powell, then she would have to admit that my sisters had been Angels all along, and then they would have to come back to Salt Lake and bring Kendra and Iris here. And remember, Kendra had just turned 14, and Iris was about to turn 13. Even then, mom knew that her time was limited with them, and she didn't want to miss a single moment. But her decision just made things so much worse."

"How?"

Beckie got to her feet and stretched. The volunteer parents had left somewhere in the middle of the story, and the two girls had the kitchen to themselves. "A few days after they got the note, a handful of people showed up and confronted my parents. From the way dad described it, they weren't an angry mob, but they weren't far off. They told my parents to leave and not come back. My parents shut the door in their faces." Beckie started pacing back and forth. Her high, clear voice wavered, and her footsteps echoed through the empty kitchen. "The next night, someone fired a gun at the windows of the houseboat. Dad told me he thinks it was a scare tactic, but Kendra was standing near one of the windows, and one of the bullets hit her in the face. My parents tried to get her to the closest hospital as fast as they could, but Kendra died on the way."

Beckie finally stopped pacing and turned back to look at Annie with haunted eyes. "She didn't even get to live to be 15." Her voice dropped into a flat monotone. "Mom killed herself later that night. Filled her pockets with stones and just walked out into the lake."

"Oh my god," Annie whispered, eyes wide.

"Dad buried mom and Kendra, then came back to Salt Lake with Iris and checked her in here. Iris is actually upstairs in the arena right now, but she hasn't spoken a single word since she got here. She just sits and stares at nothing all day long. She's broken. And she turns 15 this year."

7

A few miles away, at the mostly empty Primary Children's, Dr. Jackson Telford was standing in the middle of the room that had been Annie's. With recent events, he'd been taking care of himself less than usual. And he wasn't the only one. Half of the nurses still rotating on staff didn't even bother wearing scrubs. They all just...cared less, about personal hygiene and professionalism, now that all of the kids they used to help didn't need them anymore. Or, rather, that those kids needed so much more than Primary Children's could provide.

Standing under the bare halogen lights, Jackson looked, and felt, his age. His long silver mane of hair, of which he was so proud, desperately needed a wash. His jeans did as well. And the blue button down shirt he was wearing had been buttoned up wrong and hung loosely around his hips.

Staring around the isolation room that had been Annie's, Jackson thought about all that had transpired over the last few years, and how futile his work seemed now. Darkness weighed down his mind, and he hadn't slept properly in...he didn't know how long. Long enough.

The buzz of his cell phone where it lay on a stack of paperwork on the corner of his desk jolted him out of his reverie. Moving lethargically, we crossed the room and picked up his phone, thinking all the while *What now? What else could have possibly gone wrong?*

His caller ID showed his boss, Sam Hanson, still operating out of CDC headquarters on the East Coast. With a sigh, Jackson hit the answer button. "Hey Sam, what's up? Didn't think you guys would still be awake in your time zone."

A dry chuckle, devoid of mirth, answered that. "No rest for the wicked, Jackson. You know that better than any of us. Listen, we heard about Patient Zero being transferred to the Delta Center quarantine zone. Why didn't you run that by us, first?"

The old anger at this callous term bubbled within him. "Are you never going to call her Annie? Always Patient Zero. Everyone just a number to you guys, a statistic."

Sam cut him off. "Please, I didn't call to fight. Annie, if you insist. And we don't disagree with your decision. After all this time, I suppose there isn't anything else we can get from her. We just don't want you keeping us out of the loop."

Jackson ran a hand through his hair, unmindful of the greasy texture. "You're right about that. It just happened so quickly, and when Annie said that she was tired of living in isolation, away from her peers in the quarantine zone, I didn't think, I just said yes. It was the humane thing to do."

There was a short pause on the other end, before Sam came back on the line, now sounding as tired as Jackson felt. "Humane. Yes, well, I don't suppose you're wrong about that. It's actually the reason why I'm calling. You've been our boots on the ground throughout this longer than anyone, and now that things seem to be running smoothly in Utah, we'd actually like you to take a look at some of our more remote quarantine zones and report back to us. The major metropolitan areas are actually less of an issue for this, because infection rates are nearly at 100% due to how fast this thing spread. Ergo, parents in metropolitan areas are less likely to try to keep their kids from being tested, because they're afraid of blowback from neighbors. More remote areas around the country may be causes for concern, if parents think they can shelter their kids and not take them in for testing."

Jackson found himself nodding at that logic. "Ok, I could see that. But why me? I know for a fact that the CDC has resources beyond one aging virologist at Ground Zero."

"Because of your experience, of course. You told me in a report after the Delta Center zone opened for business, as it were, that you could look in a child's eyes and be able to tell at a glance who is an Angel and who isn't. That's the quality we need, especially because we've heard some troubling rumors in different isolated regions of the U.S."

Jackson frowned. "Where?"

"Maine, to start with. Have you ever been to Derry?"

8

February 1st, 2012.

Jackson's flight, a personal charter from the CDC, touched down in Bangor, Maine in the late afternoon. Just like in Utah, Maine wasn't yet ready to admit that spring was around the corner. Frigid air slapped him with a shock as he deplaned, pulling a gasp of frost tinged breath from him. Wrapping his long, tan trench coat around him, he hustled to the terminal to collect his two small bags.

As the sun was setting, a warmthless ball of pale red and orange in the west, Jackson was climbing into a rented Subaru Impreza (for the 4 wheel drive that was necessary with still so much snow and ice on the ground) and pointing it north, to the small town of Derry an hour away.

As Jackson drove white knuckled through the growing darkness, he fumbled on his cell phone and put on speakerphone the message that had been waiting for him from Sam Hanson.

"Thank you again for making your way east with such haste. I wanted to give you some background information. Derry is a small, somewhat isolated town in northern Maine. They have their own Civic Center that was originally intended to be made into a quarantine zone, but that plan was scrapped due to the relatively small population of pre-teens in the area. Instead, remote testing was set up in Bangor for all of the nearby towns, and Angels were then sent down to Boston. Everything seemed fine, at first, but then we started getting reports from our testing people that their numbers didn't add up. Not enough kids to match the population of Derry were being brought down to Bangor for testing. We have a suspicion

that there may be multiple Angels being sheltered by paranoid parents in the outlying regions of the town. You know as well as we do that we can't afford to miss even a single Angel, especially since after all this time we still don't have a working cure. Our only shot is to isolate the infected and give the rest of the world a chance to rebuild."

Jackson cursed under his breath at the callous, robotic quality of Sam's voice. His cursing grew rapidly in volume when a white tailed deer bounded out in front of him. A tightly controlled skid took him safely around the panicked animal, and he immediately pulled over to catch his breath.

When his heart rate was approaching normal once more, he grabbed his phone and rewound the message.

"We want you in town as an observer. You are not, repeat NOT, there in your capacity as doctor with the CDC. Just look, and listen. This town can provide us with a metric that can be used to measure what other small towns around the U.S. might look like as well. It would be folly to assume that every parent will take their child in for testing. We need a way to change that. Keep us informed daily of any new developments."

Jackson thumbed his phone off, sighed, and pulled back onto the highway, driving the rest of the way in silence as his mind ran through predictions.

9

Driving into Derry showed a tableau that he had been expecting, despite never having been there. A small downtown that consisted of two perpendicular main streets with a smattering of local businesses. A good sized park just off of the main drag, with an enormous standpipe that Jackson could only assume held a goodly part of the town's water supply. As Jackson drove slowly by, he spied what looked like a massive Paul Bunyon statue at the far end of the park, although it was dark enough by this point that he wasn't sure.

Double checking his GPS, Jackson continued past downtown, took a right at the Derry Civic Center, and shortly found himself at the Derry Townhouse, where he would be spending the next, well, however long this took.

The man behind the front desk was short and dour looking with eyebrows the size of caterpillars. When Jackson introduced himself to check in, the deskman simply grunted, double checked his computer, and handed over a room key for the third floor.

Creaking his way up the wooden stairs, Jackson found himself thinking that in this little corner of the world, nothing that out of the ordinary could possibly happen.

He was wrong.

10

February 2nd, 2012.

"Another coffee?"

Jackson looked up from his notes, hastily covering them with one arm, mindful of his 'spy' role in this job. The server standing over him with a full pot of coffee was a pleasant looking woman in her 50's, brown hair liberally salted with white, and a kind, matronly smile. Jackson smiled back and held up his empty cup. "Please."

The woman carefully poured him a refill. "You know, we don't get many visitors this time of year. Even less with the world bein' in such craziness."

The CDC virologist nodded. "Well, I'm recently retired and looking for a quiet place to settle down, maybe write a book. Had some friends swing by this part of the world for the fall leaves a few years back and raved about its beauty. Although I'm somewhat early for nature to show off."

The waitress grinned. "Oh, ayuh, we certainly do have our fair share of beauty up here. And if it's quiet you want, you couldn't have picked a better place. Just about all of our kids have been shipped off to Boston, from that virus. Now it's mostly just the old folks who've lived here their whole lives and got no notion to head anywhere else."

"Yes, that makes sense," Jackson replied with a note of naivete in his voice as if to show surprise that he hadn't thought of that. "All of the kids, then? The infection was that bad here? I would have thought that in a smaller, more remote town, the virus wouldn't have gotten such a strong foothold."

She frowned, arming sweat from her forehead. "Well, no one really knew what was going on until it had already spread.

Much like the rest of the world, I 'spose. And then next thing you know, those docs are setting up tents in the middle of town and testing all of our young ones. I got lucky myself, never did have no kids to bring in for testing, but lots of folks were pretty upset about it." She leaned in conspiratorially and lowered her voice, although Jackson was currently the only customer in the greasy spoon. "Although some of the folks in the farms on the outskirts of town didn't show up for testing. There's some that think maybe they're hiding something."

Jackson's eyebrows rose. "You really think people would do that, with how dangerous this virus is?"

The waitress shrugged. "This part of the world, folk don't much like being told what to do. Especially with their own children. Not saying I hold with that, myself, but I ken it. Anyway, welcome to Derry, Mr...?"

Jackson set his coffee cup down and then held his hand out, careful to keep his other arm on top of his research and notes. "Peters, Jax Peters." The fake name rolled easily off his tongue.

She grinned again, showing a gap in her teeth big enough to drive through, and shook his hand warmly. "Pleasure, Mr. Peters. I'm Missy, and this is my place. That's my name you see when you walk in the door. You need something else, just give a holler."

Jackson smiled back. "Thank you Missy. Thank you kindly."

As Missy turned and walked away, yelling something at the cook in the back, Jackson uncovered his notes and looked again at what had his mind racing. The statistics from the Derry testing that had gone on when Boston's quarantine zone had been opened. According to his notes, of the families in Derry with children under the age of 15, only 90% had taken their kids in for testing. Which left the possibility of 1-5 Angels still living here, depending on age.

The coffee beside him grew cold as he read through the rest of the reports, and started making notes on the most likely places to search out these hidden infected children. Assuming they were still alive.

11

February 3rd, 2012.

Jackson awoke bright and early to a slate gray sky that threatened snow but had yet to deliver. A frigid wind whistled down from the north, racing past the one window in his room and rattling the shutters.

He got to his feet with a groan, body feeling like one giant bruise. The bed in his Townhouse room left *much* to be desired. It should surely have been replaced a decade ago, at least. That, combined with the faulty heating unit and the splintered wooden floor, made him want to finish this job as quickly as possible and get the hell out of dodge.

Fortunately, on that count, at least he had a working plan. After being up until 2 a.m. the night before working through his notes, and those of the CDC testing doctors before him, not to mention enough coffee to replace most of the blood in his body, he had narrowed his search down to three farms in three different locations on the outskirts of town: the Barr family to the north, the Kitch family to the west, and the Sullivan family to the south. According to the most recent census study, all three families had had a child under the age of 15 when the CDC testing doctors had been here two years ago.

Dressing hurriedly in the drafty room, Jackson left with barely a wave to the surly deskman. Soon enough he was back at Missy's cafe, arming himself for the day with a fresh pot of coffee and a plate of runny eggs and greasy sausage. Missy was cordial, even a little flirtatious, Jackson thought in the back of his mind, but most of his thoughts were wrapped up in his chore for the day, and his cover story. He thought it would hold, if other townsfolk were anything like Missy, and loved nothing more than to share their town's history with outsiders. It was interesting, Jackson reflected as he wolfed down his breakfast that he barely tasted, how small town people around the world could be inherently suspicious of outsiders yet so willing to wag their tongues about why their small town was so great.

Breakfast finished (and with barely a rumble in his stomach that it might not have been a 5 star meal) and bill paid, Jackson thanked Missy warmly, promised he would be back later for dinner, and jumped in his car for the short drive north to the Barr farm. It was 10 a.m.

15 minutes later and Jackson was putting his rental car into park at the end of a 100 foot crushed gravel driveway that terminated in a gorgeous old Victorian house, three stories of red brick with white trimmed windows and two honest-to-goodness castle turrets on top. Jackson stared open mouthed at the renovated mansion and had time to reflect *I thought this was a farm?* before the front door was opening and a slender woman with swept up brown hair was leveling a shotgun at him.

Jackson's hands shot up in the air without conscious thought. "Don't shoot!" He managed to croak out through a throat suddenly gone dry.

The woman, older but still with a ghost of youthful beauty about her, narrowed her eyes. "First visitor we've had up here in over a year, now. And an outsider, from the look of it. Why don't you tell me your business, stranger?"

Keeping his hands up and in plain sight, Jackson launched into his cover story with slightly less confidence than he'd had on the drive up. "My name is Jax Peters, I recently retired and moved up here to write a history book about small towns. Missy said that your family has been in Derry for generations and you might be able to share some of the town's history with me."

Her eyes narrowed further. "Retired from what?"

"I taught history at Boston University, but I never much cared for the way small towns were represented. I thought they were glossed over, when they have just as much history to share as the bigger cities, like Boston and Atlanta."

The gun slowly came down inch by inch, and Jackson felt the tightness in his chest release when the barrel was finally pointing toward the ground. "I suppose that has a grain of truth to it. And Missy *is* one of the good ones." She chewed a lip thoughtfully for a second, before giving one sharp, decisive nod. "Ok, come on in Mr. Peters. I'll be happy to answer your questions."

Three hours, four cups of tea, and two scones later, and Jackson was taking his leave in a much more pleasant way than how he'd been welcomed. The woman, Sheila Barr, had been *more* than happy to have company come to visit, especially since it had been so long since anyone had come with any good intentions.

He'd spent the first two hours dutifully acting out the role of retired professor, and took thorough notes about the history of the Barr family, how they'd come to settle in Derry two hundred years ago. Over the course of the last three generations, they'd made their fortune in canny potato farming and stock market investments that had paid off tenfold.

When Sheila had caught up to the present and spoken of her husband (out on business in Bangor at the time of this 'interview') and the child they had had, Jackson had jumped on this opportunity to turn the conversation to the real reason he had come.

"If you don't mind my asking, I noticed you spoke of your child in the past tense? If so, you have my condolences."

Sheila sighed and stared down into her gold-chased porcelain teacup. "William. You heard right, professor, I used the past tense. It was the virus that took him."

"I'm so sorry," Jackson said, meaning it. He set his own teacup down and folded his hands in his lap, leaning forward. "Was he taken to the quarantine center, then, like all the rest? I noticed a distinct lack of children in town."

Sheila looked up, eyes flashing fire. "My husband and I didn't take kindly to the government wanting to take our one and only child away when we could shelter him perfectly fine here in our home. As I'm sure you've noticed, we aren't lacking for facilities here." She swept a perfectly manicured hand around the grand drawing room they were sitting in. "My husband and I knew that William had become one of those so-called Angels, impossible not to tell if you know what you're looking for. But William was already 14 when the CDC docs showed up with their testing tents, and we refused to take him in. That's why I mentioned earlier that we haven't had visitors with good intentions in quite some time. Almost had ourselves an angry mob on our doorstep last year."

Jackson nodded. "How did you dissuade them?" He asked, wondering if her shotgun had already seen action before.

Sheila carefully set down her own teacup and got to her feet, eyes cold. "I'll show you how."

Jackson followed her out of the drawing room, down a long corridor lined with pictures on both walls, through a kitchen bigger than his room at the Townhouse, and finally out the backdoor. The yard was enormous, dotted with oak and evergreen, with a giant playground in one corner that showed obvious signs of disuse.

Standing side by side on the stoop, Sheila pointed at the biggest oak in the yard, dead center in the snow covered field. At the foot of the majestic tree was a raised hump in the snow. "That's how we dissuaded the mob, professor. We just showed them where William was hiding. Haven't had a visitor since."

Jackson sighed, opening up his folder and pulling out the handwritten page of notes he'd completed last night. He put a checkmark next to the name Barr, and added the word 'deceased' in parentheses.

Next on the list was the Kitch family.

12

February 3rd, 2012.
2 p.m.

The Kitch family, living west of town just past the last of a handful of rundown motels, was a much quicker visit. Both parents had been home, and both looked as if they had aged a decade in the last few years. Jackson would have placed the ages of Dana and Zachary Kitch at no more than 50, but their seamed and sorrowed faces looked closer to 70. When they told him their story, he understood why.

He hadn't even had a chance to give his cover story. After giving them his name, Zachary had held up a hand and cut him off.

"Don't much care who you are or why you're here, stranger," Zachary had said in a tired, flat voice. *"I'm just going to tell you what I've told everyone else, and then you can go on your way. Our girl may've been an Angel; we still don't know. We had every intention of taking her to be tested, you understand? But Linda run off before we had a chance to. She was 12, and she was scared. May've been infected, maybe not, but she'd always had a fear of doctors ever since she was little and got pneumonia so bad she almost died. Doctors took care of her then, but she hated every second of it. So when I told her one night we were gonna take her in to be tested, she didn't much like the thought of it. Woke up the next morning, and she was gone. Later found her body down by the Barrens. Looked like she had been looking for a place to hide, but she had lost her footing in the dark and fallen down a crumbling riverbank. Well, that part of town, river was dry that time of year. Broke her neck and died. So like I said, we don't care much why you're here. You turn around and get right back in your fancy car."*

The door had been closed gently but firmly in his face, and Jackson had taken Zachary's advice and turned himself around.

Another checkmark went into his notebook, which left only one name. Sullivan.

13

February 3rd, 2012.
3:30 p.m.
A light snow had just begun to drift down from the forbidding sky above him when Jackson pulled to a stop in front of the last house on his list. He was nearly to the edge of Derry proper, within eyesight of Route 3 (mostly used by truckers), and there weren't too many houses this far out. The house he was looking at now was two stories of whitewashed brick, with dark windows that looked like glaring eyes.

Jackson rolled his shoulders to try and loosen the tension that was forming. He slowly got out of his car and walked up the snow-covered walkway, ready once more to deliver his cover story if needed. He raised a hand and knocked on a door that looked like it once might have been red, but with the paint peeling and faded it was impossible to be sure.

From within the house came the sound of clomping footsteps. A light went on, and a low, gravelly voice barked out "Yeah?"

Swallowing, he tried to sound as friendly as possible. "Yes sir, I'm new in town and wondered if I might have a moment of your time?"

The door opened just wide enough to show a face to match the voice: thick black eyebrows, a severely receding hairline, and a flat face that looked like it had been hit with a shovel. "Outsider? And out in this muck at that. State your business."

"Well, I'm a retired history professor, and-"

"No you ain't," the man interrupted. "Why don't you tell me true or get off my property."

Jackson cringed. Throwing caution to the wind, he did as the man said and opted for the truth. "Sir, I work for the CDC, and I've been tasked with finding out if parents are keeping their children away from testing and away from quarantine centers. That's the truth. The worry is that if children are infected, and not being sent to quarantine centers, then we'll never be able to contain this virus."

The heavy eyebrows came down in a scowl. "You really think we have a chance of containing this? Do you honestly believe that? The truth, boy."

Jackson squared his shoulders and met the man's fierce gaze with a steely-eyed look of his own. "No, I don't. But it doesn't mean we have to roll over and take it, either."

The man nodded, and swung the door all the way open. "Fair 'nough. Come on in and ask me your questions." He turned and tromped down the hallway, leaving Jackson to hurry after, shutting the door behind him.

"All I've got is water and whiskey, and I trust a man more once I've had a drink with him," the man called over his shoulder as he walked into a surprisingly clean and cozy kitchen.

"Whiskey suits me just fine, sir," Jackson replied easily.

The man snorted. "And enough of that 'sir' business. Name's Francis Sullivan. You can call me Frank." He waved a hand at a short kitchen table with two chairs, and Jackson eased himself into one of them. "I may not have the finest whiskey, but what I do have will put a little extra kick in your step." He filled two tall glasses with ice, set them down at the table, and grabbed a brown bottle with no label off of a shelf. Liberally splashing the no doubt homemade whiskey into each glass, Frank replaced the bottle and dropped down into the wooden chair across from Jackson. He raised his glass.

Jackson clinked his solemnly with Frank's, then tossed back a slug of the 'whiskey'. And immediately had to suppress a gag as his eyes watered at the strength and taste of it. Gasping for air, he managed a succinct "Good stuff!"

Frank threw back his head and laughed. "Could you guess I made it myself?"

Jackson nodded ruefully. "Yes, Frank, I suppose I could have guessed that."

Frank tossed back another mouthful, growing serious once more. "Well, Mr..."

"Jackson Telford."

"Mr. Telford, you came here for a reason. Speak your piece."

Taking another, smaller, sip of the potent brew, Jackson wasted no time. "The CDC knows that complete containment is impossible. The nation, and the *world*, is just too big. The virus appears to infect any child under the age of 15, and then kills when that age is reached. When this virus was first discovered, the world population of kids under 15 stood at just under 2 billion, and the virus had already had time to spread for several years unnoticed. Complete containment is a joke. However, as I mentioned, the CDC has to do *something*. Attempt to flatten the curve of the virus, as it were. I was there at ground zero and had a chance to study the virus from the beginning. I know how virulent it is. I also know that if 100% containment is impossible, I *also* know that we can still save some lives. That makes it worth it."

Frank nodded, eyes speculative. "And you're here because your research turned up that I hadn't taken my kiddo in for testing."

"That's it exactly. I've been to two other homes in Derry today. One family had sheltered their infected child for a year before that child passed. The other family had experienced an accidental death. The Sullivan name was the only other name on my list for this town. To be completely candid with you, and because your fine whiskey demands truth from a loosening tongue,"

Another snort.

"The fact is that the CDC wants to use the statistics from Derry as a model for other small towns as they try and figure out their next step. My guess would be sending out teams in a similar capacity that I am serving in now in order to find sheltered Angels and get them into quarantine."

"Makes sense, I 'spose," Frank said. "I appreciate your honesty, Mr. Telford. And so I'll give you an answer to your question, though it's maybe not the answer you were expecting. Do you notice any signs of a female influence in this house? Any pictures of a loved one hanging in the hallway you came down?"

Jackson opened his mouth to respond, but Frank held up a hand. "Rhetorical question. The answer is, my wife and I have been separated for years, and she has custody. Now, I'm guessing you found your three families with missing Angels from census reports, would that be right?"

"That's correct," he answered, head cocked in confusion.

"That there is your answer. My wife and I have been separated, but not legally. She still lists this place as her legal residence, which I have given her permission to do. But her current residence is in Boston, so she can be closer to our daughter, who is in fact in the Boston quarantine center."

Jackson set his glass down carefully. "Why didn't you both go, if you don't mind my asking?"

Frank shrugged. "Oh, I still go down and visit most weekends. But Derry is my home. Like most folks who grew up here, this place gets a hold of you. Hard to leave, easy to come back. So the wife is staying in Boston with her 'friend'," a wry smile to indicate the truth behind the word. "And to be within arms reach of our girl. And I'm up here, keeping my own world from crumbling through sheer force of will. And my fine whiskey, of course." He slammed back the rest of his drink.

"Thank you for telling me your story, Frank. I'm sorry for the intrusion, but this new information helps greatly. Honestly, your situation hadn't crossed my mind. I'll have to rethink the census approach." Jackson made as if to stand up, but Frank waved at him to stay seated.

"Stick around for another drink, and I'll give you one more story that may help your investigation. 'Sides, it's nice to have an open conversation ain't filled with suspicion like the rest of this town seems to be mired in."

Jackson resettled himself, curiosity getting the better of him, and accepted another heavy splash of moonshine whiskey.

Once he was seated again, Frank leaned forward intently. "You said you had three families on your list. I 'spose you're talking about the Barrs and the Kitchs, right?"

Jackson nodded, eyebrows going up in surprise. "That's right. How did you know?"

Frank grinned. "Small town, Mr. Telford. Everyone knows every damn thing that happens in a town this small. 'Specially the dirty laundry. Now, I know the Barrs. Hoity toity family, noses up in the air, like, but it don't mean I disagree with their call to keep their son home. He wasn't much longer for the world anyway, with how the virus works, so who can blame them for keeping him home for the little time he had remaining? And the Kitchs, well, it's a damn shame what happened to them. But they ain't the only families here that got hit with anger and suspicion, and that's the important thing for you to take back to the CDC. It ain't just about the families with hidden Angels. It's about the families with regular kids that *act* like Angels."

Jackson took a gulp of his freshened drink, feeling it burn it's way pleasantly down his throat and settle in his stomach, radiating warmth through his body. "You're talking about naturally intelligent children, prodigies, who might be regarded with suspicion. But that's exactly why we have the testing zones set up everywhere, so that we can nip that suspicion in the bud by proving who *doesn't* have the virus."

"That may work in the bigger cities," Frank said with a frown, twirling the ice around in his glass. "But I think you'll find small town mentalities are a little different. When suspicion takes root in a place like Derry, or a hundred other small towns in our country, it takes more than a medical report to make that suspicion go away. Fear, like this damn virus, is infectious. Gets in a person, deep, and drives people to do things they normally wouldn't. See, you take a single intelligent person, and that person can be rational, they can use their brains to work their way through a thing. But you put that person together with a dozen others, the logic takes a flying leap. Group think takes over. Mob mentality, understand?"

"I understand very well. Precisely what we've been working tirelessly to control."

Frank laughed mirthlessly. "Can't control a mob, doc. And that's exactly what we had here in Derry only a few months ago. We're talking old testament, here." A short pause to take a gulp of whiskey. "There was a family in town. Mom, dad, son. The kid was 13, and somehow he escaped being infected. When the testing docs were here, he got himself tested, came up clean. Went home, did the self-quarantine thing until all the local Angels had been gathered up and carted off. Problem is, the kid was a prodigy, like you said. My daughter went to school with him before the virus hit; that's how I know so much about him. He actually tutored my girl in a few of the subjects she struggled with. I think she was a bit taken with him, truth be told. Childhood crush, you ken?"

Jackson nodded, fascinated.

"Well, people in town knew he had been tested. Clean. But he was one of the only kids left in town who was, and he was too damn smart for his age, to boot. Suspicion started slow. Whispers across fences. Dark looks when the family came around town to go to a movie, or out to dinner, normal family stuff. The whispers got louder, until the parents noticed and got scared. Stopped going out. Kept their kid home. 'Cept that turned out to make things worse, because then people got it in their heads that they were keeping him home because he *was* an Angel, that he had somehow cheated the test, got a false clean report. I'm sure you can guess what happened next."

"Small town lynch mob," Jackson said quietly.

"Got it in one." Frank finished off his second whiskey. "The leader of the mob was a younger guy. With a pregnant wife. Was terrified that his new baby would get infected. So he got all his like minded friends together, went to the poor kid's house, and demanded that the boy be turned over to them. The parents refused of course. So that mob full of individually intelligent people burned their house down around them."

Silence fell.

When Jackson found his voice again, he asked the one question he had left. "Why wasn't this in the news? This should have been nationally reported!"

Frank crossed his arms and looked at Jackson with pity in his eyes. "Like I told you, small, backwater towns like Derry are different from the big cities. 'Specially here in Derry, we've always been good at sweeping our dirt under the rug. Day after this happened, that same mob that had burned the house down was already hard at work cleaning up the charred debris. Life has a way of just going back to normal. This is the information your CDC needs to hear, doc. It ain't just the Angels that the world needs to worry about. It's the suspicious fools, the regular folk that can turn into a mob at even a hint of a reason to. That young man, the ringleader? He was a good man. Used to teach at the high school. All the kids liked him. But his wife was pregnant, and he was scared. Fear changes us all, doc."

14

February 3rd, 2012.
7 p.m.

Jackson was back in his drafty room at the Townhouse, head still buzzing from the homemade whiskey as well as everything he'd heard that day. His computer was open in front of him, and his fingers were a blur as he typed up his report to send to the CDC. As he typed, that now-familiar feeling of helplessness was drawing tight around him.

He emailed his report to Sam Hanson at 9 p.m., then immediately went out and walked down the block to a corner market to buy himself a bottle of real whiskey.

As soon as he got back to his room, he got busy drinking himself to sleep, trying desperately to push away the ghosts that surrounded him.

15

September 19th, 2012.
Annie and Beckie stood side by side, watching silently as a doctor pulled a white sheet over Iris's lifeless face.
"At least she's at peace, now," Beckie said softly.
Annie put her arm around her friend's shoulders.

16

As 2012 came to a close, the worldwide death toll was approaching 100 million. The CDC and WHO weren't any closer to finding a cure. The world was giving up hope that a cure would ever be found.

Part 10: The Trial Con't (The Year 2018)

1

After child psychologist Eric Ellington had been questioned, court was dismissed for the day. The jury, sequestered in a nearby Radisson Hotel, was encouraged to review all of the evidence so far submitted, and to do so with as objective an outlook as possible (if such an outlook *was* possible).

Jeff and Gabriel, after a formal handshake during which Jeff had to restrain himself from crushing the little man's hand, parted ways, each going home to prepare for the next day's witnesses.

Calvin Michaels, given the nature of his crimes against humanity which he had already pled guilty to, was given over to the care of the court for the night. This meant that he got a county clerk's office to bed down in, as the judge was worried that if Calvin left the building, he would be lynched almost immediately.

Jeff went home and spent the evening going over his examination of his two planned witnesses for the next day: CDC epidemiology department head Samantha Hanson, and CDC director Richard Matheson. He set to with a will, going over every detail with Kristi, who might catch something he might have missed. He didn't go to bed until after midnight, exhausted but confident.

Gabriel Conklin, defense attorney, spent his evening in the company of a bottle of Merlot and John Grisham's latest court fiction. He was asleep by 10 with nary a concern fluttering through his mind.

Gabriel was single and had no children of his own.

2

The next day dawned clear and bright, with a hint of heat in the air even at 7:30 a.m., when Jeff arrived back at the courthouse, grande latte in hand.

Gabriel, looking hungover only if you knew the signs to look for, arrived at 8:45.

The honorable Judge Erikson called the court back in session promptly at 9 a.m.

3

"You Honor," Jeff intoned with a firm voice that carried to every corner of the large courtroom. "I'd like to call to the stand Dr. Samantha Hanson."

Sam Hanson, short and slender and wearing a somber gray pantsuit for the trial, stood from her place in the audience and made her way forward to be sworn in. Her heart was pounding in her chest at the worry of the questions she was going to have to answer, but her steps were sure and she held her head high. *You're not the one on trial,* she kept telling herself. *Just answer the questions and get the hell out of here, back to the comfort of the bottle of Jack Daniels waiting at home.*

"Do you swear to tell the truth, the whole truth, and nothing but the truth, so help you God?" The bald, muscular bailiff asked her loudly.

Sam gulped, and the hand she had placed on the bible trembled. "I swear."

Judge Erikson looked over to Jeff. "The prosecution may begin."

Jeff stood and walked forward. He was aware of Sam's unease, and knew why, so he tried to keep his facial expression and voice as kindly as possible. "Dr. Samantha Hanson, will you please tell the court of your role within the CDC at the time of the Angel Virus pandemic?"

"I was the department head of epidemiology, and provided oversight and guidance to the departments of virology and genetics as they pertained to epidemiology." Sam answered clearly, tension undetectable.

"And for the sake of clarification, can you explain the purpose of the department of epidemiology, in layman's terms?"

She nodded, feeling more sure of herself. "The department of epidemiology deals specifically with the incidence, distribution, and possible control of diseases."

"Thank you. So it was you that Dr. Jackson Telford reported to?"

"Yes."

Jeff glanced over at the jury box. "We've already heard from Dr. Telford about what the CDC was able to discover about the nature of the Angel Virus, its virulence, and how it was nearly undetectable in the beginning. We've also heard his expert medical testimony on how the virus was created not by nature, but by man." Jeff didn't need to look over at Calvin Michaels, seated once more behind the defendant's table; every person on the jury swung their eyes over to glare at him.

Jeff continued. This was the critical part of his examination. "Dr. Hanson, in your capacity as department head at the CDC, when did your people first become aware of the Angel Virus?"

"In early 2009, the CDC began receiving reports of unexplained deaths from different hospitals around the country." Sam paused to take a drink of water. Even just remembering those early days gave her the chills, thinking about how even then they had been helpless before the storm that was already raging. "Our immediate response was to gather information from every hospital, send out teams of our own investigators, and bring in the president's medical team to keep them apprised of the situation."

"This was early 2009," Jeff restated, to emphasize the timeline. "Nine years ago. What did your preliminary information gathering yield?"

"Very little, at first," Sam admitted. "As everyone now knows, the virus kills without explanation when the patient turns 15.

My department did our own autopsies and studies, but what made it so difficult in the beginning was that we didn't know what we were looking for. We desperately needed a live subject, but again, we didn't know how to find one. That was what made the Angel Virus so terrifying. The way that Angels were able to live under the radar until it was too late."

"Objection!" Gabriel's nasal voice rang out. "Your honor, the witness lacks sufficient basis for her opinion."

Jeff turned an incredulous look on Gabriel even as Judge Erickson rapped his gavel once. "Overruled, counselor. Witness is here to provide expert witness testimony and has not deviated from that to my mind. Prosecution may continue."

Jeff shook his head and had to take a second to reorganize his thoughts. That was part of what made Gabriel Conklin a tough opponent in court. He wasn't the most intelligent of lawyers, but he was cunning, knew how to throw monkey wrenches into examinations at key moments. "When were you first able to examine a live patient?"

Sam took another sip of water, wishing that there was a splash of something stronger in her glass. "Later in 2009. We found hospital records that matched up with the same investigation we were doing, or at least appeared to."

"And who was your live subject?"

"Patient Zero," Sam answered softly. "Orphan Annie."

Silence fell in the courtroom. Jeff, expertly reading the room, let it draw out for several moments. Finally, he continued. "What did the CDC do next?"

"We dispatched Dr. Jackson Telford and a team to Salt Lake City to find and study Patient Zero. We knew that every bit of information we could learn about this new virus could help us try to fight it." *Yet even then, we were fucked,* Sam didn't add.

Jeff turned to the jury box and spread his hands wide. "Ladies and gentlemen of the jury, you've already heard Dr. Telford's testimony about the virus itself, and how rapidly it spread. We now have expert testimony proving that the CDC, and our own government, did everything they could, but the virus had already spread too far and too fast. The evidence continues to stack up against the defendant, Calvin Michaels. By the time humanity was even *aware* of this threat, it was already too late. This man," a sweep of one hand encompassed the defendant. "Not only doomed a quarter of our population, he ensured that we didn't even have a chance to fight it." Jeff turned back to Sam, and the judge, as the jury members began murmuring quietly to themselves. "No further questions, your honor."

4

After a five minute recess, Gabriel Conklin took to the floor to begin his cross examination. He didn't waste any time with niceties. "Dr. Hanson, by your own admission, your department began live study research in 2009, correct?"

Sam nodded nervously. Jeff had prepped her for Gabriel's aggressive questioning style, but it didn't make her any less uncomfortable now that it was happening. "That is correct."

"That was nine years ago. You're telling me that in nine years, the combined efforts of the CDC and, as I understand it, the WHO weren't able to make any progress whatsoever in finding a cure?"

"Objection!" Jeff rapped out. "Your honor, the CDC isn't on trial for a lack of developing a cure."

"Sustained."

Gabriel smirked. "Your honor, I'm simply trying to establish a timeline. Dr. Hanson, I'll back up. You said that in 2009, you finally 'discovered' Patient Zero and made the connection that she might be a so-called Angel, and provide a live study. Correct?"

"Yes."

"You also said that up until that point, you just had reports from country-wide hospitals to go on, and the information wasn't enough in order to provide a proper diagnostic of the disease. Why is that?"

This time Sam needed a gulp of water. "As we know now, the virus doesn't survive the death of the patient. It's truly a symbiotic relationship, with simultaneous death."

Gabriel's smile turned sly. "And how did you find out about Patient Zero? Did the hospital here in Salt Lake contact you?"

"No," Sam said quietly.

"Could you speak up for the court, please?" Gabriel demanded.

"No! There was no previous contact. The CDC has technological tools at our disposal in order to gather information even when said information isn't willingly forthcoming."

Gabriel turned his smile on the jury. "So you were hacking hospitals."

Sam's temper flared. "I'll have you know it was all perfectly legal. A subsection of the Patriot Act allows us to access information relevant to protection of U.S. citizens. Looking for information about the Angel Virus falls under that."

Gabriel waved a hand as if shooing away a fly. "Yes, yes, the Patriot Act can be interpreted in many ways. Regardless, you got your information. You got your live patient. You said that you then sent a CDC team here to Salt Lake to 'study' your live patient. How did you go about doing that?"

"Using presidential influence, we got a court order for the release of Patient Zero into our custody. She became our first quarantined patient." Sam dropped her eyes, ashamed at being forced into making this admission, and how it made her look.

"And this was in 2009?"

"Yes."

"Could you be more specific? *When* in 2009 did you steal Patient Zero away from her family?"

"Objection!" Jeff nearly shouted, coming to his feet. "Badgering the witness!"

"Sustained." The judge said immediately. "Watch your language, counselor, or I'll hold you in contempt of court."

Gabriel held up his hands defensively. "I'll rephrase. Dr. Hanson, what month did your CDC team put Patient Zero into quarantine?"

Sam reached for her water glass and saw that it was empty. "Mid June."

"And when did the national quarantine go into effect?"

Sam closed her eyes. "End of August."

Gabriel leaned forward exultantly. "You're saying the CDC knew for two and a half months that a quarantine could potentially be the only answer to halting the spread of the virus and yet did nothing except quarantine one little girl?"

Sam's eyes shot open, blazing. "Sir, at this point the CDC was still confident that with a live patient to study, we would be able to accurately diagnose and map the disease, and discover a cure or, at the least, a vaccine. As everyone saw from the eventual global quarantine, it sparked riots in several cities that took days to put down, and in the end it didn't actually change a thing. Yes, the CDC knew that quarantine *might* be necessary at the time, but wanted to exhaust every other option first. As both myself and Dr. Telford have already attested, we have never before come up against a virus like this before. We were woefully unprepared, but still hopeful that we could figure it out in time to *stop* a global panic."

Gabriel's mouth twisted. "But you didn't. No further questions, your honor."

Part 11: Society Crumbling (The Year 2013)

1

January 1st, 2013.
The day Annie turned 10, the global death toll passed 100 million.

2

Over the course of 2012, the CDC had kept Jackson busy with trips similar to Derry made all over the country. Anywhere the CDC heard a rumor of unrest over possible hidden Angels and community uprisings, that became Jackson's next stop, sometimes with a team if the rumors were dark enough.

Jackson became used to living out of his suitcase. He also became stronger bedfellows with whiskey.

In early 2013, the CDC heard something new, this time from the West Coast. A nurse who lived and worked in Seattle, in the quarantine center established at the CenturyLink Field (home of the

Seahawks) reached out to the CDC hot tips line (which was always flooded and rarely of any help) and said she had an Angel who *didn't die when he turned 15*.

Sam Hanson personally called the nurse back on the spot.

3

April 2, 2013.
8:30 a.m.
NURSE: *Hello?*
SAM: *This is Dr. Samantha Hanson, of the Centers for Disease Control and Prevention. Is this the nurse who called in about the Angel who lived?*
NURSE: *Yes! My name is Rebekah Carroll, I've been working at the Seattle quarantine center ever since we got up and running.*
SAM: *Tell me about the boy. First of all, did he test positive when he was first admitted into your center?*
NURSE: *Well, that's the thing. Seattle's quarantine center has always been chaotic, as I'm sure so many of the other big city centers have been. In the very beginning, when we were being flooded with children to be tested and hadn't yet set up a streamlined process for testing and admitting, there were many kids who weren't blood tested, they were just eyeballed. I'm sure I don't need to tell you that 99% of the time you can look in a kid's eyes and just KNOW. That ageless look that they all have.*
SAM: *-sigh- Yes, I'm familiar. So you think that this boy was admitted clean. However, what I want to know is, how could he have spent so much time being surrounded by infected children and not become infected himself?*
NURSE: *The boy, whose name is Jose Corkhill, was admitted last year at age 14. I had a few personal interactions with him myself, but didn't notice anything out of the ordinary. He didn't quite have the same ageless look, as you know many of the older infected don't, but he was beyond bright, and seemed right at home with all of the other Angels. And we just have so many here that it can be easy to let the individuals get lost in the crowd. Again, I'm sure you are well aware.*
SAM: *Yes. We're all aware of that here.*

NURSE: *Ok, well, two days ago, Jose turned 15. And he was fine. So I myself, with one of our main doctors, pulled him aside and finally did a formal blood test. He's completely clean of the Angel Virus. Which to us suggests that he has some kind of immunity. If true, that could be a game changer, wouldn't you think?*

SAM: *-speaking rapidly- Where is Jose now?!*

NURSE: *His parents were in town from Spokane, which is on the east side of the state and where his family lives. They were here to say goodbye. But when Jose lived, and we tested him and found him clean, they obviously demanded he be released so they could take him home. We had no reason not to. So we released Jose and the family headed back to Spokane.*

SAM: *Do you have their information, and home address?*

NURSE: *Of course.*

SAM: *I want everything you have on Jose, his family, his blood test, the time he spent in the center, medical history, EVERYTHING you have on him. How quickly can you get me that?*

NURSE: *I can email you later this morning. Do you think we've found something that could turn the tide on this, doctor?*

SAM: *Time will tell. Thank you, Rebekah, for all of this. If we find out more, the CDC will be in touch.*

4

April 2nd, 2013.
12:30 p.m. EST.

Jackson had just returned from a trip to Ohio, to look into a series of threats made to a farming family who was suspected of hiding an Angel. It had ended up being a dead end: no Angel had been hidden away; it was just another example of society's growing distrust and suspicion.

He had walked back into his own house, which he saw so little of these days, and barely had time to sit down on his bed with a sigh of relief when his cell phone rang. The sigh of relief turned into one of dismay when he saw the Caller ID.

"Yes? This is Jackson."

"It's Sam. Don't get comfortable, we're sending you right out again. No team this time, although we do have some connections at the local hospital who will be helping you out. I believe the hospital is called Sacred Heart."

A groan. "Ok Sam, where to this time? And what's the situation? The usual?"

"Actually no." Her voice sounded excited for once, and that brought Jackson's interest up. "A 14 year old in one of the Seattle quarantine centers. He recently turned 15." A dramatic pause. *"And lived."*

Jackson shot to his feet. "What? You're sure? This information has been validated?"

"I just got an email from the nurse who treated him in Seattle. I'm running through the boy, Jose's, medical history and quarantine charts, and it checks out. The short of it is that he was admitted without formal blood testing, but despite being in a quarantine center surrounded by Angels, he didn't get infected. He turned 15, was tested, the test came back negative, so his parents scooped him up and took him to Spokane, on the east side of the state. You'll be flying from here to Seattle, then a short flight directly into Spokane. We already have a place rented for you, as well as a car. I'll forward along all of the relevant information."

Jackson blinked and started pacing, mind racing a mile a minute. "Is this it, Sam? Do you think we've found a natural immunity we can use for a vaccine or a cure?"

"Let's not get ahead of ourselves," Sam cautioned, though the excitement in her voice betrayed her sense of hope. "Just get out there, talk to the family, test the kid, you know the drill. Let's find out what's really going on with this."

"When is my flight?"

5

April 2nd, 2013.
5:30 p.m. PST.
Jackson's puddle hopper of a plane touched down at what for him, on east coast time, would have been whiskey o'clock. But in his excitement, he hadn't even had a drink on either of his flights, nor did he have his usual burning desire to hit the local liquor store before continuing on to his newest assignment, as had been his routine for the last year as his assignments got more and more bleak.

After deplaning and collecting his bags (which he hadn't even bothered to unpack from his last trip; he planned to do laundry as soon as he got settled) Jackson made his way to the rental car counter next to baggage claim. Going through the usual paperwork routine, he was finally given the keys to an ugly tan 2009 Toyota Tercel. He barely saw it as all of his thoughts were centered on the job ahead of him.

What brought his mind back to the present was the view of Spokane as he drove in. The freeway east from the airport and into the city slanted down into the bowl of downtown Spokane, and it was lit up in reds and golds from the late afternoon sunset. The handful of skyscrapers surrounded by bright green trees took his breath away. It was a little jewel of a town, and it filled him more than ever with a feeling of hope that he hadn't felt in years.

Jackson carried that feeling nestled within him like a glowing seed as he drove down into the city, then got off the freeway, turned right, and made his way up into the neighborhood called the South Hill (which was very appropriately named). His AirBnB was just a couple blocks from Sacred Heart Hospital.

After getting settled, ordering food in, and doing the necessary laundry, Jackson turned in with nary a thought for grabbing a drink to help him sleep.

Right now, at least, he didn't need it.

6

April 3rd, 2013.
9 a.m.

Dr. Jackson Telford had already been up for two hours and gone through two pots of coffee as he reviewed all of the information on the Corkhill family that Sam had forwarded to him. Typing on his computer, he brought up the tab on the family.

FATHER: Jose (Sr.) Corkhill (age: 52)
MOTHER: Tammy Corkhill (age: 50)
BROTHER: Trae Corkhill (age: 30)
BROTHER: Mateo Corkhill (age: 20)
PATIENT: Jose (Jr.) Corkhill (age: 15)

Scanning down, Jackson saw they lived in the Mead neighborhood, which, according to his GPS, was roughly a half hour north from the South Hill, on the other side of Spokane. He clicked from that tab over to the information sent over from the nurse at the Seattle quarantine center, once again going over all that she had said to Sam in their brief phone call.

Jose Corkhill. Inpatient at Seattle quarantine center (CenturyLink Field). Not blood tested upon admission at age 14. Spent a year in the quarantine center. Turned 15 and didn't die. Blood tested. Results negative. Reason??

Taking another sip of coffee, Jackson leaned back in the rickety wooden chair and turned his thoughts back to Annie, and the Oritt family. Specifically to Maddy. Just like Jose, Maddy had spent years in close contact with an Angel, from the age of 12, and never got infected.

So what does this mean? He thought. *Natural immunity? We tested Maddy and nothing out of the ordinary came up. At the time, Jessica and I speculated that maybe it had to do with puberty. If Maddy didn't get infected because she simply hit puberty early. Is it the same with Jose? But then why wouldn't we have heard of this before now?*

He shook his head. There was an easy answer to that one. The kids who would have hit puberty early and been lucky enough to avoid getting infected were a very small percentage of the infection rate, and there were a multitude of reasons they might have slipped under the radar. First of all, despite the chaos of the quarantine centers, especially in the beginning, most kids *did* get blood tested, and not just eyeballed. So if a child was tested and it came back negative, they would have been released back to their parents, who surely would have quarantined their kid at home until they were 15 and safe.

A second possibility, and a much darker one, is what Jackson had seen in small towns all over the U.S. over the last year. Kids who were *suspected* of being Angels, who were then singled out and attacked in their various communities.

"Well," Jackson said to himself as he pushed himself back from the table in the nook of his little kitchen. "No time like the present to find out."

Sam had already assured him that she had reached out to the Corkhill family, and they were more than willing to meet with him and discuss the situation. They were so overjoyed that Jose had lived that they wanted to share it with the world.

Informally dressed in jeans, a Motley Crue t-shirt, and cowboy boots, Jackson grabbed his computer tote bag and notes and hopped in his ugly Tercel, whistling to himself as he started up the car and headed across town.

7

April 3rd, 2013.
10:30 a.m.

Jackson knocked on the wooden door of a very handsome townhouse in the tucked away cul-de-sac. The house was two stories tall, white with black trim around the windows, and a gabled roof. It had a warm, welcoming feel to it.

The young man who answered the door was tall, lanky, and had a wild mop of jet black hair that fell around his face. Seeing Jackson, he broke into a broad smile. "Hey, you the doc?"

Jackson smiled back. "That's right, I'm the doc. I'm guessing you're Mateo?"

The young man laughed. "That's me. Man, you've done your research on us. Here to see the miracle kid?"

"Mateo?" A woman's voice from inside the house called out. "Is that Dr. Telford?"

Mateo turned back and shouted. "Yeah, ma! Here for Jose!"

A short, handsome woman in her middle years walked up and gently shouldered Mateo aside. She looked up at her son. "Well, don't keep him waiting outside! Where are your manners?" Turning to Jackson, she looked him up and down before opening the door wide. "Please, come in, doctor. My name is Tammy, I'm Jose's mother. He'll be right down."

Jackson stepped forward into the house. "Thank you, Tammy. And you can just call me Jackson; I don't stand on formality much."

Tammy led Jackson down a hallway lined with family pictures, chattering away all the while. "I'm sure you already know, but our family has been in such a dark hole as Jose's 15th birthday approached. And then a miracle! We were there in Seattle to be with him when, you know, and then he lived! My boy lived! I mean we prayed and we prayed, but so many have already died that we didn't put much stock in our own prayers. And now he's been returned to us. Our whole community is talking about it!"

Good things, I hope, Jackson thought privately to himself, ashamed at his own negative response. This should be a cause for celebration, but Jackson had seen too much hate and suspicion already that it was hard to take a 'positive community reaction' at face value.

Tammy led him into a cozy dining room and got him seated, asking him if he needed anything to eat, to drink, was he comfortable, all the while with a face-splitting smile on her face. It warmed Jackson's heart to see so much love in such a dark time.

As Jackson was waving away Tammy's offers of food and drink, Jose strolled casually into the dining room, and Tammy immediately turned her attention to her 'miracle son'. Jackson took the opportunity to study the young teen.

Already well into his growth spurt, Jose looked to be about 5'7", and walked with a natural grace that implied some kind of athletic prowess. The family resemblance between Jose and Mateo was easy to spot. Both had the same dark brown eyes that appeared to be laughing at something no one else could see, the easy smile, the lanky frames. Possibly the only difference was in their hair: Mateo's was jet black, and Jose's was dark brown, although just as long, coming down past his shoulders.

Finally fending off his mother, Jose sat down at the table opposite Jackson and studied him right back unabashedly. "So, the CDC wants to know if I'm a real miracle or not, huh?"

Jackson flashed him a grin. "Straight to the point. Man after my own heart. That's pretty much why I'm here, yes. The CDC has been doing everything within its power to find something, *anything,* that can help us figure out a way to beat this thing. It's been years, and you're only the second child we've found who didn't get infected before the age of 15, despite close proximity to other Angels."

Mateo dropped down in a chair next to Jose. "You mean Jose isn't the first?"

Right on the heels of his older brother, Jose burst out "Who else?"

"A girl in Utah. Had a younger sister who was infected, but despite the fact that the girl in question was 12, she never caught it."

Tammy sat down on the other side of Jose, suddenly making the doctor feel like he was the one being questioned instead of the other way around. "Do you know why?" Tammy asked.

Jackson held up his hands and shook his head. "We tested her extensively, and all we could determine is that she was negative for the virus, and perfectly healthy in every other way. The girl is now 22 and doing just fine."

"How about that," Mateo mused, before turning and punching Jose lightly on the shoulder. "Maybe you're not a miracle after all!"

Jose laughed. "What do you think I've been telling you all this whole time?"

Tammy made shushing noises to her sons. "So what now, doctor? You want to test Jose I imagine?"

He nodded. "Yes ma'am, with your permission. I already have a team of local doctors standing by at Sacred Heart, ready whenever you are."

Jose stood up. "Ok."

Jackson laughed. "Just like that?"

The teen shrugged. "Hey, if you can figure out something from me that could help other people, then we should get started, yeah?"

Five minutes later Jackson was driving down Division Street, heading back through the heart of the city to the hospital, with three members of the Corkhill family in a minivan behind him.

8

April 3rd, 2013.
Noon.

Tammy and Mateo had been left in the waiting room while Jackson led Jose through the hallways of Sacred Heart to a large operating room.

Jose looked around with a quiet gravity that made Jackson understand why the medical staff at the Seattle quarantine center had been so quick to label him as an Angel. He didn't quite have the ageless look in his eyes, but his whole demeanor marked him as mature beyond his years.

"This seems like a pretty big room for just drawing blood and doing some rudimentary tests," Jose remarked casually, hands stuffed in the pockets of his jeans.

Jackson, now wearing a doctor's lab coat over his informal clothes, nodded. "Well, there are a lot of people here who want to help. You've created quite a stir, you know."

The boy laughed, showing gleaming white teeth in his tan face. "You don't have to tell me. I just hope you're able to get some good information out of my blood."

Another doctor and a nurse walked in, and the informal conversation cut off abruptly. Jackson, once more in doctor mode, made introductions all around then got down to business.

Over the course of the next six hours, Jackson and his temporary team of Sacred Heart doctors and nurses ran every test they could think of.

Blood testing.
Blood typing.
EKG.
EEG.
CBC.
CAT scan.
MRI.
Whole genome microarray.
The list went on and on.

Through it all, Jose was calm and collected, betraying not a single twitch or tic of nervousness. Jackson's respect for the boy grew with each passing hour.

Finally, at 6 p.m., Jackson brought the testing to a halt. "I think that will do it for today," he said, helping Jose up and out of the MRI machine. "If there is anything unique to be found, one of these tests will find it. We are going to fast track every single test in order to get the results as rapidly as possible, for obvious reasons. I'm hoping to have something to share by tomorrow afternoon at the latest."

"Whatever you need, doc. I'm just along for the ride," Jose said, still wearing the same calm, unruffled look that he'd had on his face the whole day.

Jackson shook his hand warmly. "Whatever happens, just know that we're all thankful you survived. And you have all of our thanks that you were willing to put yourself at our mercy, so to speak, to see if we could learn anything new."

"What kind of miracle kid would I be if I didn't want to share the love?" Jose responded with a laugh.

Jackson laughed along, leading Jose back out through the maze of hallways to the waiting room.

The whole Corkhill clan was waiting for them when they came out. The oldest brother, Trae, looked like an older, more handsome version of Mateo, with the same jet black hair, although his was pulled back in a tight ponytail.

The father, Jose Sr, had his hair cut short, with an intimidating mustache framing a serious face. The intimidating look vanished when he saw his son. Jose Sr, smiling broadly, got to his feet and walked over to meet them, Tammy by his side, with the two older brothers a half step behind them. He held out his hand to Jackson.

"Dr. Telford!" Jose Sr had a deep, basso voice. "I've been hearing all about you. Thank you for coming."

Jackson shook his hand. "Please, thank you all for being willing to help us out. And thanks to your son for putting up with six hours of rigorous testing! I was just telling him that we should have results one way or another by tomorrow afternoon, and we will be in touch the minute we do."

"Thank you sir," Jose Sr replied sincerely. Dropping Jackson's hand, he turned to his sons. "Alright boys, I think it's time we clear out and let the professionals do their thing. I, for one, am starving."

Each member in turn thanked Jackson and shook his hand, and then in a whirlwind of babbling voices, they were out the door.

Jackson, still smiling, turned around and headed back into the interior of the hospital, intending to grab himself a cup of coffee and work around the clock if necessary. He was too excited to do anything less.

9

April 4th, 2013.
1:30 p.m.

True to his word, Jackson had worked around the clock with the different teams running the different tests. And the results?

Nothing out of the ordinary whatsoever.

Just like Maddy.

Trying to swallow the bitter defeat he was feeling, as well as the need for a stiff drink, Jackson made his phone call to the Corkhill family and informed them that Jose Jr was a perfectly healthy, normal 15-year-old, and thanked them again for their time. The Corkhills weren't nearly put out as he was; they were simply happy that Jose was alive. Jackson couldn't blame them for that.

Shortly after, Jackson placed a call to Sam Hanson.

"Hello?"

"Sam, it's Jackson. I have an update on the Spokane front."

"And?" Her voice was taught with excitement.

"Not a single thing out of the ordinary. Just like Maddy Oritt."

A long pause. "No miracle cure, then."

Jackson sighed. He was doing that a lot these days. "Not here, at least. I think our earlier supposition was correct: that there is a demographic of children who reach puberty before the age of 15 and that's why they're not contracting the virus. It's nothing to do with natural immunity."

"Then we just keep looking," Sam replied fiercely. "We have to. We can't give up, Jackson."

Jackson's shoulders slumped, but his voice was firm. "Agreed."

"Come on home, doctor. I think you've earned yourself a reprieve from all of this flying around. It's the least we can do for you."

"Yes ma'am. Be seeing you all soon."

10

The CDC, true to its word, allowed Jackson Telford to take paid leave for the remainder of the year. However, that didn't mean they weren't staying busy. As well as sending teams of doctors out to continue investigating possible hidden Angel situations, they were now also investigating children who might have hit puberty early and thus escaped infection. They didn't find many, but they found enough to substantiate the theory that yes, the Angel Virus attacked the thymus gland directly while it was still functioning at full power before puberty struck. What they still couldn't figure out, however, is that once a child was infected, why, *why* did they die at the exact moment they turned 15?

11

The year 2013 passed by with society sinking down into a lull of grim acceptance. The death toll continued to rise, but with all of the quarantine zones running as smoothly as possible in all corners of the world, the rest of humanity was simply trying to get on with at least a semblance of normality. High schools still ran regular school hours, and most students even showed up. Grownups got up, went to work, went home. Martial law remained in place, but in something of a dormant phase. Families, those family members that remained in each unit, at least, tried to get back on a normal schedule. Which included the occasional vacation.

Air and water travel was once again operating smoothly, with the added check in procedure of having all children tested if they were under 15.

12

January 1st, 2014.
Annie turned 11.
Global death toll: 300 million.

13

July 1st, 2014.
10 a.m.
"Kids, get off your phones! The line's moving." Abigail said with fond exasperation as she and her wife Fran attempted to herd their two kids forward to where cruise passengers were being checked in.

The Vega family had arrived in Seattle the night before, flying in from the East Coast, and spent the night sightseeing around the beautiful city. Beautiful, at least, if you stayed downtown and avoided the grim quarantine zone at CenturyLink Field.

Abigail, short, black, and with short black hair was a study in contrast to her wife Fran, who was tall, white, and with hair blonde enough to do justice to a Valkyrie warrior of old. The two had first met in Seattle, and had been excited to show the city to their kids, who had only ever experienced locales on the East Coast.

Robby, who was 15 and generally exhibited the bored disinterest of a world-wise teenager, hadn't shown any excitement until they had gone to the top of the Space Needle. Then his bland facade had dropped away and he had nearly thrown his tall, lanky body at the glass wall as adrenaline pounded through him seeing the world drop away beneath.

Dayna, their 14 year old daughter, was the exact opposite of her brother. *Everything* about Seattle had excited her! Pike Street Market, Town Square, the Museum of Pop Culture, Dayna couldn't get enough.

And now, on the 1st of July, Abigail and Fran were thrilled to be taking their kids on their first ever cruise up the inside strait of Alaska! It was all any of them could talk about ever since school got out the month before.

Robby deigned to look up from his phone long enough to shuffle his feet forward a few steps. He peered around the people standing in front of him to see how far it was to the front, and what he saw there pulled his mouth down into a grimace of frustration. He turned to look at his moms. "Another testing checkpoint? Again? Are we ever not going to have to do this?"

Abigail and Fran shared a long look. Abigail was the one who answered. "One day, Robby, I'm sure. In the meantime, just be happy you're already 15, ok? That means you just have to show your ID. This year, Dayna is the only one who has to be tested. But it's just a formality. We had her tested last year and she was clean, and everyone knows that all of the infected have all been gathered up and sent to the quarantine camps. Nothing to worry about, ok?"

"More like leper colonies," Robby muttered under his breath, eyes dropping back down to the game on his phone. Beside him, Dayna gulped and her face turned white.

"Hey!" Fran barked out. "Watch your language. You know I don't like that term." She turned to Dayna and hugged her close. "Don't worry, Dayna, we all know you're fine. And soon you're going to be on your first cruise ship!"

Slowly but surely the line inched forward. Most of the cruisers ahead of them were retirees, and largely passed by the checkpoint with nary a pause.

When the Vega family finally got to the front desk, Abigail produced all four of their passports for inspection and approval. The desk clerk, a young man with the same bored expression on his face as Robby, gave Abigail's and Fran's a perfunctory glance, but spent a little more time going over Robby's and Dayna's. Finally he looked up and handed three of the four passports back. "You three are good to go. Just one needs to clear the checkpoint, and then you can head on up to the ship."

Dayna, with a tremble in her lower lip, allowed herself to be led over to the medical testing tent that had been set up to the side of the front desk. A kindly older woman with a ready smile invited her to sit down in an empty chair. Dayna, trying to force herself to breath evenly, allowed the doctor to take a small vial of blood, which the doctor took behind a curtain to whatever testing equipment they had back there.

Someone had once explained to Dayna that it had to do with something called a centrifuge, which allowed them to find whatever was, or wasn't, in her blood, that would give her a negative or positive result.

The seconds ticked by like hours, and when the doctor came back out, the kindly look on her face was gone, replaced by sad resignation. She avoided Dayna's eyes, and instead addressed herself to Abigail and Fran. "I'm so sorry. Her test came back positive. She'll have to be escorted to the quarantine center."

The announcement hit the entire family like a ton of bricks.

Robby dropped his phone in his surprise, and his mouth dropped open.

Abigail could only stare uncomprehendingly.

It was Fran who was the first to break the silence. "NO! That's impossible! We just had her tested last year and she was fine! Test her again!"

The doctor shook her head sadly but firmly. "I ran her blood through the centrifuge three times. I'm sorry, but she's infected."

Dayna started to scream.

14

An hour later, Dayna was finally getting herself under control. The family was sitting off to one side in a secluded area of the check-in terminal. A polite distance away stood the doctor and a soldier, both of them looking extremely uncomfortable.

"I don't want to die," Dayna whispered, arms crossed tightly and head lowered.

Abigail, with an arm around her shoulders, gave her a squeeze. "Don't you worry, honey. I'm not going anywhere." She looked over Dayna's head at Fran. "Can I talk to you for a second?"

Fran nodded, and the two women stood and walked a short distance away. Robby moved over to the seat Abigail had just vacated and put an arm around his sister, face still wearing a shocked expression. Dayna leaned into him and started sobbing quietly.

"Listen," Abigail began, once they were out of earshot. "I think you should still take Robby on the cruise. I'll go with the doctor to take Dayna to the quarantine center."

"What?! You can't be serious!"

Abigail nodded firmly. "Dayna has another 7 months before she turns 15. More than enough time for you to give our son a fun trip before coming back here and helping me deal with this. We both know that the road ahead is going to be an incredibly hard and heartbreaking ordeal. Why not give Robby a ray of sunshine before he has to start wrapping his head around his sister's death sentence?"

Fran dashed a hand across her eyes. "Dammit, you always were the logical one. Ok, what you're saying makes sense. But are you sure he would even want to go? The poor kid is in shock!"

Abigail offered a wan smile. "He's 15, and as easily distracted as he'll ever be in his life. This could be good for him. You're the one who is going to have the challenge, making sure that he has fun."

A humorless laugh. "Christ. Ok, let's ask him and see what he says."

The two women walked hand in hand back to Robby and Dayna.

"Dayna? Sweetie? It's going to be ok," Abigail said gently. "Come on, let's go talk to the doctor."

Dayna, still sniffling, got up and joined Abigail, and the two headed toward the nurse.

Fran dropped down next to Robby. "How are you holding up, kiddo?"

He shook his head, eyes wide. "I don't get it. It just doesn't make sense. I mean, how can it happen to our family? We've followed all the rules."

Fran sighed. "I know we did. But you've heard the reports on the news. Not everyone else follows the rules, and our family has to pay for that."

"It's not fucking fair!"

For once, she didn't call him down for his language. If there was ever a time for cursing, this was it. "I know, kiddo. I know. Listen, your mom had an idea. Abby thinks you and I should still go on the cruise, and she'll take Dayna to the quarantine center and stay with her until we get back next week."

Robby turned an incredulous look on her, and Fran had the guilty thought that at least one of her kids was safe. "Still go? After this?"

Fran nodded once. "There's nothing we can do, now. But life goes on, and you are going to have a long and fulfilling one. We both know that's what Dayna would want for you."

He looked away, expression troubled. "Well...I mean, I guess. Are you really sure it's ok?"

"I'm sure. And as soon as we get back, we'll go straight to the stadium to meet up with them and spend all the time we can before..." She let herself trail off, unwilling to say the next words.

Robby twisted in his seat to look at Dayna and Abigail speaking with the doctor. The soldier was still with them, but was looking anywhere else, obviously painfully uncomfortable with his role in the situation.

He looked back to Fran. "Ok, mom. I guess I'm game. Can we at least say goodbye?"

"Of course!"

The next ten minutes passed by in a blur for all of them. There were hugs all around, and tears. Dayna squeezed Robby until he thought his ribs would burst, her tears falling heavily on his shirt and in the crook of his arm where she had buried her head. And then, just like that, Abigail and Dayna were going one way with the doctor and soldier, and Fran and Robby were heading to the gangway.

Abigail looked back over her shoulder for one last glimpse of her wife and son before they disappeared into the ship.

That was the last time she saw her son alive.

15

The ship, called the Norwegian Joy, was on the smaller side of cruise ships, but was still an impressive sight to behold. Boasting nine levels, two above deck swimming pools, six hot tubs, gym, spa, five restaurants, two theaters, and an arcade, it was exactly the distraction that Fran hoped it would be, for Robby's sake.

That first day, a Saturday, Robby mirrored Fran's emotional state: shock and bewilderment. But when they awoke Sunday morning on the gentle swells of the Pacific, Robby took one look at the open ocean and his expression turned to one of awe. For that one moment alone, Fran was thankful to Abigail for pushing them to do this.

Their cruise would go for a full week. The first day would be a day at sea, chugging up the distant coastline. Day two would see them in the fishing town of Ketchikan, which was the first of three Alaskan stops, day after day. Day five was another day at sea, and then day six would be their last port, at Victoria Island, BC. Then back home, next Saturday.

That first day at sea, Fran gave Robby free reign to explore the ship, for his sake and for hers. If he went off exploring, it would relieve Fran of the burden of putting on a strong face when all she wanted to do was cry.

And explore, Robby did. He spent the day running around the ship, eating at the buffet until he thought he would burst, then off to run around some more. In the arcade, he made friends with some other kids near his age, and was soon tearing around the ship in a gang of long limbed teenagers. He kept the secret of his sister's infection to himself, and lost himself in the fun of newfound friendship.

He met back up with his mom so they could have dinner, but as soon as the last dishes were cleared, he was off again, this time to change into a swimsuit and hit the hot tubs and pools with his new gang, to watch the sun set in a blaze of purples and reds from the open air deck on top of the ship.

By the time he finally made his way back to the stateroom he shared with his mom, she was already fast asleep, with the aid of a xanax.

It wasn't until Robby was curled up in his own bed opposite Fran's that thoughts of Dayna finally returned full force.

Robby cried himself to sleep that night.

16

When Fran and Robby awoke the next morning, well after the sun had already cleared the horizon, the Norwegian Joy had docked in Ketchikan.

Fran, still groggy from the xanax, slowly levered herself out of bed. Robby, moving with the natural energy of youth, had already bounded to his feet and shoved the window curtains open. Spread out before his eyes was the popular tourist destination, with a large sign at the entrance of the dock proclaiming that Ketchikan was the 'Salmon Capital of the World'. Whether or not that's true, Robby couldn't care less. He had eyes only for the colorful town spreading out into the hills of Alaska.

Ketchikan, built at the southernmost entrance to Alaska's Inside Passage, looked as if it was built into the very landscape. Towering green trees dominated the horizon, growing wild up the sides of the mountains. The town itself was awash in color, with buildings painted brilliant shades of purple, blue, orange, and pink. Robby's eyes flickered here and there as he tried to take it all in.

"Mom, look! Look how cool this place is!"

Fran had to smile at the excitement in his voice. "Don't worry, kiddo, we're going to see all of it. I've got us booked on a walking tour of the place, with a lumberjack competition at the end."

Robby turned to her. "Lumberjacks?! Badass!"

Again, Fran let the obscenity slide by. She just didn't have the energy to call him down.

At that moment, they heard an announcement over the loudspeaker in the hallway outside their stateroom, stating that the gangways were down and passengers could now leave the ship to explore Ketchikan, but to make sure that everyone knew the all aboard time: 5 p.m.

"Come on, mom, let's go! Come on!" Robby, voice slightly muffled as he pulled on a dark blue long sleeve shirt, was still loud enough to be heard clearly. The next stateroom over probably heard him, too.

Fran couldn't help but laugh, which felt nice. "Slow down, Robby, we still need to grab a little grub before we head out. Don't worry, we have plenty of time. Our tour doesn't start until 1, and the lumberjack show is at 3."

Robby pulled out his phone. "Yeah, but it's already 11! We gotta go!"

Fran allowed herself to be prodded into movement, pulling on the first clothes that came to hand and only taking time to brush her teeth before Robby was literally pulling her out the door and down to the main restaurant on the ship.

An hour and a half later, and Fran was walking down the gangway after Robby, who had already sped ahead and was waiting for her on the dock, bouncing on his toes.

Robby, for his part, knew somewhere in the back of his mind that he was moving so quickly because he was trying to outrun his own thoughts. But in the front of his mind, all he cared about was seeing the whole town before they had to get back on the ship. He chafed at the bit while he waited for Fran to make her overly slow (to his mind, at least) way down the gangway. He had already located the part of the dock where different locals stood with numbered signs held high over their heads, signaling where different tours would start.

"Quick, mom, we're supposed to be gathered with everyone else at least 15 minutes before the tour starts! What's the number of our tour?"

Fran laughed again, pulling the tour tickets out of her back pocket and giving them a quick glance. "Looks like we're tour number 15. And it's only 12:40, Robby, don't worry. We've got plenty of time. They're not going to leave us behind."

Mother and son joined the throng of cruisers standing patiently in a group in front of the tour guide holding the number 15 over her head. She looked to be a native Alaskan, somewhere in her forties, with an easy smile and a long braid of dark brown hair hanging over one shoulder. She was in the process of answering a few questions from tourists as she waited for the tour to start.

Promptly at 1 p.m. (*Finally!* Robby thought) the tour guide began.

"Hello everyone! My name is Shila, and I'll be your tour guide for the next hour. I'm going to take us on a walking tour of beautiful Ketchikan, and tell you all about our amazing town and its history. If you have any questions, please don't hesitate to ask!"

The group of twenty cruisers led by Shila started off at a brisk walk off the dock and into the town proper. Robby, eyes wide as he drank in the sights, only caught snatches here and there from the tour guide, such as:

"...known as the salmon capital of the world, and indeed we provide many different fishing opportunities for anyone interested..."

"...located in the midst of the Tongass National Forest..."

"...native American totem poles everywhere, including one rising tall right over there..."

"...thriving art scene..."

"...town is the beginning of the Last Frontier of America..."

"...due to our remote location, and the strict testing measures in place for tourists, we haven't had a single Angel infection here..."

As the group meandered its way through the small town, past businesses, restaurants, and tourist traps, Robby was entranced. The totem poles that they passed stretched into the sky, depicting fanciful carvings of animals. Each building, often standing cheek by jowl with the next, was even more brilliantly colorful than from when he first viewed them from the ship. And the air! It was so clear that it seemed to refresh his lungs, his body, with each breath.

But what caught the 15-year-old's attention the most were the girls. Beautiful local girls sitting at counters of shops that they passed, or serving food at the restaurants. To Robby's budding teenage libido, he couldn't help but grin. And, wonder upon wonders, when girls would catch him looking, they would smile back.

Fran noticed, and wore a small smile herself, happy to see Robby having such a fun time.

By the time the tour wound to a close at 2, with the group being deposited back at the dock, Robby was fairly certain that he was in love with at least five different girls.

As the tour group dispersed, some heading back to the ship, but most meandering into town to take advantage of the few hours they had left before all aboard, Fran glanced at her watch.

"Well, we've got about an hour before the lumberjack show. Was there anything else you wanted to do? You hungry?" This last was mostly a rhetorical question; Robby was 15 and that meant he was always hungry. Which made his answer a surprise.

"Actually, mom, I thought we could go back to one of the shops we passed and get souvenirs for mom and Dayna?" He blushed slightly when he said this, and Fran suspected there was an ulterior motive.

She was proven right when she and Robby walked into one of the numerous little arts and crafts shops that dotted the main thoroughfare through town. Sitting behind the counter was a gorgeous young girl who looked to be about Robby's age. She even had his same usual bored look on her face and she was paging through a book and chewing gum.

As they walked in, Robby turned to Fran. "Hey mom, maybe you could go look for something? I'll just, uh...I'll ask that girl if she has any recommendations?"

Fran grinned mischievously. "How about I talk to her first, see if she's single? Maybe I need to meet her mother, too."

Robby blushed from chin to crown. "Mom, geez! Just go look in the back, ok?"

Fran laughed and wandered off, rolling her eyes. As she walked through the store, she glanced back in time to see Robby shaking the girl's hand. They were both grinning at each other. She rolled her eyes again, then started looking through the shelves for something Abby and Dayna might like.

For Abigail, Fran picked out a flower made out of strips of wood masterfully woven together. For Dayna, she found a book of local fauna and flora. Dayna had recently exhibited an interest in wildlife, and she and Abigail hoped that Dayna might become some kind of biologist someday.

That thought brought Fran up short. *There won't ever be a 'someday' for Dayna. Oh, Lord, why?* She hurriedly wiped away a few tears and tried to paste a smile back on her face before walking back up front.

Fran approached the counter in time to hear that Robby was trying to deepen his voice as he talked with the local girl, and that she appeared to be eating it up. She had to clear her voice twice before Robby noticed she was there.

"Oh, hey mom! This is Olivia. She was just telling me about Ketchikan. Olivia, this is my mom."

"Pleased to meet you Olivia," Fran said, still with that fake smile plastered on her face.

Olivia barely registered Fran's appearance; her eyes were all for Robby. But she did manage to get Fran's purchases rung up and bagged. Fran left the store, giving Robby a chance to say goodbye.

A minute later, Robby came bouncing out of the store. "Mom! Guess what?"

"What, kiddo?"

"She totally gave me her number!"

This time her smile was genuine. "Way to go, stud. Now come on, we don't want to be late for the lumberjack show."

The two of them hurried back through town toward the dock. The lumberjack show was a block away, and featured two teams of lumberjacks going head to head in such competitions as chainsaw speed and accuracy, axe chopping speed, and axe throwing. The audience was divided in two down the middle of the three tiered bleachers, with each half cheering for one of the two teams.

Robby's eyes were as big as saucers from the first minute, all thoughts of girls forgotten for the moment as he drank in the action and the noise from their front row seats. Even Fran got caught up in the moment, enjoying the skill necessary for the events, as well as the humorous 'trash talking' between the teams of lumberjacks.

Near the end of the show, just after the axe throwing and before the final relay competition, Fran felt a tugging on the sleeve of her sweater. She turned to see Robby with an expression of consternation on his face.

"Mom? I feel kind of-" His eyes rolled back in his head and he toppled forward onto the ground.

Fran screamed, and the show came to a screeching halt. Several of the lumberjacks rushed over to see what was going on. Fran, hands over her mouth, watched in horror as one of the lumberjacks gently turned Robby over and felt for a pulse.

In the sudden silence, the lumberjack's quiet voice reached every ear. "He's dead."

Fran fainted.

17

She slowly came back to her senses in a hospital room. There was a doctor hovering over her. "What...what happened?" Her mind was a complete blank.

The doctor looked away, then back to her. His eyes were full of sympathy. "You're in a room in the Ketchikan emergency room, Mrs. Vega. You were brought here after you fainted at the lumberjack show."

The events of the day crashed back into her with the force of a tidal wave. Fran bolted up in bed, head whipping this way and that, searching for Robby. "My son! Where's my son?!"

The doctor put a firm hand on her shoulder. "He's gone, Mrs. Vega. From all indications, he was infected with the Angel virus."

She shook her head, long blonde hair whipping around her face. "No, that's impossible! He was 15! HE WAS 15!"

"We don't know how it happened. Please believe me, we are currently running every test we can. We will tell you more as soon as we know."

Fran continued to thrash around, striking out at the doctor. When she started screaming for Robby, an orderly came in and gave her a shot. Her last thought before blackness took her was *Not Robby, too, dear god, not Robby*...and then she was drifting away on a sea of sedation.

18

That day in 2014 marked the first recorded case of someone past the age of 15 contracting the Angel Virus. After intensive study, it was found that Robby was a late bloomer, and hadn't yet hit puberty. Dayna had infected him just before he boarded the cruise ship with Fran, but due to his being on the cusp of puberty and his already shrinking thymus gland, the infection was delayed, and prolonged his life by two days. This gave Robby enough time to infect Olivia, the local girl at the shop where he and Fran got souvenirs. Olivia, oblivious to what had happened, went on to infect her friends in Ketchikan, who then spread it to the rest of the prepubescent population of the small Alaskan town.

Part 12: The Trial Con't (The Year 2018)

1

"You honor, I call to the stand Dr. Richard Matheson." Jeff's voice, steely and authoritative, had each of the juror's leaning forward in anticipation. This was to be Jeff's final witness before the defense would have a chance to bring forth witnesses of their own, and all wondered what possible new information could still be brought to light after everything that had already been said.

Dr. Richard Matheson, director of the CDC and on the health advisory staff to the White House, rose to his feet from his seat behind the prosecutor's desk and made his way to the stand with a firm step, exuding control and confidence. The director was around 5'7", but carried himself in a way that made him appear taller. More impressive. His short, military style haircut was steel gray, and a trimmed mustache adorned his upper lip. His eyes, dark blue, had a way of piercing through a person when his glance took you in. Every member of the jury was immediately intimidated.

After being sworn in, Jeff launched into his line of questioning without preamble. "Dr. Matheson, could you explain to the jury your role as the CDC director, as well as your position with the White House?"

Face empty of emotion, Dr. Matheson explained in a monotone voice that he oversaw every operation of the CDC, and used his knowledge to help advise the White House on past and current threats to national and global health, as well as work to come up with solutions to said threats.

Jeff nodded. "And when the Angel Virus was discovered by your epidemiology department, their department head, Dr. Samantha Hanson, testified that the CDC was doing everything they could to study this disease and look for a cure or a vaccine. The defense as much as accused her, and the CDC, of not being willing to quarantine sooner. Can you speak to this?"

Dr. Matheson turned his cold eyes on the defense table, and Gabriel Conklin, always so cocksure and unshakable, found himself being weighed and measured in that gaze. And found wanting.

Dr. Matheson turned back to Jeff. "The CDC knew from the beginning that quarantine would be like putting a bandaid over the hole in the Titanic after striking the iceberg. We knew from day one that it would fail."

Several members of the jury gasped.

Jeff nodded as if Dr. Matheson had confirmed something he already knew. "Then why quarantine at all?"

"I personally asked the president that very same question. The answer is that we had nothing, repeat, nothing in the way of a cure or a vaccine. The Angel Virus was an unthinking, unfeeling killing machine, and nothing we tried would stop it. As has been stated previously, once the Angel Virus became known to us, it was already too late. Every projection we had, every model, every statistic showed an exponential infection rate that had already spread so far that there was no stopping it. However, quarantine served a different purpose. It helped keep society calm, and in the end, it only served that purpose for a limited amount of time. The last two years have shown us a darkness and brutality that hasn't been seen in millennia, and we are just now *barely* starting to put ourselves back together."

"Can you speculate what would have happened if quarantine measures hadn't been put into place?"

Dr. Matheson barked out a humorless laugh. "Without quarantine, my people speculate that the final death toll would have been closer to three billion than two. Humanity is an emotional animal, and mob mentality on a large scale is one of the most terrifying things in the world. Look at every big riot that has happened in human history, and you will see good, decent people mixed in with the bad, because a kind of hive mind takes over. *That* is why we established quarantine measures. The animal that is humanity can be pacified if shown a measure of control, and that's what we did. It might be the smartest decision the president made over the course of his time in the White House."

"Doctor, how long have you been director of the CDC?" Jeff asked, switching lanes smoothly in his line of questioning.

Dr. Matheson, aware of the change of approach, knew where this was going. "Fourteen years."

"And in your time served, you've seen a variety of new, biological threats that nature has thrown at us, is that correct?"

Dr. Matheson nodded. "Several. Avian flu. Swine flu. Zika virus. Just to name a few of the more well known outbreaks."

"Do these viruses share anything in common?" Jeff asked innocently.

Dr. Matheson turned his gaze once more on the defense bench. "They weren't man made."

Gabriel Conklin had to swallow before speaking. "Objection your honor, speculation!"

The judge shook his head. "Overruled, counselor. I'll remind the court that your client has already admitted guilt."

Gabriel muttered something under his breath but kept his peace.

Jeff, with a cold smile on his face, continued as if unaware of the interruption. "Doctor, in your years of studying the Angel Virus, what made you first suspect that it was a man made disease?"

"We became suspicious very early on in our study of the Angel Virus that it was man made for one simple reason: the Angel Virus doesn't mutate. It acts exactly the same way in every single infected young person. Once contracted, that person will die on their 15th birthday without fail. In every virus that nature has thrown at us, the virus is a mutating, living thing. Why do you think we have such a problem with the ordinary flu year after year? It changes. It mutates, finds new ways to attack the body. And then you have the infected themselves to consider. With every other kind of virus we've discovered, no two people will have the *exact same symptoms in the exact same time frame*. Consider AIDS. Yes, the way it attacks each person is extremely similar, and yet some people are able to live with it, and some aren't. Some people experience the entire gamut of symptoms, some don't. Some die fairly quickly, some are able to live long, full lives. But the Angel Virus behaves the exact same way to every infected person. And you can only contract it if you haven't yet reached puberty. Every single one of these observations points to a created virus, not a natural one."

"One last question, doctor. When you and your people first began to suspect that this was a created virus, what was your reaction?"

"Incredulity," Dr. Matheson said quietly, and his monotone finally broke as anger entered his voice. "What kind of a sociopathic, xenocidal bastard would unleash something like this on the world?"

"Objection!" Gabriel practically shouted, coming to his feet behind the defense table. "Your honor, his emotional response has zero relevance to this case!"

"Sustained," Judge Erikson responded, a troubled look on his face.

Jeff smiled. "Withdrawn. No further questions, your honor."

Judge Erikson turned to Gabriel. "Your witness, counselor."

Gabriel, his greasy smile tinged only slightly with unease, got to his feet and sauntered around to stand in front of the witness stand. "Dr. Matheson. I'd like to speak to the fact that you admitted that even at the presidential level, you believed quarantine would fail."

Dr. Matheson nodded and refrained from reaching across the short distance and strangling this pompous little man until his head popped off of his body like a champagne cork. "Yes."

"And you *speculated*," Gabriel loudly emphasized the word. "That society needed a solution, even a failing one, in order to keep itself in working order."

"Yes."

"But you admit that you don't actually *know* how society would have reacted if you had simply continued looking for a *real* solution and didn't basically offer up false hope in the form of new age leper colonies."

Dr. Matheson cocked his head and studied Gabriel as though looking down at an interesting looking cockroach. "Do you have children, counselor?"

Gabriel blinked. "I...what? No."

"Then you have absolutely no idea what kind of fear was driving this thing forward. And we know, we don't speculate, we *know* how fear can affect a person's decision. And their actions."

"I-"

"I lost three grandchildren to the Angel Virus, counselor," Dr. Matheson continued in his monotone, eyes boring through Gabriel. "I was on the front lines in ways that you can't even consider. So yes, I believe that my people and I, in our speculation as we strove to find a solution, made the right call."

"You-"

"And furthermore, even with the quarantine centers in place, the CDC, the WHO, and every world government continued until the very end to study the virus and try to find a vaccine, a cure, *anything*, and we came up with nothing. Don't you dare sit in your ivory tower and judge the decisions we made when you have absolutely no comprehension."

Gabriel turned to Judge Erikson. "Permission to treat the witness as hostile?"

Judge Erikson waved a hand and tried not to roll his eyes. "Feel free, counselor."

Gabriel turned back to Dr. Matheson. "All of that information aside, the *fact* of the matter is that you and your people did make a decision based on speculation and not information."

"Yes."

"Said decision affected the lives of people worldwide."

"Yes."

"Wouldn't you say that in effect, you were playing God with people's lives?"

Dr. Matheson's stone facade finally broke as he barked a laugh right in Gabriel's face. "You client has already admitted guilt, and you ask *me* that?"

"Answer the question!" Gabriel snapped, face turning red.

"You want an answer? Ask the president."

Part 13: Society Collapsing (The Year 2015)

1

       January 1st, 2015.
       Annie turned 12.
       Global death toll: 500 million.

2

       Quarantine centers had been running worldwide for nearly six years. It was widely believed that most (if not all) infected children were currently quarantined. Humanity was still scared, but the pandemic had been raging for long enough that it had become another part of life. Kids who turned 15 were no longer throwing crazy parties and indulging wildly in ways that they normally wouldn't, because it was now common knowledge that if you were a late bloomer and reached puberty after the age of 15, it meant you were still susceptible to infection and death. This was the positive, silver lining aspect of suddenly not knowing if age 15 really was the cutoff age or not.

The negative effect of not having a cut and dried expiration date on your potential age of infection meant that suspicion, of your neighbor, of your community, came back in full force. Air and water travel, while still running, had begun testing any person age 18 and under, and even then many people still refused to travel. The world economy, which had only recently begun to show signs of healing, dropped once more into the red zone.

The official global death toll, which only took into consideration those Angels who died at quarantine centers and were formally quantified by the census bureau, had passed 500 million. This number was exquisitely terrifying, and was almost too much to wrap the mind around.

But.

Worse was the knowledge that 500 million was still only a quarter of the nearly 2 *billion* prepubescent children who had been alive when the Angel Virus began. Which meant that the quarantine centers around the world were still trying desperately to provide living space for nearly 1.5 billion children.

Overcrowding was a foregone conclusion, despite world governments making use of every sports arena, ever community gathering space, any building large enough to retrofit into a suitable living space for Angels waiting to die.

In the early months of 2015, another government summit was held. It was decided that as a new stop gap solution, they could start using old prisons that were only currently being used as historical attractions.

Kilmainham Jail and Cork Gaol in Ireland.

Port Arthur Penitentiary in Tasmania.

Robben Island, off of Cape Town, South Africa. Once home to Nelson Mandela.

Alcatraz, set on a foreboding island in the bay off San Francisco.

Just to name a few.

This solution was widely accepted in the beginning, because parents of Angels were simply happy that new places were being opened to ease the overcrowding situation. But as the months of 2015 passed, unrest began to grow.

Parents didn't like the fact that their children were waiting for their turn to die in prison.

3

As the parents of the world began to chafe about the inhumaneness of their children being housed in old prisons, another issue came to light, one that had yet to see the light of day in lieu of broader concerns.

The fears of the children.

Specifically, children who, over the course of the Angel pandemic, continued to act out, were caught, and punished accordingly.

Children who were sent not to quarantine centers, but to juvenile hall.

4

April 20th, 2015.
2:30 p.m.
Primary Children's hospital.

Jessica Gardner had just gone on break, and was heading towards her office to place a call to Jackson Telford. After the CDC had recalled Dr. Telford to use as their personal detective and errand boy as the crisis continued, he had still kept in touch to keep Jessica in the loop of the inner workings of the CDC. The bond they had shared during their time with Annie, something akin to soldiers spending time in the trenches together, had imparted in Jackson a sense of duty to keep Jessica and the Oritt's apprised of any new information coming to light. Which was why Jessica had found out before the rest of the world about 'late bloomers', kids who were 15 but were still susceptible to the virus. He had also kept Jessica informed of the various communities he visited where parents were sheltering Angels instead of giving them up to the quarantine centers, although she could have guessed that this would happen.

What was about to happen was *not* something that Jessica or Jackson could have predicted, but in hindsight after the fact, kicked themselves for not thinking of it earlier.

Jessica entered her office and dropped down into the swivel chair behind her desk with a sigh of relief. Just because the staff at Primary Children's had few actual patients these days didn't mean there wasn't the usual administrative work to be done, as well as staying on the front lines of information on the Angel Virus. Not to mention that Jessica's department, the neonatal intensive care unit, or NICU, was one of the few departments that continued to have work, with new mothers coming in. Work, like death and taxes, was a constant for medical professionals.

Her phone rang just as she was reaching for it, as if it were a living thing and anticipated her presence. Jessica gave a start in her chair, suddenly fearful of who was on the other end. Then she gave herself a shake, told herself not to give in to the doom and gloom attitude that everyone else tended to exude day in and day out, and snatched up the phone.

"This is Jess Gardner, NICU."

"Jess? It's Jenna, over in the ICU. We just admitted a 12-year-old boy, a stabbing victim. I think you need to come down here."

Jessica frowned, wondering briefly why the ICU would be contacting her directly, but she didn't question the other nurse. "I'll be right over," she replied.

Ten minutes later, Jessica was staring through the observation window of one of the ICU's operating rooms as a team of doctors and nurses worked to save the boy's life. Jenna, the admitting nurse and not part of the operating team, saw Jessica watching and hurried over with a clipboard in her hand.

"Is he going to make it?" Jessica asked without looking away from the surgery in progress.

Jenna, a pretty, young nurse who had just started her internship at Primary Children's a few months earlier, bobbed her head, brown ponytail shaking back and forth in her nervous excitement. "The doctor said he should be fine. The knife, or shiv or whatever you call it, went in under the ribs, but missed any vital organs."

At the word 'shiv', Jessica whipped around. "Where was this boy stabbed?"

"The juvenile detention center in south Salt Lake. That's the reason why I called you. The boy, just before they wheeled him into the OR, said something under his breath about 'not being an Angel'. Well, all of us here know that you've worked so closely with the Angel Virus, so I was told to call you down so you would be on hand when the surgery was done."

Jessica's eyes narrowed, and an ugly premonition stirred in the back of her mind. "I thought all juvenile detention centers were treated with the same amount of caution as quarantine centers. Testing before admission. Is that no longer the case for some reason?"

Jenna was shaking her head before Jess stopped talking. "All the kids get tested, even if they're 17 because of, well, you know, Alaska?" Jess nodded impatiently, waving a finger in the air as if to say *get to the point*. "Yes, well, um, this boy," Jenna looked down at her clipboard. "Moe is his name, he got tested the same as everyone else, and he's negative for the virus. That's what makes the stabbing so odd. According to the officer that our ambulance medics talked to at the detention center, Moe was stabbed because an older boy *said* he was an Angel."

Jessica groaned and shut her eyes, leaning back against the wall. "Christ, not another one of these."

"Another one of what?" Jenna asked innocently, showing her young age and inexperience.

"Were you here when Dr. Telford and a CDC team were here studying the virus and the infection rate?"

"Nooo…"

Sigh. "Right. Well, the CDC has been investigating all over the country, looking for parents who might be harboring Angels and therefore keeping the rest of us in a state of danger of infection, specifically new mothers with new children. It's been happening more than you'd think, for reasons I'm sure you can guess. However, that's not the only issue that's come to light. If you've been keeping up with the news, which, if you haven't, I wouldn't blame you, considering how bleak it always is…point is, there has been a rise in the last two years of kids being accused of being Angels, and then attacked.

"And it's getting worse."

5

The boy, Moe, age 12, came out of surgery an hour later. As Jenna had said, the shiv had missed all vital organs, luckily for him, and so the doctors had been able to stitch him up without complication.

Shortly after being wheeled to a private room (of which Primary Children's had an excess of) Moe groggily opened his eyes.

Jessica, sitting next to his bed, smiled reassuringly at the young brown haired boy.

"Where," Moe slurred, still feeling the effects of his recent sedation. "Where am I?"

"Primary Children's hospital," Jessica answered softly. "Do you remember what happened?"

Moe looked around the room, struggling to focus his eyes. "I remember the other boys yelling at me," he said slowly as memory returned. "They were calling me an Angel…"

"Freak!" Paul shouted in Moe's face. "Angel freak! Here to infect the rest of us?!"

Moe was slowly backing down the aisle, bunk beds on either side of him. Blood trickled down the side of his cheek from where Paul had hit him, and fear made his eyes as wide as dinner plates.

Four other boys, all of them older and bigger than Moe, were tight behind Paul, faces screwed up in anger and fear.

Paul, 17 years old and about to 'age out' of Juvenile Hall, stood a full foot taller than Moe, and his fists were clenched tight. "My kid brother got infected by one of you, and I could see in his eyes when he changed! I can see it in yours, too!"

Moe had his hands up, palms out, pleading. "I got tested," he whimpered. "I'm not an Angel, I swear! I'm not!"

Somewhere in the building, alarm bells started going off.

Paul put a hand behind his back, and suddenly he was lunging forward.

Moe felt something punch into his gut, through *his gut, and then he was falling, and falling…*

"Then everything went black, and I woke up here." Tears leaked down his cheeks as Moe told Jessica his story, and she felt a vise close around her heart.

"You're going to be ok," Jessica told him, fighting down tears of her own. "I promise. The surgeons took good care of you, and nothing serious was damaged."

Moe looked over at her, eyes still full of fearful anticipation. "Do I have to go back there when I'm better?"

Jessica shook her head violently. "Absolutely not. And we're going to make sure those other boys don't hurt anyone else." But even as she said this, Jessica was wondering. *Could* they actually do anything to stop the hate, stop the attacks? Every day, things just seemed to get worse and worse. *Was* there any end in sight?

6

After the incident at the juvenile detention center in south Salt Lake, contact was made with other cities, other detention centers. New measures were put into place in order to separate kids, and keep a closer eye on potential fights and flare ups. But there were just too many kids and not enough staff to keep an eye on every child at all times, and they weren't willing to put each child into solitary confinement, as that was deemed inhumane.

Children died. Not Angels. Just children.

And society continued to spiral.

7

The rest of the world wasn't faring any better. In August of 2015, rumors began to circulate, rumors of parents talking about storming the new prison quarantine centers. Despite everything that governments were doing to reassure people of the steps they were taking to retrofit the old prison museums to be as warm and accommodating to the Angels now occupying them, all people could focus on was the word 'prison'.

Suspicion of neighbor and community turned into a shared hate, of the governments who were allowing their children, Angel Virus notwithstanding, to be imprisoned. Who decided which Angels would be allowed to stay in the 'nice' quarantine centers, and which Angels would be shipped off to old, broken down, falling apart prisons to live out the rest of their short lives in such horrible locales?

For years, the governments had been trying to erase the slang term for their quarantine centers that had spread with the speed of word of mouth from the very beginning: leper colony. It was an unflattering, and downright damaging, term, and all wanted to put as positive a spin on things as possible. But with the opening of the prison centers, the term 'leper colony' came back with a vengeance.

In neighborhoods all around the world, in every language, posters began to appear, with messages like "ANGELS NOT LEPERS" and "CHILDREN NOT PRISONERS". The hatred built, grew, like a living thing.

Armed forces were dispatched to each prison center to enforce the peace, and visiting hours for parents became limited, precious commodities.

Which only made things worse.

8

September 19th, 2015.
6 a.m.

Dr. Jackson Telford was silent on the drive from San Francisco International Airport to Pier 33, where he would be taking the ferry over to Alcatraz Island to observe the conditions of the prison quarantine center as part of a peacekeeping mission to show U.S. citizens that the Angels were being taken care of in a humane way.

Jackson was currently riding in the back of a large black sedan, being driven by his National Guard escort. It had been explained to him that this was for his safety. While the National Guard hadn't yet had any physical altercations with the public, there had been vocal threats and spray painted messages, and they were taking every precaution to ensure that it didn't come to outright violence.

As the sedan rolled smoothly through the city and the light early morning traffic, Jackson sat flipping through the outline that he had written down while on the flight over, running numbers through his head and trying to figure out the best next move for the CDC and the U.S. If there was one.

2003: Annie born. Presumably starts spread of virus w/ no one knowing.

Adopted sister Maddy (12) doesn't contract virus. Hits puberty early?

2009 (beginning): First (known) death due to Angel Virus. CDC begins investigation.

2009 (end): global death toll: unknown.

U.S. death toll: 300,000.

Quarantine centers opened.

2010: Global death toll: 5-10 million.

2013: Global death toll: 100 million.

2015: Global death toll: 500 million.

Overcrowding of quarantine centers prompts new sites to be established.
Old prisons converted to quarantine centers.

"Sir?" the National Guard driver said from the front seat, looking at Jackson in the rearview mirror. "We've arrived."

Jackson looked up from his notes, absentmindedly running a hand through his thick mane of silver hair. His pale blue eyes sharpened as his mind came back to the present, and he looked around with interest.

Pier 33, part of the long stretch of waterfront that made up Fisherman's Wharf, was already bustling with activity despite the relatively early hour. In the briefing Jackson had read on his flight over from the East Coast, he had learned that all of Fisherman's Wharf had been taken over by the National Guard.

Pier 39, just west of where they sat parked now, had been converted into the testing site for all incoming Angels, even if the children had already been in the care of a different quarantine center before being shipped here. The government was requiring testing at all new facilities.

Pier 41, further west, was being used as housing for the National Guardsmen so that they would all be on site at any given time, in the event of an emergency (or, it was loudly whispered, an uprising).

Pier 33 held the dock that the two ferries put in at, to ferry Angels to their new home, and to facilitate the travel of doctors, nurses, and visitors back and forth, as well as Guardsmen.

At other quarantine facilities, parents and other community members were allowed to volunteer their time, as teachers, as cooks and food handlers, basically in whatever capacity would help benefit the Angels and pass the time. Not so at the prison facilities.

Society at large had been upset about the use of prisons for quarantine centers from the word 'go', and so various world governments had deemed it wise to use their military not just as guards for these facilities, but also as the caregivers. Parental visitation was largely limited.

Jackson had read all of this on his flight, but it was another thing entirely to see it first hand. The camo of the soldiers and white coats of the doctors and nurses were all he saw, wherever he turned his head. It was a sobering sight.

At least with the other quarantine centers, there's an attempt made at normalcy, he thought to himself. *This...this just looks like a government lockdown. It's no surprise that people are upset. But then, could the government have done anything different?* He shook his head sadly. *This was a bad idea. It should have never come to this, using prisons for children.*

He slowly climbed out of the black sedan, joints creaking and reminding him that he wasn't a young man anymore. His driver got out as well, and led Jackson through the pier and down to the dock. Jackson saw two large trucks off to his left being unloaded by several soldiers, stacking up boxes of what appeared to be bulk foodstuffs in one pile and toilet paper in the other. Jackson shook his head again, following his soldier escort in silence.

Once on the ferry, Jackson got his first look at the foreboding island that sat ominously in the distance across the bay. Light fog drifted just above the water, giving the scene an ethereal otherworldliness.

After casting off and beginning the short ride across to the island, Jackson's escort began to tell him about the facility.

"Since we opened last month, we've brought 1500 Angels here for quarantine. The government has spared no expense in order to make it as hospitable and comfortable as possible." The soldier was young, probably not even old enough to drink, and his voice was a clear tenor that carried only a hint of a tremble, betraying his lack of comfort with his assignment here. "The Angels are all in the cell house building in the center of the island. We've converted the barracks into moderately comfortable housing for onsite Guardsmen, medical staff, and caregivers, who help out with food distribution, teaching, and supervision. Not that the Angels really require supervision." He forced out a laugh. "Hell, these kids are better behaved than some of the soldiers I've been stationed with."

Jackson turned away from his study of the approaching island to look at his escort. "What about recreation? Are they provided with the same options as the regular quarantine centers?"

The soldier nodded jerkily. "Yes sir. The island has a recreation yard, minus the barbed wire, of course." Another forced laugh. "And we have a theater, too, so the kids can watch movies and play video games!"

"Tell me about parental visitation."

The soldier gulped, looking away. A red flush suffused his young face. "Well, see, with the situation being what it is, and with the ferry only going back and forth at scheduled times during the day, we only allow one to two dozen parents to visit each day, for two hours at a time."

Jackson's jaw dropped. "You have 1500 Angels at this facility, and you only allow up to two dozen parents each day? Are any of you actually surprised that people are upset?"

The soldier shook his head; his helmet very nearly went flying with the force of it. "Doctor, you know it ain't up to us. We're just following orders! Government says to limit parental visitation, and we do it."

Jackson sighed wearily and turned his gaze back on the island that now loomed large in front of them as the ferry prepared to dock. "I know, son. I know."

Leading Jackson off of the ferry, the soldier made a sharp right and headed up a steep hill that took them past an old brick building on the left. The soldier pointed out that that was where all the staff were housed at any given time, and that they rotated out every two days.

Another two hundred yards and they turned left, now heading straight toward the cell house where the Angels were living. A doctor in a white coat met the two of them just outside the cell house, a massive, two story stone and brick building with bars over the windows.

The soldier turned to Jackson and touched a finger to his helmet. "I'll leave you here, sir. Dr. Adams will take over your tour; he's been with this site since day 1."

Jackson thanked him, and the soldier gratefully made an about face and quick-timed it back down the hill.

"Dr. Telford, right?" Dr. Adams said, holding out his hand. The facility doctor was a big man, standing just over 6'4", and with the broad shoulders of a veteran weightlifter. His short hair was cut military style, and had more pepper in it than salt. Jackson immediately guessed that he was a military doctor rather than a civilian.

"Please, call me Jackson," he said, shaking his hand cordially. "No need to stand on formality with me. The CDC just wants to learn more about how the prison quarantine facilities are being run."

"Gladly, and you can call me Douglas. We figured there would be an inspection, formal or not, and I'm happy to give you a tour and answer any questions you have. Would you care for breakfast? Most of the kids aren't up yet."

Jackson's stomach grumbled in assent, reminding him that he hadn't eaten since the night before. "Breakfast would be greatly appreciated, thank you! Lead the way."

Douglas led the two of them past the cell house to the old warden's house, which had been converted into a mess hall for the staff. They breakfasted on usual military fare: scrambled eggs, bacon, toast, oatmeal, and several cups of coffee for both doctors.

Over the course of the next two hours, Douglas told Jackson all about their start up and operation on the island. First, the government sent in their people to do a top to bottom upgrade of the entire island. Electricity and plumbing had already been set up for tourism, but everything was gone over with a fine tooth comb to make sure it would be suitable for the number of people that would be making this place their home. Next, a complete scrub down of every building, and each cell was prepared for the coming occupants. Bunk beds, blankets, pillows, dressers, TV's, games, every amenity the regular quarantine centers had.

"Yes, it's a prison," Douglas was saying, taking a sip of his third cup of coffee. "But believe me when I say that the only real difference between our quarantine site and the sports stadiums that have been in use to date is the fact that we are, for the most part, military run. But that is a matter of necessity, as I'm sure you can understand."

Jackson nodded, setting his own cup down. "I understand. It doesn't make me like the need for it, but I, and my colleagues at the CDC, *do* understand. But I'm sure you appreciate that to the general public, it's not about understanding the inner workings, it's about public image."

Douglas cocked an eyebrow. "If the CDC has any better ideas about where to house them-"

Jackson held up his hands. "No, we don't. But it doesn't alleviate our worry about how the public is reacting. Part of the reason I'm here is to take all of this information and attempt to use it to assuage the public, and avoid further conflict."

At that very moment, alarm klaxons around the island began to wail.

9

September 19th, 2015.
10 a.m.

A soldier, older than Jackson's escort that morning, came running into the mess hall. His head whipped around and he saw Jackson and Douglas sitting in the corner. He sped over to them, throwing Douglas a hasty salute that Douglas returned.

"Sir, there's a mob of people approaching Pier 33!"

Douglas shot to his feet. "Armed?"

"Yes sir. Some, at least. Others appear to just be carrying signs. You know the ones that have been popping up all over?"

Douglas turned to Jackson. "You'll probably want to see this, doctor. I assume this is what the CDC has been worried about? Well, so have we."

The two doctors followed the soldier out of the mess hall and back down the steep concrete path to the dock, where the ferry was waiting for them. As soon as they were aboard, they cast off.

"How has the National Guard prepared for this contingency?" Jackson asked calmly as they began to cross the bay. After everything he'd seen, nothing much surprised him anymore.

Douglas, just as calmly, answered without looking away from the mainland. "Usual riot control. Tear gas, rubber bullets, plastic riot shields to keep the mob at bay."

"That soldier said some people were armed. What is the standard riot procedure for civilians firing on your soldiers?"

Douglas's mouth pulled down in a grimace. "We are authorized for maximum force if necessary."

"And who decides when it becomes necessary?"

Douglas finally turned and met Jackson's eyes. "I do."

They heard the first gunshot echo across the water five minutes before they reached the pier.

10

As soldiers tied the ferry up at the dock, Douglas was already striding quickly up the ramp and towards the sounds of chaos coming from ahead. Jackson hurried quickly to keep up.

Turning a corner, the street beyond Pier 33 came into view, and Jackson found that he could still be surprised, after all. The entire street, and the intersecting street beyond, were packed shoulder to shoulder with what could only be described as an angry mob, numbering in the hundreds if not the thousands. Many carried signs over their heads, proclaiming the words 'ANGELS NOT LEPERS' and 'CHILDREN NOT PRISONERS'. Another gunshot, and Jackson saw a tall man in the front of the crowd firing a pistol, not at the line of National Guardsmen, but into the air. The man carried a bullhorn in his other hand, and Jackson saw from 100 yards away as he lifted it up to his mouth.

"THE U.S. GOVERNMENT'S ACTIONS HERE ARE INHUMANE, AND ILLEGAL. WE DEMAND THAT OUR CHILDREN BE TAKEN OUT OF THIS PRISON AND RETURNED TO THEIR NORMAL QUARANTINE CENTERS." The angry father, for what else could he be, punctuated this statement by firing another round into the air.

Douglas cursed under his breath as the two men continued forward to the front line. "How in the hell didn't we hear word of this organizing?" he muttered.

A soldier in full riot gear - helmet, bulletproof vest, and shield, with a rifle slung at a slant across his chest - came rushing up. "General!" he said, throwing a salute that Douglas returned. "They came out of nowhere, from side streets. We got lined up as quickly as possible, sir. Someone almost took that guy's head off when he raised his gun, but he just fired into the air, so we stood down to wait for orders. We have tear gas and rubber bullets trained on the mob, sir."

Douglas finally pulled up to a halt a scant 50 yards away from the line of soldiers, and Jackson was able to catch his breath and survey the scene.

The mob held their own line another 20 yards further on, filling the street as far as he could see in either direction. Roughly half of the civilians carried signs, but Jackson's sharp eyes caught many holding pistols, and some had rifles as well. Every one of them had the look of death in their eyes.

Jackson turned toward Douglas, fear churning in his gut. "General, Douglas, whoever you are, you know this can only end badly. Just talk to them, tell them you'll do it, tell them whatever you have to in order to de-escalate this!"

"I can't do that, doctor," Douglas said tiredly, before he straightened up and squared his shoulders. "You know as well as I do that we just don't have any other place to put these kids. Those civilians out there know that. That makes this confrontation a foregone conclusion. I just didn't think they'd be able to take us by surprise like-" He cut himself off and turned to the soldier who was still waiting there. "Private, find me a bullhorn, double time!"

Less than a minute later, Douglas was raising a bullhorn to address the crowd. "GO BACK TO YOUR HOMES. THESE CHILDREN ARE BEING WELL TAKEN CARE OF AND WE HAVE NO, REPEAT, NO OTHER PLACE TO PUT THEM. DISPERSE PEACEFULLY AND-"

A bullet took Douglas high in the forehead. A splash of blood arced through the air, and then he was falling, with a look of surprise on his face. He was dead before he hit the ground.

The world erupted in chaos.

The line of soldiers, seeing a gun fired into their midst, immediately opened up with everything they had. Canisters of tear gas flew wildly into the mob, bursting with yellow fog. Bullets, rubber and metal both, punched into the first line of civilians, then the second. People went down screaming.

The mob returned fire with anything they could find close to hand. People who had brought their own firearms immediately started shooting back. Other people had brought rocks. Still others picked up tear gas canisters and, through fits of coughing and crying, threw them right back at the soldiers.

Jackson, in shock, knelt down next to Douglas and checked for a pulse even as blood pooled under the general's head.

Another soldier came sprinting up to Jackson and grabbed his arm, screaming in his ear about running for safety. The soldier went down with three rounds in his chest, one of which managed to punch through his bulletproof vest.

Jackson managed to make it to cover behind a storage shed at the edge of the pier, tears streaming down his face from the gas that blanketed the area. Everywhere people were screaming, soldiers and civilians alike. The gunfire went on and on and on.

An eternity later, silence fell. Jackson climbed to his feet, legs shaking, and peeked around the corner of the storage shed. Bodies littered the pier, bodies in camo, bodies in black, bodies in civilian clothes. The whole world seemed red. Blood coated the street, the sidewalk, the bodies. Soldiers were tending their own as the civilian mob, what was left of it, limped away, disappearing like ghosts into the tear gas fog. The silence was broken only by the moaning of the injured.

Feeling like a ghost himself, Jackson stumbled over to Douglas's body, his face still frozen in a look of surprise. "You could have done better," Jackson said quietly, staring down at the dead man. "You should have done better." He turned and walked past the soldiers, letting them take care of their own. He crossed the no man's land of the street that had become a warzone, looking for survivors among the mob, to see what help he could offer.

11

Over the remaining months in 2015, more prisons were mobbed and attacked. Civilians died. Soldiers died. Nothing changed. The prisons stayed open because there was nowhere else to put the quarantined Angels. But humanity fought on, because it had found a common cause at last.

Before the prison riots of 2015, humanity had been scared, suspicious, and angry, but it had been on a more individual level. Neighbor was suspicious of neighbor. But now people had an outlet for their anger, and that anger grew into a connecting force that brought people together. Anger grew, and became hate.

Hatred of the world governments for how they were handling things.

Hatred of the health organizations, like the CDC and the WHO, for not finding a cure.

And finally, that hatred turned its eyes on the cause of the world's upheaval.

The Angels.

12

At the end of 2015, the global death toll stood at just under 700 million. The next year, hell on earth began.

Part 14: The Trial Con't (The Year 2018)

1

Jeff watched the cross examination of Dr. Richard Matheson with a calm outward demeanor, but inside he was exulting as Dr. Matheson tore Gabriel down. *About time someone called that weasel to account*, he thought, holding in a smirk.

When Dr. Matheson coldly told Gabriel to go ask the president himself, the courtroom erupted, some people cheering, some jeering. Judge Erikson had to call for order several times before everyone calmed down, and then announced a short recess while the defense got their witnesses in order for the next part of the trial.

"You honor," Gabriel said, before the judge had a chance to rap his gavel. "With all due respect, the defense doesn't require a recess. I have only one witness, and he's fully prepared to give testimony now."

Judge Erikson eyed him shrewdly, before glancing over at Jeff. "Prosecution?"

Jeff shrugged. "No objection, your honor."

The judge set his gavel down. "Call your witness, counselor."

Gabriel looked over at the jury box, then back to the judge. "Your honor, the defense calls Dr. Calvin Michaels to the stand."

The courtroom was so quiet you could have heard a pin drop as Calvin Michaels climbed to his feet with dignity and walked over to the stand to be sworn in.

Dr. Michaels, at first glance, looked nothing like the monster the jurors assumed he would. He was 45, 5'11", with a trim build and wearing an impeccable black 3 piece suit that looked tailored to fit him like a glove. Neatly trimmed brown hair, gentle brown eyes, and a finely trimmed beard gave him the look of a Wall Street banker, or a CEO of a Fortune 500 company. He certainly didn't look like a man who had wiped out a quarter of the planet.

But then, one of the jurors thought to himself with a frown, *Nobody suspected Ted Bundy at first, either.*

As Dr. Michaels was being sworn in, Jeff was watching Gabriel with interest. Gabriel's face was slowly losing its usual weasely smirk. He stood up straighter, adjusted his suit jacket, and a pensive look was in his eyes as he stared at his client. If Jeff didn't know any better, he would say that Gabriel looked like he was just now starting to take this seriously, as a professional.

What could that possibly mean?

"Dr. Calvin Michaels," Gabriel began, voice clear and confident, but without the usual arrogant cast. "As has already been mentioned in this case, you've turned yourself in."

"Yes," Dr. Michaels replied quietly.

"You've admitted guilt."

"Yes."

"And yet, you demanded, in return for your guilty plea, a chance to have your day in court, as due process requires."

"Yes."

"Can you tell the court why you made that request?"

Dr. Michaels didn't look at the jurors, although he must surely have felt those twelve pairs of eyes boring into him like augers. "To explain."

Gabriel cocked his head. "Do you mean to say you intend to explain how you created the virus?"

Dr. Michaels shook his head. "No. I mean to explain why I stood back and let the virus take its course."

"So you *didn't* create the virus."

Another shake of the head. "I did not. My daughter, Annie, was born with it. It should have killed her, but instead, she was given a blood transfusion from her twin, Grace, that saved her life, at least for a time."

"I'm confused, doctor. Could you clarify for the court what you are admitting guilt to?"

Dr. Michaels sighed sadly. "If the court will be patient with me, I'll explain exactly what happened."

Gabriel looked up at Judge Erikson, who nodded. "Proceed, Dr. Michaels."

"My field is genetics, and I specialized in neonatal study. I created tests that could show whether a fetus had any diseases and/or defects, and even come up with ways to fix and heal any such complications. When my wife was pregnant, God rest her soul, I ran every diagnostic at my disposal, wanting to ensure that my children would be born healthy, just like any other parent wants.

"One of my tests showed that both twins carried life threatening diseases. I can't tell you what they were, because there isn't a name for them, but it had to do with chromosomal defects that affected their immune systems. I performed prenatal surgery and attempted to use groundbreaking technology to fix their DNA, and reforge the broken links in their chromosome chains. I did this not only to try and save their lives, but also because the childbirth of two such sickly babies would have threatened the life of the mother, as well.

"With Grace, I was successful. The chromosomal defect was altered, reforged into complete chains, and her immune system immediately strengthened. With Annie, however, it didn't take. It might have made things worse; I honestly don't know. My point is, when we delivered Grace first, she was the picture of health, a perfect baby girl. But Annie..." Dr. Michaels paused and looked down, taking a deep breath. When he looked back up at Gabriel, his eyes were shiny with unshed tears. "Annie's birth was long and arduous. My wife didn't survive. Annie herself was born with several physical defects, and internal organs that were already beginning to shut down even as she drew her first breaths. She would have died that very night if I hadn't suggested a blood transfusion from Grace, the healthy twin. My wild thought was that maybe, just maybe the genetic manipulation I had successfully performed on Grace would work on Annie via her blood.

"And lo and behold, it did work. Better than I could have dreamed. Overnight, Annie was transformed, sickly to healthy. At first I was ecstatic, seeing God's hand at work in this miracle. And yet a voice in the back of my head wondered. The pragmatic doctor in me couldn't just say 'Praise God!' and let it go at that. I had to know for sure.

"That night, as the doctors and nurses in the NICU were going crazy over the 'miracle baby', I got hold of a vial of Annie's blood and ran my own specialized tests, and found right away what the world wouldn't discover for years. Annie's chromosomal defects that should have led almost immediately to a full shutdown of all internal organs hadn't been healed by Grace's blood. Rather, Grace's blood, and the truly miraculous properties within, simply coated over the defects in Annie's blood. Grace's transfusion supercharged Annie's thymus gland, allowing Annie to start producing her own enhanced T cells and boost her own immune system exponentially.

"I saw right away from the tests I ran that this 'cure' would only last until Annie's thymus gland began to shrivel and slow production of T cells at puberty, like all other children in the world. I knew in that moment that Annie wasn't cured, her death had simply been delayed."

The entire courtroom was hanging on Dr. Michaels' every word, fascinated. At long last, questions were being answered.

Gabriel, the only one in the room to have already heard the story, continued with his questioning. "Did you know then that Annie's disease was infectious?"

Dr. Michaels sat up straight. "No, I did not. I didn't learn about the virulence of the Angel Virus until the rest of the world did, in 2009."

"Let's table that for a moment," Gabriel said smoothly, ignoring the bombshell this comment caused in the courtroom. "Going back to the birth of your children. You disappeared that night with Grace. Why didn't you take Annie, as well?"

"I couldn't. Grace, being perfectly healthy, wasn't under surveillance. Annie, going through her miracle transformation, was. There was no way I could get close to her. It was the hardest decision I ever made in my life, up until that point at least, leaving Annie behind."

Gabriel frowned as if something new had just occurred to him. "Dr. Michaels, *why* did you run off with Grace? Why not stay and try and help Annie further?"

His shoulders slumped as if under a great weight. "I ran tests on Grace that night, as well. I had to know the extent of what my prenatal genetic manipulation had done to her. You see, I hadn't just fixed Grace's chromosomal defects. Grace was born perfect in every single way. Her very blood potentially carried a cure not just to Annie's disease, but to other diseases, too. I knew beyond a shadow of a doubt that if, *when*, other doctors realized the same thing, Grace would never be left alone again. She would be studied like a lab rat. Medical organizations would all want their hand in figuring out how to use Grace to cure everything under the sun. I didn't want that life for her, because it is no life a child should have to endure. So I took her, and I left."

Gabriel nodded and began pacing back and forth in front of the witness stand, hands clasped lightly behind his back. "Let's go back to 2009, when you attest that you learned of the Angel Virus with the rest of the world. What was your reaction?"

"The same as the rest of the world, I expect. Absolute horror. The one emotion that was mine and mine alone, however, was guilt. That I was responsible. That it was my own child who was spreading this contagion."

"You said that Grace's blood could have held the cure to all world disease as we know it. Did it cross your mind that Grace could have been the cure that the CDC and the WHO were looking for all along?"

Dr. Michaels nodded. "I surmised that Grace could have been a cure to others, even though she had failed to completely cure Annie. This is because Annie was born with her disease, and shared at least a partial genetic blueprint with Grace. I believe that is why Annie wasn't fully cured. However, it meant that it was possible, probable even, that Grace could be a real cure for all of the other infected Angels."

Gabriel stared hard at Dr. Michaels. "You came to this conclusion and yet did nothing? Why?"

"Because," he answered sorrowfully. "I also came to the same conclusion that Dr. Richard Matheson and his team at the CDC did. That by the time we found out in 2009, it was already too late. The virus had been spreading for six years, and Grace doesn't have enough blood in her body to have saved us from the coming storm.

That is what I'm admitting guilt to, Mr. Conklin. Staying silent and letting the virus run its course, though it meant sitting back and watching billions of children die."

Part 15: Hell On Earth (The Year 2016)

1

January 1st, 2016.
Annie turned 13 years old, and she celebrated with her parents, who brought in a cake, and Beckie. Everyone avoided talking about the prison riots that were happening around the world. Conversation was kept light. Jeff and Kristi remarked frequently on how tall and beautiful both Annie and Beckie were getting.
Annie and Beckie, for their part, tried to keep their own increasingly alien natures hidden. Neither of them attempted to finish anyones sentences, or provide a word choice when someone was struggling to come up with the proper term. Neither of them attempted to lead the conversation, or talk about how the attitudes of the Angels around them were spiraling.
Neither of them brought up their fears that the prison riots were only the beginning.

2

January 5th, 2016.
Boston, MA.

Fran and Abigail sat on opposite sides of the long leather couch in their quiet three bedroom house. The house that, until recently, had always been bursting with noise and energy.

No more.

After Robby had died in Alaska, Fran had taken a flight directly back to Seattle to break the news to Abigail and Dayna, who had already been admitted into CenturyLink Field, the local quarantine center. The two mothers had then petitioned the government to have Dayna transferred to one of the Boston quarantine centers so she could at least be closer to home. This request was approved, and they were flown back to Boston, where Dayna was admitted into Agganis Arena.

Either Fran or Abigail or both visited Dayna every day, until just a few months ago when Dayna turned 15.

She died in her mothers' arms.

Since that day, Fran had withdrawn into herself. She stopped working, didn't leave the house, and often refused to eat unless Abigail forced her to.

Abigail, for her part, was just as broken-hearted, but she had always been the pragmatist of the two, and she was able to work through her grief while still living her life, and putting food on the table for the two of them.

Nights were hardest for both of them. Being alone in the empty house that was suddenly too big, too silent...Abigail felt Fran pulling away from her as well as everything else. Tonight Abigail had resolved to do something about that.

"Fran, honey," Abigail said, scooting over closer to her wife.

Fran didn't respond. She just sat there, staring at nothing, lank blonde hair hanging in her eyes.

"Honey, I miss-"

"Dayna shouldn't have ever gotten infected," Fran said suddenly in a flat voice, devoid of emotion. "If all those parents with infected children had just done what they were supposed to do and sent their *Angels* off to the quarantine centers, both of our kids would still be alive."

Abigail blinked, pulling back a little as Fran wrapped her arms around herself and started to shake back and forth ever so slightly.

"If the infected children had just been disposed of when they were found out, our family would still be whole," Fran whispered.

"What do you mean, 'disposed of'?" Abigail asked with real concern. She'd never heard Fran speak like this.

Fran's head whipped around and her blazing eyes pinned Abigail to the couch. "The Angels should have been killed. Immediately. They were going to die anyway, right?" Her voice dropped back down to a whisper. "Should have just killed them off…"

3

January 12th, 2016.
Derry, ME.
Frank sat alone in his little house on the outskirts of town. He was in his kitchen, sitting at the same table where he had told Jackson Telford the story of Derry, and the boy who was killed by an angry mob. In front of him was a bottle of moonshine whiskey that Jackson would have recognized immediately. Next to the moonshine was a disassembled gun that Frank had been cleaning.

In his hands was a letter from his estranged wife, still living in Boston with her 'friend'.

Frank had already read the letter several times, and could probably recite it word for word at this point, but still he couldn't stop himself from bringing the single handwritten page back up to his eyes and reading it again.

Frank,
I don't know how to say this, and I'm sure you've already guessed, but our daughter is dead. You were never good with remembering birthdays, but I'd assume you remember hers well enough. It was last week. I was there when she died. She was at peace, she said, and didn't want us to grieve her overlong. Said she understood why you didn't come down more. Maybe she understands, but I sure don't.
I'm not coming back to Derry. I'm sure you've guessed that, too. I've spoken to a lawyer, and will be sending paperwork for you to

sign. I'm not trying to be cruel, if you can believe that. Just moving forward.
I hope you're well, Frank. I really do.
Take care of yourself.
Katherine

Frank carefully set the letter down to the side of his gun, picked up the bottle of whiskey, and took a long slug. Wiping his mouth, he got back down to the business of cleaning his gun.

And thinking about what he was going to do next.

4

January 17th, 2016.
Spokane, WA.

Jose and Mateo were playing video games and talking about current events with the casual air of indifference that comes so easily to young people.

"You been hearing about these prison riots?" Mateo asked as he landed a combo on Jose's character.

Jose cursed as his player went flying through the air. "How can I not? It's the only thing on the news right now. I still can't believe how crazy people are getting. I mean, it's not enough that their kids are dying, now the parents are taking up arms and starting a war against the very people trying to take care of their kids? It makes no sense."

Mateo finished killing Jose's player and set his controller down, reaching over for his beer. He had just turned 21 and was never far from a drink. "Humanity, my dude. We're all just a bunch of crazed wild animals when you get down to brass tacks." He took a long pull from his beer, belched loudly, and wiped a hand across his mouth. "Trust me, this *is* turning into a war. I'm just happy we don't have a quarantine center or a prison center here in Spokane. It pays to be away from the action."

Jose nodded thoughtfully. "That's a good point. In fact, walking around downtown, sometimes I forget about everything that's going on. Things here still seem pretty normal, if you don't look too closely. Besides the lack of kids, it's just people going about their business."

Mateo burped again and reached for his controller. "The only downside of *not* being where the riots are going on?"

"Yeah?"

"I could sure go for some looting in all the craziness. We need a new Xbox!"

The two brothers laughed at that, and just went on playing their game as the world spiraled around them.

5

January 25th, 2016.
Salt Lake City, UT.

Beckie's dad, Steven, sat in a circle of people in the basement of a church. The sign outside the door read ANGEL SUPPORT GROUP.

"My name is Steven, and I'm the father of an Angel," he said, looking around the group of angry, tired looking parents.

"Hi Steven," they responded robotically.

Steven had to fight down a manic laugh that suddenly wanted to burst out of him. The world was falling down all around and here he sat in a goddamn *support group*? He got a hold of himself with difficulty. Beckie had suggested he go, and he would do anything for her. Clenching his hands together, he started opening up.

"When this whole thing started, I had a wonderful family. Beautiful wife, and three amazing daughters. You know what happened next. All three were under age 15, and all three got infected. I wanted to take them to the quarantine center, like you're supposed to, but my wife was against it. Ran off in the night with my two oldest. I got my youngest, Beckie, into the Delta Center, and then I went after them. Well, we holed up for a while in our houseboat, but the locals found out. An angry mob came calling, and a gun was fired. My oldest took a bullet, and she died on the way to the hospital." Steven gulped, looking down as his eyes filled with tears. "My wife killed herself that night."

Sounds of sympathy from the group, many of whom had similar stories.

"I brought my other girl back up to Salt Lake and took her straight to the Delta Center, where she died. My youngest is still alive, at least for a little while longer. I guess I don't know what I'll do when she dies."

Silence fell.

A man across the circle from Steven, a big guy with thick arms and a trucker hat, growled softly, rolling a toothpick around his mouth. "Did any of you stop to think that this could have been avoided if the Angels had been killed off in 2009 when this whole thing started?"

The group leader tried to quiet him down, but the beefy man shook off the restraining hand. "I'm serious, dammit! My little girl didn't get infected until two years ago! She was 14, and she died two months later, in that God-forsaken stadium. If the so-called Angels had been put down like rabid dogs when they were first discovered, how many of our children would still be alive today? Yours?" His finger stabbed out at Steven, who flinched back. "Yours? Or yours? Mine for damn sure would be alive right now! Quarantine center? HA! It's a time bomb, is what it is. As long as a single infected kid is still breathing, the world is in danger. I'd say it's past time someone did something about it!" The big man got to his feet and stormed out of the room, leaving behind several people putting their heads together and speculating, wondering…

The next day, Steven went to go visit Beckie, and he told her what had been said at the meeting, and how it worried him. Beckie put on a brave face and tried to assure him that everything would be fine, but as soon as he left she immediately sought out Annie. The two of them went to find somewhere relatively private where they could speak alone.

"…and then my dad said the guy got up and stormed out. But people were still talking about what he had said. Dad said the couple next to him were agreeing that something needed to be done. About all of us."

Annie shook her head sadly. "Then we were right. The prison riots were only the beginning. I think the world is going to try and kill us. And you know the worst part? I don't think they're wrong to do so. That man was right when he said that if even one Angel is alive, we threaten the rest of the world."

Annie told her parents everything when they came to visit the following morning. Next thing Annie knew, she was being bundled up and taken back to Primary Children's, to be put back in self quarantine 'for her own safety'. She didn't even have a chance to say goodbye to Beckie.

6

February 1st, 2016.
Salt Lake City, UT.

Early that morning, just before sunrise, a nondescript white van pulled into the service entrance of the Delta Center. When the guard at the gate asked the big man in the trucker hat what he was delivering, the man shot the guard in the face and continued on into the sub level parking lot directly under the stadium. He parked, got out of the van, and walked away. In the back of the van, four large cylinders sat ominously, each with a small metal cube on top that was blinking red.

Thirty minutes later, each red light turned green simultaneously.

The Delta Center exploded.

Hell on earth had begun.

7

March 15th, 2016.
Boston, MA.

Abigail awoke that morning to find the other side of the bed empty. That wasn't so odd, in of itself, as Fran had been getting up in the middle of the night unable to sleep and gone to the living room, where she tended to pass out on the couch.

Abby got out of bed, stretched, and tossed on a threadbare black robe before padding down the hall and down the stairs to the kitchen. She put on a pot of coffee before going to poke her head into the living room to see if Fran was awake.

The living room was empty.

An ominous feeling settled over her, raising the skin of her arms in goosebumps. "Fran?" she called out.

No response.

Abby walked back into the kitchen and noticed a folded piece of paper on the kitchen table. Stomach in knots, Abby snatched up the paper and unfolded it. In shaky writing that was barely recognizable as Fran's, it contained only two lines.

There's something I have to do.
I'm sorry.

"Oh dear god," Abby whispered, sinking down into a chair and putting a hand on her forehead. "Fran, what are you doing?"

Later that day, four different vans that looked identical to the one that had driven down under the Delta Center approached the four different stadiums that Boston had converted into quarantine centers. Fran was driving one of them. Frank, down from Derry, was driving another.

Working with precision, each van approached each stadium at exactly the same time. Since the Delta Center bombing, security had been increased at all of the U.S. quarantine centers.

But not enough.

From four different places around Boston, gunfire could be heard echoing across the city. Less than five minutes later, all four quarantine centers went up in flames. None of the drivers of the vans escaped with their lives.

But then, none of them had intended to.

8

April 29th, 2016.
Seattle, WA.

Security had been augmented with military force at every quarantine center in the U.S., and at most of the major centers around the world, as well.

At CenturyLink Field, once home to the Seattle Seahawks, an entire platoon of National Guardsmen had been deployed to ensure the safety of the Angels inside. Everyone breathed a little easier, knowing that they were being protected by real soldiers, and not just a limited force of security guards.

Except.

Three of the soldiers were parents who had lost children to the Angel Virus. Those three had managed to pull guard duty together that evening on the loading docks, where semi trucks regularly came and went to drop off food and other necessary supplies to keep the 70,000 Angels within happy and healthy (or at least healthy, if not happy).

As the sun was setting, the three guardsmen let in a semi that was carrying something very different. The entire truck was packed floor to ceiling with dynamite, enough to level a city block.

The soldiers directed the semi to the driveway that led down to the unloading dock underneath the stadium. The driver parked, set the timer on the explosives, and then he and the three soldiers vanished into the night.

An hour later, 70,000 Angels died.

9

January 1st, 2017.
Global death toll: 1.5 billion.
10 p.m.
Annie was sitting in her quarantine room in Primary Children's hospital, watching the TV with a look of calm acceptance on her face. The reporter was announcing the most recent bombing, at London Stadium in England.

"-confirmed that 80,000 Angels were killed in the blast, along with the eight bombers. This brings the global death toll-"

Annie shut the TV off and set the remote down on the table next to her before picking up her diary and a pen. She had decided to start this diary back in 2009, as she wanted to leave something of herself behind for her family.

She opened up the leatherbound book, uncapped the pen, and began to write.

Today I turned 14. That means I have just one year left to live. I find myself unafraid as the end approaches. At least I will be free.

So many people died last year, and not just Angels. Reporters are calling it 'hell on earth'. I think it is an accurate name. I begin to believe that Angels do *need to be exterminated. After all, we're going to die anyway. If the end comes sooner rather than later, maybe that means the whole world will have a better chance at putting itself back together.*

I am back in self quarantine. It's the only reason I'm still alive. Do I deserve to still live? The virus started with me. Sometimes I wonder if I should have ever lived. Maybe I should have died in childbirth.

I know these are dark thoughts. But then, these are dark days, so it feels appropriate. But I do not want you, my dear family, to read this account and think that I was filled with only negativity and foreboding as my days wind to an ending on this earth. I am also filled with happiness at the life I got to experience, thanks to all of you. You were the best family anyone could have ever asked for. You raised me with love, and affection, and acceptance, even when you knew how different I was. You always made me feel like an Oritt, not an adopted child. I love you all with my entire being.

Annie paused, reaching up to wipe away a tear. Sometimes she felt amazed that she still felt emotions so keenly, when her mind had become such a logical machine as the Angel Virus progressed within her.

So many have died already, but we are not out of the woods yet. I fear that when my time comes, one year from today, I will be the only Angel left. I suppose there is something poetic about that. I brought the Angel Virus into the world, and I will take it with me when I go.

I wish I could tell the world how sorry I am. I know it's not my fault, but it's hard to not feel guilty regardless. But you always tell me not to feel guilty for things out of my control, so I'll try, for your sakes.

I will forever be thankful for everything you've given me.

Annie slowly capped her pen, closed the diary, and lay down to sleep.

10

Annie's prediction came true. Over the course of 2017, hell on earth spread like a malignant tumor all over the world. Quarantine centers everywhere were targeted one by one, with bombs, with gas, with fire, with guns. The Seattle stadium wasn't the only center to have its own military force let the bombers in, not by a long shot. Too many parents had lost children to the virus, and they vastly outnumbered those who hadn't. No matter how much security was increased, the Angel killers always found a way.

Always.

By summer of 2017, the global death toll was just under 1.8 billion.

By December, Annie was the only Angel left in the world.

11

January 1st, 2018.

Jeff held Kristi in his arms while Jessica slowly pulled a white sheet over Annie's face. Jacob, Maddy, and Alex all stood in one corner of the hospital room, staring on helplessly.

So passed the Angel Virus from the world.

Part 16: The Verdict (The Year 2018)

1

"Dr. Michaels, there's one question that hasn't been answered, that no one has been able to figure out, not the CDC, not the WHO, nobody. Why did the Angels die exactly on their 15th birthday?" Gabriel asked.

"That blame can be laid at my feet, as well," Dr. Michaels answered quietly. "When I performed genetic manipulation on Grace and Annie, I knew that even if my chromosomal repair was successful, it was still no guarantee that they wouldn't have issues with their immune systems. I wrote in, if you will, genetic markers to increase thymus gland production of T lymphocytes and B lymphocytes, but I wrote in a single additional genetic marker to cut off increased production at age 15. The thymus gland begins to atrophy and decay at puberty anyway, but just in case my girls hit puberty early, as many girls do, I wanted to make sure they had at least until they turned 15 to have maximum usage of their thymus glands, to ensure a healthy adulthood.

"That is why the Angels died on their 15th birthday," Dr. Michaels continued. "At age 15, the supercharged thymus gland shut down, and Annie's virus took over, causing instant organ failure and death."

"One further question, Dr. Michaels. Why turn yourself in at all? As you attest, the Angel Virus was a freak accident, and not truly your fault. Your only guilt, to your mind, is from inaction."

Dr. Michaels cleared his throat. "I had to explain. I *needed* the world to know, to at least provide what peace can be had from the truth. About me, about the Angel Virus. And about Grace."

At that moment, a young girl in the audience of the courtroom stood up, and every eye was drawn to her.

Jeff's eyes widened when he saw the girl. "Annie?" he whispered.

"This is my daughter, Grace," Dr. Michaels said. "This is the other reason why I felt compelled to be here. Because, you see, despite having turned 15, Grace still carries within her blood a possible cure to any disease we've ever encountered. Despite her thymus gland stopping increased production of T and B lymphocytes, she still has within her the perfection of the Angel Virus, without the virus. Grace volunteered herself for testing, to see if her blood, and her enhanced immune system, could be replicated and made viable for the world's use.

"So much death over the last decade, caused inadvertently by my own hand. I know my life is forfeit. I want to leave this world with a chance for living instead of dying."

Grace sat back down amid the tumult of crashing voices that Dr. Michaels revelation had created.

Judge Erikson called the courtroom back to order. When all was silent once more, the judge looked over at Jeff. "Your witness, counselor."

Jeff, face pale, just shook his head. "No questions, your honor."

Judge Erikson nodded as if he had expected that response. "Then we will have a recess while the jury deliberates their verdict." He banged his gavel, and the twelve members of the jury got up and filed out of the courtroom. Dr. Michaels was escorted by the bailiff back to the room deeper within the courthouse where he had been sequestered during the trial.

2

Jeff met up with Jessica on the front steps of the courthouse in the hot afternoon sunlight. He still looked stunned.

"I just can't believe...I really thought it was Annie for a moment, come back to us," he said softly, staring off into the distance.

"So did I," Jessica said, nodding. "What do you think will happen now?"

Jeff shook his head, coming back to the present. "I don't think the jury will take long. They'll come back with a guilty verdict, Dr. Michaels will be sentenced to death, and that will be the end of it."

"Justice," Jessica said under her breath.

Jeff nodded, but he looked troubled.

3

As Jeff had predicted, the jury took less than 15 minutes.

After everyone had come back in and been seated, the judge called for their verdict.

The jury foreman, a distinguished looking older man in a tweed jacket, stood with a paper in his hands. "On the count of kidnapping, the defendant is found guilty."

Grace, sitting in the audience, shuffled nervously as people around her commented quietly to each other.

"On the count of criminal conspiracy, the defendant is found guilty."

Jeff tensed, waiting for the final pronouncement.

"On the count of genocide, the defendant is found...not guilty."

"WHAT?!" Jessica shouted, jumping to her feet with outrage written on her face.

The entire courtroom exploded in noise as people spewed their incredulity at the jury.

The foreman, unperturbed, sat down calmly.

Judge Erikson had to bang his gavel several times, shouting for order.

Finally, when the courtroom had settled down, Judge Erikson glared out at the people seated in the audience. "The next person who speaks out of order will be held in contempt of court. Do I make myself clear?" Dead silence. "Good. The court accepts the verdict. A date will be set for sentencing." Another bang of the gavel, and court was adjourned.

"Not good enough," Jessica said, getting to her feet and pulling something out of her purse. Time seemed to slow as every head in the room turned toward her.

"Gun!" Someone screamed.

The bailiff reached for his own firearm.

Jessica leveled her small pistol at Dr. Michaels from ten feet away. Her first shot took him in the neck. Her second blew the top of his head off. Before she could pull the trigger again, the bailiff finally got his gun out and put a round in her chest. She went down amid a chorus of screams.

Jeff shoved through the mass of panicked spectators and reached Jessica's side. "What did you do?" he said through clenched teeth. "For the love of God, why?"

"Justice," she said with her last breath. She died with a smile on her face.

Epilogue (The Year 2018)

Dr. Michaels' murder was the only subject on the news for days. All over the world, people talked about it, argued over it. Some called Jessica a killer. More called her a saint, providing the justice that the world deserved.

Eventually the world moved on, beginning the long and arduous healing process. New children were born, new families were started. Slowly, communities began to come together again. Hatred and suspicion faded away.

One night, near the end of that fateful year, Kristi sat alone in her favorite reading chair in the living room. She had Annie's diary in her hands. Slowly she opened it up, flipping to the last page Annie had written, the night before she turned 15, and began to read.

I'm not afraid. Short though my life was, you all filled it with adventure, enough to make me feel like I experienced a long and happy lifetime. I will always be grateful for that.

I don't know what comes next, but that's part of the adventure, isn't it? One last adventure.

I love you all, and I'll always be with you. Forever.
Tears began to stream down Kristi's face.
She took a deep breath.
And closed the book.

Made in United States
Troutdale, OR
11/11/2024